Not often do you come across a book that is both entertaining and engaging from the off. You are captured by the charming, delightful character that is Miss Daisy and the wonderful way that this book is written enables you to create each scene vividly in your mind, bringing colourful characters to life.

This book is a lovely example of escapism which should be made available on prescription on the NHS.

Phil Evans: Comedian, writer and presenter.

What a tonic *Miss Daisy Conquers Britain* is. I loved it. It's like stepping back in time. It's full of charm, verve and a sense of fun. What I especially love is how fast moving the story is, there's never a dull moment as we follow the escapades of Miss Daisy, her owner and one asthmatic dog as they make their way to John O'Groats and then back to Lands End. Is there no end to the trouble that they seem to get into? All I can say is I want a car like that, oh and you may as well throw in the dog as well. What an absolute joy.

Wynne Evans, Broadcaster & Opera Singer

To Liz

I hope you enjoy

Miss Daisy
Conquers
Britain

Best Wishes
Ed P...

Matador
9 Priory Business Park,
Wistow Road, Kibworth Beauchamp,
Leicestershire. LE8 0RX
Tel: (+44) 116 279 2299
Fax: (+44) 116 279 2277
Email: books@troubador.co.uk
Web: www.troubador.co.uk/matador

ISBN 978 1784621 179

British Library Cataloguing in Publication Data.
A catalogue record for this book is available from the British Library.

www.missdaisydiaries.co.uk
Twitter @missdaisydiary
Facebook http://www.facebook.com/missdaisydiary
You Tube http://youtu.be/p8xiaykG4pM

Typeset in 11pt Aldine401 BT Roman by Troubador Publishing Ltd, Leicester, UK

Matador is an imprint of Troubador Publishing Ltd

Printed and bound in the UK by TJ International, Padstow, Cornwall

To my grandchildren, Dewi, Josh, Freddie, Seren, Phoebe and Zak; who when they are old enough to read for themselves will realise just how bonkers their aging ancestor is. And of course to my oldest grandson Toby who still hasn't quite realised what a challenge Miss Daisy is going to be when she belongs to him.

Preface

I couldn't resist it. I'd decided that she should come back and write another book even before we'd finished her first one. She's as cantankerous and curmudgeonly as ever and Her Ladyship's ebullience even more exasperating. Their 'Odd Couple' relationship is as thriving as it has ever been. Add to that Oscar The Asthmatic Barking Dog as an unplanned for passenger and three definitely is a crowd.

This time Miss Daisy tells her story over just ten days, describing events after Her Ladyship has announced that it would be jolly good fun if they attempted the John O'Groats to Land's End run. But with the prospect of a near 800 mile drive just to get to the top of Scotland, Miss Daisy braces herself for what is as good as doing the famous John O'Groats to Lands End twice. Unlike her last book, Miss Daisy would like to stress that this narrative is a work of complete fiction. With one or two notable exceptions any similarity between characters in this book and the real world are purely incidental.

Once again, I would like to thank the wonderful Ed Tanguay for his cover and book illustrations. I'd also like to thank Yvette Brown who tirelessly rearranged Miss Daisy's words so they actually made sense.

Finally for those of you contemplating retirement and

wondering what on earth you are going to do with all this time on your hands, think about investing in a car like Miss Daisy, It will be tremendous fun and you'll never find yourself stuck in a queue, because you'll be the cause of it!

Prologue

'Miss Daisy, meet Doctor John. He's the gentleman who will undertake
your heart surgery.' I get the feeling he thinks Her ladyship is away with the
fairies. He looks sympathetically at me.

A Tale of Two Ends!

'It was the best of times, it was the worst of times, it was the age of wisdom, it was the age of foolishness.' Actually it's nothing like that as far as I am concerned. What I can say is that it is regularly the worst of times and certainly the age of foolishness, especially when it comes to my companion, she of ample form and with three-score-years-and-eight under her belt. I call her 'Her Ladyship.' That's because of her haughty and opinionated manner and, of course, her propensity to come up with ridiculous ideas, usually involving me. I still recall with horror her notion that she and I were going to drive around the world to mark her sixtieth birthday. It took some seven years and a disaster-ridden two-thousand mile drive around Spain to Santiago de Compostela and back for her to decide that perhaps it wasn't such a good idea after all.

Since then it appears that, finally, I am to be allowed to enjoy retirement in my quiet corner of Pembrokeshire. Her Ladyship appears to content herself with gentle sojourns around the locality and occasionally straying into a neighbouring county. There hasn't even been a mention of a trip to the continent since we came back from Spain. I'm nearly eighty, you know, and I find that most reassuring. This is how I like things to be.

I suppose I should also mention Her Ladyship's dog, Oscar, 'The Asthmatic Barking Dog,' as she calls him. He's known me for years but he still insists on lifting his leg against my wheels at every possible opportunity. Ghastly creature. I mean, I don't do anything to upset him, so why does he have to go and piddle on me? He wouldn't like it if I dribbled on him, oh no, no, no, no.

I'm sorry, I haven't introduced myself, have I? How do you do? I am Miss Daisy, a child of the Austin family, born on the 15th of March 1934 at Longbridge in Birmingham.

As I said, Her Ladyship appeared to have settled down so I could finally enjoy life. Well, that was how it was until a few days ago...

'Happy New Year, Old Girl. A very Happy New Year.' Her Ladyship appeared in a good mood. She'd thrown open the garage door and a chilly blast worked its way around my chassis. I waited patiently for her to shut the door again. She didn't.

'Brrrrr, it's a bit of a chilly morning, isn't it? Tell you what, though, at least it's sunny and dry. Do you fancy going on a little run? Could be fun, Old Girl. What do you think?'

As long as we are not heading off into the wild blue yonder I've always loved the idea of a 'little run' as she calls it. I felt it would warm me up a bit. If it wasn't for the cold it could have been a spring day.

'Then, of course, this will be your last drive for a while,' she said, almost as an aside, as she rolled me out and turned my crank handle a few times. She turned on my ignition and hauled out my choke, securing it in place with the usual three clothes pegs she keeps in the glove pocket. 'An important accessory, Old Girl,' she said. 'You never know when you might need a clothes peg when driving a car.' She was wittering away again, but I couldn't stop wondering what she'd meant by 'last drive for a while'.

'Right now we're off to the Preselis for lunch. We're meeting a few friends. You'll enjoy that.' For once I wasn't interested in where we were going. I wanted an answer to my question. What did she mean 'last drive for a while'? Then, without any explanation, we were off up into the Preseli mountains.

I was no wiser when we returned home and she was peering under my bonnet. 'Hmmm, yes, it's going to be quite a job. But I think we should get it done before we attempt the JOGLE.' Now that confused me even more. The JOGLE? What was that when it was at home?

'Oh sorry, Old Girl, I haven't told you have I?' No, actually she hadn't.

'Well, Old Girl, since this year is the 90th anniversary of your ilk, I thought we would join the Austin Seven run from John O'Groats to Land's End to mark the event.' I saw that familiar twinkle in her eye that suggested there would be no stopping her. She must have sensed my concern because she tried to reassure me.

'It's not going to be that bad, Old Girl. Hang on a minute.' She left the garage and moments later returned.

'This is a globe of the world, Old Girl. Look up here.' She pointed to a spot near the top. 'That's John O'Groats, all the way up there. Now the run goes all the way down to… there, there it is, Land's End. You see? It's downhill all the way and it's only about nine hundred miles. You'll sail down and it's not nearly as far as that trip we had to Spain. It'll take us a few days to get to John O'Groats and then it's only four days to get to Land's End. It's a piece of cake – honestly.'

It's all very well her pointing at a globe where I see a shape that looks rather like an old woman riding on the back of a pig. Where exactly is this John O'Groats anyway? Is it foreign? I don't know where Land's End is either. What if they're both foreign?

'But before we embark on that little trip I think you're in need of some heart surgery, so I've arranged to have your engine rebuilt. We can get all that sorted out before we go. How about that then?'

Well, I was speechless. Let's face it, I'm always speechless. Have you ever heard of a vintage motor car that could talk? I'd hoped beyond hope that she'd given up on any more crazy long-winded trips. I was, however, encouraged by her remark about my having heart surgery. Then she was gone, closing the garage door behind her.

A couple of weeks have passed and I am still quietly pondering these matters when my garage door flies open to reveal Her Ladyship standing there in some old overalls. As usual, she is a sight to behold. With her is a gentleman.

'Miss Daisy, meet Doctor John. He's the gentleman who will undertake your heart surgery. To do that, Old Girl, we're going to have to take your engine out so he can do it properly. It'll take a couple of months won't it John?' The Nice Doctor forces a smile. I get the feeling he thinks Her ladyship is away with the fairies. He looks sympathetically at me.

'It might be three months actually, just to be safe.' Her Ladyship butts in.

'Yesss, so don't be alarmed, to get your engine out we're going to have to remove a lot of other bits first.'

They wheel me out into the yard and start to take off various parts of my anatomy. I have to say that I am feeling rather tired. I think I need a snooze. Suddenly I am brought out of my slumbers by an enormous electrical spark jumping off my starter and the sight of The Nice Doctor John whipping his hand away.

'I think it would be a good idea if we disconnected the battery, don't you?' The Nice Doctor John nurses his hand. He reaches for a spanner and goes around to my side. I can't see what he is doing and to be honest I don't really care anymore. I'm sure that I'll feel a lot better after my heart surgery. But oh gosh, I'm so tired.

'Do you really talk to this car?' I hear The Nice Doctor John ask Her Ladyship.

'Of course I do. We're old friends now. I've always talked to her.'

What does she mean 'old friends'? Oh golly gosh, I'm so, so tired. I think I'll have a little snooze…

Chapter One

*'Fifty eight, nine, come on, Old Girl, you can do it, just one more!' Her
Ladyship is becoming very excited. 'You're already going faster than you've
ever been before. Sixty! That's it! You've done sixty!*

Running In... Please Pass!

'Good Morning, Old Girl. And how are you feeling then?'
What? Who's that? Where am I?

'Tell you what, Old Thing, I'll leave you here for a while and let you fully come round. You've been away for quite a time having your surgery but I'm assured you'll soon feel really good. I was going to take you into town to do some shopping but obviously you're not up to it.'

'Now I remember. I've had my engine done, haven't I? I'm back at home with Her Ladyship and The Asthmatic Barking Dog. Her Ladyship's mobile phone interrupts my clearing thoughts.

'Hello? Who's that? Oh hello, John. Hang on a minute, I'll put you on speaker.' 'Pam... to put it simply enough for even you to understand, do not take Miss Daisy anywhere until I've been over. I've found a bit of her suspension here and she's not safe to drive at the moment. Okay?' Oh, I remember now, It's The Nice Doctor John, the one who conducted my surgery.

'That's fine, I was going to give her a bit of a rest, she still looks quite tired.'

'I'll be over in an hour. You will be there won't you?' Her Ladyship mouths an obscene word. She had planned on going shopping and she really hates having her plans disrupted.

'No, that's fine, I'll be here.'

Two hours have passed and not only am I feeling wide awake, I'm raring to go. The Nice Doctor John emerges from groping with my undercarriage.

'There, that'll be fine now. She's all ready to take you on the John O'Groats to Land's End run… after you've run her in, of course. It's only a few weeks now isn't it?

'Yes, three to be precise.'

Oh! I had forgotten that bit. The whole reason for my surgery was to get me fit to attempt 'A JOGLE,' as Her Ladyship calls it.

'That engine looks absolutely superb now,' she says. 'Like brand new. And with an oil filter. After 78 years she has an oil filter. No more having to scramble underneath her three times a year to fiddle with her bottom, drain the old oil and put new stuff in. So what do I need to do about running her in?'

'She won't need a lot. A few hundred miles will do. You'll feel her urging you to put your foot down, but keep her speed below forty-five and, most importantly, don't labour the engine.' The Nice Doctor John puts his tools away and turns to go. 'I'll put my report in the post along with my bill.'

Her Ladyship blanches. She always does when anyone mentions any sort of payment required from her.

Two days later she's back in my garage waving an unopened letter at me. She stands beside me wearing a posture that suggests it is my fault that she has to cough up a sum of money for something that has been done to me. She slowly opens the envelope and unfolds the contents, glancing occasionally at me. Putting the report aside, she opens her mouth, totters backwards and catches her shoulder on one of the shelves on my garage wall.

'What the ff…lipping heck?' She says. 'What? Oh my God, this'll take ages to pay off.' She turns back to me. 'This is your fault. If you hadn't been burning oil this work would never have needed to be done.'

That's right, blame me.

'I think I'd better check my bank account. But not now. Come on, Old Girl, let's take you for a run. It's a nice day, let's see what you can do.'

I start very easily. No more fiddling with my petrol pump, although she did have to crank my handle a few times. It seems ages since I felt like this. We head off to the petrol station. I want to go faster but Madam is holding me back.

'Steady on, Old Girl. We have to keep your speed down for a while, but I will let you go faster. All in good time. Your engine's much quieter than it used to be. I'm very impressed. I think the JOGLE will be a doddle.'

We swing into a petrol station and pull up neatly beside a pump. Her Ladyship, obviously feeling delighted with herself, hops out and trips over the plinth that the pump stands on. A gentleman at the neighbouring pump comes over and helps her to her feet.

'Are you all right? That was a nasty fall.'

'Yes thank you,' she responds, in a sharp, shrill voice suggesting that she is in pain but doesn't want to give that fact away. Embarrassed, she just wants to fill me up and get away as quickly as possible. She grabs the nozzle and thrusts it, rather violently I think, at my tank. Only then does she realise that she hasn't removed my filler cap and she's already squirted petrol over my bodywork.

'Oh for heaven's sake,' she says as she removes the cap and starts to fill me up properly. She starts muttering quietly to herself. Never a good sign. I think she's stressed about something.

'That's a very nice car. What is it?' asks the man who helps her up.

'An Austin Seven touring car,' Her Ladyship replies as she taps the last drips from the nozzle into my tank. '1934, she's just had her engine rebuilt. Here, have a look.' She opens my bonnet.

Oh good grief, do we have to go through all this every time anyone compliments me? The man seems to lose interest rather quickly. I spot an unhappy looking wife. So does he.

'I'd better go,' he says. He climbs in his car and is gone. Was that his wife wagging her finger at him and shouting? I've always felt that I am a good judge of people. I've had so many owners over the last, gosh how many years is it? Seventy eight? Yes seventy eight years and they were all so different. He's rather like Mister Chalk who bought me from 'Don't Worry Beatrice' just after the war. I liked him, but he was always being hen pecked by his wife. A bit like this man? No possibly not. I think this man's been between some other woman's sheets and has been caught, as humans say, *in flagrante delicto*. I think that watching him talking to Her Ladyship convinced her that he was flirting once again. Poor devil, he's in for a bad day.

'Thirty six pounds, Old Girl,' Her Ladyship snorts as she returns from paying. 'Bloody thirty-bloody-six bloody pounds to fill you up. That's a third of what you cost when you were new! Mind you, that's nothing compared to what you've cost me to have your engine done.'

So that's it. She's still fuming over the cost of my surgery. Well, it was she who chose to have the work done. I might have been burning a bit of oil but I was fine. Perhaps not as powerful as I feel now, but we went around Spain without any problems. That is apart from my dynamo, my sparking plugs, my carburettor, my brake lights and my oil leak. A normal trip really. So she can only blame herself.

A day or two later Her Ladyship throws open my garage doors. 'Here, look at this, Old Girl. I think it's a good idea to fix this sign to the back of you to warn others why you're going slowly.'

She holds the sign up. It says RUNNING IN. PLEASE PASS. What is she thinking? I know it's supposed to explain why we are going slowly but, let's face it, we're always going slowly... new engine or not.

'There, that'll do. It's a lovely day. Let's go for a good run. The Nice Doctor John said that we should get four to five hundred miles under your bonnet before we head to sunny Scotland. Where's that dog?'

If Your Ladyship cares to look at my front wheels, you'll see The Asthmatic Barking Dog sunning himself.

'There you are dog,' cries Her Ladyship, opening my door and folding the seat forwards. 'Come on, hop in.' Refusing to be hurried, The Asthmatic Barking Dog lifts his head. The dust of the yard stays attached to the side of his face. He takes a tired look at Her Ladyship and very slowly sits up and stretches his head as high as he can. Still without any sense of speed, he clambers onto all fours and vigorously shakes his head to remove the dust, at the same time making his ears slap against his neck. It sounds like one of those ratchets that are used by fans at football matches.

'Oh stop fart-arsing about Oscar, get in the blooming car.' I'm convinced that Madam gets even more impatient as she gets older. Still in no hurry, The Asthmatic Barking Dog decides to take the long way round to the open door, pausing to piddle on my nearside front wheel before passing around my rear end and sniffing at my number plate.

'Oh for God's sake, just get in.' He plants his front paws on my running board and tries to clamber in, without success. Her Ladyship grabs his rear end and heaves him up so that he can hop onto my rear seat. He breaks wind into Her Ladyship's hand before settling down ready for another snooze.

'You dirty, filthy, stinking creature! You could have held that back until I'd pulled my hand away!' The Asthmatic Barking Dog briefly looks up, unconcerned, before going back to sleep.

Her Ladyship clambers into my driver's seat, starts me up and we're off.

'Right, Old Girl,' Her Ladyship shouts as we drive along. 'We need to get a good distance under your bonnet today, and then we'll do that trip up to the Country Park. By then we should have done the necessary mileage for The Nice Doctor John to change your oil. Then we'll be ready to attempt the JOGLE'. I have to confess that I do feel good and I am keen to go faster but, unusually, Madam is controlling my speed. For once, is Her Ladyship looking out for me? Well maybe, but I think it's more to do with her investment in my engine.

We've travelled about seventy miles past Carmarthen, Newcastle Emlyn then on towards Cardigan when first I, then Her Ladyship, notice a strange noise coming from my engine compartment.

'We'd better pull over, Old Girl,' Her Ladyship announces as she swings me into a parking area and switches me off. She opens my bonnet and closely examines my engine. I do love this. She puts on an air of pretending to know what she's doing, when in truth she hasn't a clue. 'Hmm, well everything looks okay. Your engine is still spotless. I can't see anything wrong. Let's start your engine and I'll see where the noise is coming from.' She starts me up and the noise seems to have gone.

'Oh it can't be that serious, Old Girl. The noise has gone away. Time, I think, to turn for home, but let's go a different route.' She closes my bonnet, hops back in and we're off.

'It seems fine now, Old Girl, I expect something was catching on something else, it couldn't have been that serious. Anyway, I'm going to see if you can go any faster than you used to. I think we've done enough miles now to have a little go. There's a nice bit of straight road coming up ahead.'

We round a bend, I feel Her Ladyship press my accelerator pedal to the floor, I respond and surge forward.

'Come on, Old Girl! Oh well done! That's it, we're up to fifty. You've always been able to do that. So let's see what you've got left. Fifty five, oh well done, Old Girl. Come on now, let's see if you can you give me sixty!'

Everything is starting to shake, rattle and roll. Fortunately that noise we heard earlier seems to have gone away, but for all I know the noise my engine is making is drowning it out.

'Fifty eight, nine, come on, Old Girl, you can do it, just one more!' Her Ladyship is becoming very excited. 'You're already going faster than you've ever been before. Sixty! That's it! You've done sixty! Well done, Old Girl, that's amazing.' That's a mile a minute!

What on earth are you thinking about? I can hardly hold myself together. I dread what it might be doing to Your Ladyship's anatomy.

She allows me to slow down again, thank goodness. There's a sharp bend coming up and I spot a triangular sign with the word 'Ford' written on it. Unfortunately, it's half covered with weeds and undergrowth and Her Ladyship doesn't appear to notice it. She's still elated by the speed we've just reached and I have a feeling that she's after a bit more excitement.

'Let's see how fast you can take this bend, Old Girl,' she shouts above my engine noise. 'Down a notch!' What is she on about? 'Into the crown of the bend and foot to the floor… aaaargh!'

A large plume of water leaps up from my front wheels. It pauses for a few seconds before gravity decides to return it to earth. My driving compartment is now placed firmly between the flying pool of water and its natural home – the road. The Asthmatic Barking Dog wakes with a start and wonders why it seems that he has just been for a swim. It didn't make sense, he had been dreaming about chasing cats. Her Ladyship pulls into the side of the road and emerges from the driving seat. I can't see any single part of her that isn't soaked.

'You would have thought,' she says as she flicks a drip of water from the tip of her nose. 'You would have thought that they might have put up a sign warning us of the ford. I'm soaked, and judging by the look of you, so are you. Let's get home. I'll have to get both of us dried out before next weekend.

We reach home and she parks me outside in the sunshine. 'I'm going to get changed,' she says, with as much dignity as she can muster. The Asthmatic Barking Dog, still dripping, strolls onto the lawn in search of a warm patch of ground where he too can dry out. Before she even reaches the house, Her Ladyship's phone rings. I am surprised it's even working after that soaking. Mind you, it is quite an old phone, and my experience tells me that old things are far more reliable than new things. Anyway, Her Ladyship is not inclined to keep up with the most modern technology.

'Hello? Oh, hello John.' It's The Nice Doctor John again. I imagine he's checking up on me.

'Yes, we've been out today and added,' she glances at my speedometer, 'gosh a hundred and fifty miles to Miss Daisy's clock... she's going really well actually. What? Yes, not a drop of oil. There was a funny noise at one point but it went away and hasn't returned. We've got a run to Pembrey next weekend. That should take us over the four hundred mile mark and we can change her oil. What? The noise? I'm sure it's nothing to worry about. Anyway it hasn't returned. No, that's fine too. Tell you what though, we reached sixty on the way home. Then we flew into a ford and we're all soaked. What? Oh come on. It was only for a little while and we slowed down as soon as we hit the magic Six-O. No John, it won't happen again, I promise.'

She hangs up, looking rather deflated. Forgetting that she's soaked to the skin, she grabs a chamois leather and starts to wipe me down.

'Oh dear. It looks as though we've lost our Running In sign

already. I expect it was washed off, Old Girl. I'm very impressed with your engine though. Do you think we should attempt the JOGLE as a non-stop run?'

No, that's not a good idea. Indeed we shouldn't be attempting it at all.

A week has passed since our swim and in spite of being rolled outside every time the sun decides to emerge, I still feel damp. Her Ladyship throws open my door with a significant degree of enthusiasm.

'Good morning, Old Girl, what a lovely day for a bit more running in.'

It's a chilly, but a bright and sunny day. One of those lovely spring mornings. I was hoping to spend a day basking in the sun. But it seems that is not the plan.

She whips open my bonnet. 'Not a drip of oil anywhere. No discharge at all. Your nether regions are spotless. You won't need a nappy anymore.' She chuckles as she closes my bonnet. I don't find that very funny.

'Right, let's go. We've got a vintage car club meeting at a very unusual venue today.' She hops in, starts up my engine and we are on our way.

After about 35 miles we arrive at a very large building that says 'Go Karting' on it in big letters. Go Karting? I remember those things, children used to make them out of old wooden boxes and pram wheels and whiz past my chassis in a most unnerving manner. I can hear the sound of revving engines. Oh, of course, nowadays they have engines, don't they? Where are the children? Oh no, surely she's not serious, she's not going to go-kart herself is she? This woman has finally, completely, lost the plot.

'Won't be long, Old Girl. I've just got to show these chaps that we women are as competitive as drivers as they are.' She disappears inside the building and I suppose I must wait quietly here while she makes a fool of herself.

It isn't long before I hear a roar of engines again. The roar continues for about ten minutes and then it seems to die down, except for one engine that I can still hear. Other club members start to trickle out of the building. They get in their cars and head off. Where are you all going? What have you done with Her Ladyship? The sound of that last engine eventually stops and, moments later, Her Ladyship appears.

'That was fun, Old Girl. I showed 'em how to drive. Ten laps we did.' Oh yes? I believe you.

'The people who run this place have said that I can take you onto their little track. Would you like to have a go?' No thank you. I am not a racing car. Let's go home. The big doors of the building start to open.

One of the marshals comes out. 'Are you sure you want to do this? That old car isn't really suitable for a track like this.'

'Oh we'll only do a couple of laps. I know this Old Girl will enjoy it.' Oh I will, will I?

'All right then, just a couple of laps. Come on then.' Her Ladyship gets in and we roll through the big doors and pull up at a white line. Another Marshal comes over.

'Right,' he says, 'You've done the course in a kart. You've experienced the sharp bends in that. This thing's much higher and the track is quite slippery. Don't push it.' What does he mean 'This Thing'?

12

'Okay.' Her Ladyship says this with a degree of anxiety. Is she suddenly regretting her decision?

A klaxon sounds, Madam struggles to get me into first gear and we are off. We are into second before we hit the first bend. She doesn't go to third. Instead she's concentrating on getting me around this first, almost hairpin, bend. We are barely round that when she yanks my steering wheel the other way and we swing round a sharp left-hand bend. I feel my wheels start to slide towards the pile of old tyres that surround the track. She regains control and we are into the straight. Into third gear now and we are accelerating. Is she sure she should be doing this with my new engine? Brakes, down into second. Very sharp bend coming up Your Ladyship. Can you hear me? Very, very sharp bend. I lose grip of the track and we glide gracefully into the tyres.

She slams me into reverse. Into first and we shoot off again. She has a most determined look on her face. It's as if she's possessed. Right-hand bend… left-hand, a gentle one this time… sharp right and we shoot over the starting line. Thank God, only one lap to go. But unfortunately, having done one lap, Her Ladyship seems hell bent on attempting this last lap even faster. I can't do this! You are supposed to be running me in!! My tyres are screeching on the track this time. Oh no. Here come another pile of tyres… Ouch! Off again. Sharp left, ah the straight, up a gear, brakes… BRAKES! At last. Right! Right! Swing me to the bloomin' RIGHT!! Thank you. We are over the finishing line. Thank God, I'm still alive. Her Ladyship is sitting there, gripping my steering wheel and breathing heavily. Eventually, she gets out.

'Wow, that was fun wasn't it, Old Girl?'

Excuse me? That was definitely not fun. It was worse than that so-called gentle roll down the side of the Cantabrian Mountains trying to get my engine started two years ago. Never, never again. Please.

'I really enjoyed that,' Her Ladyship addresses the marshal. 'Thank you. Come on Old Girl, let's go home.'

'Right, Old Girl, let's get this trip done and dusted.' My garage doors are rattling on their hinges again, Her Ladyship having thrown them open with demonic force.

'Then I can change your oil and we're ready for John O'Groats. Dog? Where are you? Get off your arse and get into the car.'

The Asthmatic Barking Dog seems more enthusiastic than usual, but he still has time to lift his leg against my rear wheel. Then he literally leaps straight onto my rear seat. You would have thought that after his soaking he would rather stay at home.

'Right, let's go!' Madam starts my engine and we head down the drive. As soon as she pulls us onto the road the noise that mysteriously arrived and then disappeared, returns.

'Sod the thing,' shouts Her Ladyship as she turns me around and heads back up the drive again. This time she leaves my engine running to examine every part of it.

'Ah! I think I've found it! It's your fan, Old Girl. The bush seems worn. I think it needs some more grease.' She switches me off and goes into the garage and grabs a grease gun. She brings it over, thrusts it onto my nipple and pumps vigorously. Do you mind? Warm your hands first.

'That should do, Old Girl. Let's go.'

We head off up the road. The noise seems to have lessened, but it's still there. 'I expect the grease needs to work through from your nipple, Old Girl. The noise will soon go away. Pembrey, here we come!'

A few minutes pass… 'Blast, I've left the picnic basket behind.'
She turns to The Asthmatic Barking Dog. 'That means I've left your
treats behind too.' We start to drift across to the other side of the
road. Oooooh dear!

BLAAAAH. The horn of the approaching oil tanker causes Her
Ladyship to turn back to see that we are heading at speed straight
towards it.

'Oooooh whoops!' She swerves me back onto the left side of the
road and waves an apology to the tanker driver.

'Sorry, Old Girl, wasn't concentrating. Now where can we turn
round? God Almighty, at this rate we'll never get there.'

Ten minutes later we embark on our journey for the third time.
The fan noise, although quieter, is still there and I'm beginning to
have a horrible feeling that we are never going to get to Pembrey.

Unlikely as it seems, we've made it to the Country Park. Her
Ladyship starts to look around.

'I wonder where the others are,' she says. 'They said they'd be
here somewhere. Ah, there they are… Hellooo! Hello, here we are.
A bit of a problem getting going, but this engine is fantastic.'

'You are a bit late aren't you?' It's The Nice Mister Arthur, the
man who came to Spain with us last year. He understands
significantly more about me than Madam ever will.

'What's that noise?' He lifts my bonnet. 'Good grief, it's your
fan. Switch off quickly.'

'Why, what's the problem?' Her Ladyship looks decidedly shifty.
I've seen this before with you-know-who. She allows something

serious to build up, not having a clue what's going on, and then as the reality of the situation descends on her she goes very quiet.

'Your fan is about to chew up your radiator core and if it does, you ain't going nowhere. Look...' He grabs my fan blade and rocks it to and fro. 'It's actually about to touch the radiator, and if it chews that up, well, much more driving in this state and you won't be able to do the JOGLE.' Is there a god out there looking after me? Could this be the perfect reason for me not to have to go?

'We'll disconnect your fan. That should be fine to get you home.'

'Won't she overheat?' Her Ladyship seems concerned.

'No, she'll be fine, but try not to stop and leave her ticking over for too long and don't overwork her on the hills.'

Her Ladyship nods acquiescence. The Nice Mister Arthur starts to attack my fan assembly with a spanner. Then as he whips my fan belt off, something occurs to Her Ladyship.

'But we're off to Scotland in a few days. I'm not sure I'll get a new fan assembly fitted by then.' Her ladyship looks dejected. I almost feel sorry for her, but inside I'm delighted. There's a real chance that I might not have to take part in this madcap trip now.

'Try ringing round, there may be someone with another fan assembly you can borrow for the run.' The Nice Mister Arthur closes my bonnet and pats it.

'Good idea, I'll do that.' Her Ladyship whips out her mobile phone and dials a number. 'Blast, it's on answer-phone. He's not in. I know who I can try,' she selects another number and dials. 'He's not in either. Oh, I remember, he said he'd be away this weekend. I know, I'll try Roger.' She taps her phone and gradually a big smile appears on her face and she nods at The Nice Mister Arthur.

'Hello? Roger, is that you? Can you help me? I have a problem with Miss Daisy's fan assembly and I'm wondering whether you have one I could borrow?' Her Ladyship wanders off, chatting away happily on the phone. She suddenly spins round and with a big grin on her face, she strides back.

'Oh, thank you… Yes I'll get on the road now. I should be with you in an hour or two. Yes, about four o'clock… I'll see you then.' She hangs up the phone and tosses it onto the back seat. The Asthmatic Barking Dog opens one eye to inspect this intruder into his domain. Deciding it's friendly, he starts to lick it.

The journey to The Nice Mister Roger passes without problems and we make it on time. He appears, triumphantly waving something in his hand.

'Let's have a look then.' He opens my bonnet and peers at my silent and motionless fan assembly. 'Ah… we have a problem. It's the wrong size. You have the short fan assembly but this is the long one.' Her Ladyship looks crestfallen as she sees the JOGLE slowly drifting from her grasp. Me? I'm elated and can hardly hide my delight.

'No problem,' The Nice Mister Roger stands back. 'I'll make you a new one. I'm sure I've got some brass I can turn on the lathe. Don't worry, you'll be on your way soon. The first thing we need to do is to take the old one off, so I have something to model the new bush on.' With a little help from Her Ladyship, The Nice Mister Roger loosens my radiator so he can take off the damaged fan assembly.

'We now need to heat the piece up so I can drift the old bush out of its aluminium assembly.' He fires up a blow torch and heats it all up. He then gets a metal bar and a hammer and whacks the brass bush. There is a crunching sound.

'Ah… We now have another problem. We've broken the aluminium pulley assembly.' Her Ladyship stares at The Nice Mister Roger with a look that says 'what do you mean, we?'

'We can make you another one of those as well.'

Several hours pass as The Nice Mister Roger, working at his

lathe, creates first a new brass bush and then a new pulley assembly. Bits of brass and aluminium shavings fly everywhere and then, triumphantly, he places the newly built part in place and reassembles my radiator.

'Right, before we start, let's fill the thing with plenty of grease.' The Nice Mister Roger grabs his grease gun, presses it firmly onto my nipple and starts pumping.

'It's not going in that easily,' he says. 'It's probably because it's a tight fit.' Her Ladyship nods vaguely in agreement, her mind is elsewhere although she seems impressed by his pumping action.

'There, it's oozing back out of the nipple now. That'll be enough.' I can't help but agree with him.

'Right, let's start her up.' Her Ladyship clambers in… choke… ignition… starter. I fire into life. The Nice Mister Roger stares lovingly at my fan assembly, obviously proud at the work he's done.

'Perfect. That'll last you. It's tailor fitted and much better than if you'd bought one. Time for you to get off home now.' He opens the workshop door. It is pitch black outside.

'Gosh,' says Her Ladyship. 'I'm going to have to use her headlights and they're not the brightest stars in the firmament by any stretch of imagination.' She puts me into reverse and we roll out. As the light of the workshop fades, I spot the usual two little yellow balls on the drive about six yards in front of me – my headlight beams. How on earth Her Ladyship will get me home with the help of those I really don't know. Her Ladyship thanks The Nice Mister Roger profusely, turns me around and we drive off up a very dark road, heading for home.

'Gosh, Old Girl.' Her Ladyship is slumped forwards peering over my steering wheel into the darkness, pointing me towards the two little yellow balls which run along the road ahead of us. 'This isn't fun and it's blooming cold.' A modern car roars past us, blaring his horn. Her Ladyship swerves me to and fro in shock.

'Bloody idiot,' Her Ladyship snorts. 'What's the matter with the man?'

One of the yellow balls I've been religiously following is now starting to blink. It looks as though I'm sending out a distress message in Morse code. Her Ladyship and I become transfixed at this flickering. That's strange, there now seems to be a blue halo adding its influence to my yellow balls, and that's getting brighter.

A loud wail brings us both out of our mesmerised state and now we are brightly illuminated by the blue flashing. Is this an alien invasion?

'Oh, hell's teeth. That's all we need. Come on, Old Girl, we need to pull over.' Her Ladyship steers me into the side of the road. The aliens seem to stop as well. Oh, it's not aliens. It's a pair of Pembrokeshire's finest.

'Good evening, Madam,' a police officer bends forwards to peer into me. 'Should we really be out in this old car at night?' Cheek! Old indeed.

'No officer, we shouldn't,' Her Ladyship sounds far too tired to be arguing with a policeman. 'The thing is, this 'old car' as you call it is going to attempt the John O'Groats to Land's End run in a few days time and a problem occurred with her fan assembly while out driving today. It needed to be fixed straight away so I went over to a friend's place in Tenby to fix it. If I hadn't, we would have had to withdraw from the run.' The policeman looks at Her Ladyship very thoughtfully. I know what he's thinking. He's thinking Her Ladyship has been at the gin.

'Have you been drinking alcohol madam?' Her Ladyship is affronted. For once she hasn't.

'Certainly not!'

'Hmmm.' He's wondering whether to believe her or haul out the breathalyser. He looks at his watch and decides to accept Her Ladyship's statement. I presume he's off duty soon and doesn't fancy a load of form filling. He turns and proceeds – that's what the police say isn't it? I was proceeding in a northerly direction, M'lud! In this case it is a westerly direction as he walks to the front of me. My winking headlight intermittently illuminates his trousers.

'And what about this flashing headlight, Madam?' He pauses briefly. 'Remarkable, it's still flashing and you're not moving.' I can't help it, I am of a nervous disposition when in the company of a police officer. 'Are you going to have that fixed before going on this, umm, run?' He returns his gaze to his flashing trousers as if trying to decipher the message.

'Yes I am. But to be honest, you can see how faint they are. I normally avoid driving at night for that very reason. But it will be fixed. I promise.'

'All I can say, madam, is you're either very brave or completely foolhardy. It's a long trip for an old vehicle like this. You do know they've forecast snow later this week?'

'Ah, yes, but this little car is brilliant in snow. Narrow wheels and all that. The engine has undergone a complete rebuild as well. She's going like a little bomb.' The policeman stretches himself to his full six feet two inches and grins.

'Let's hope she doesn't turn into a big bomb.' He laughs at his own joke. I am really going off this man. 'Will you be all right getting home?'

'Yes thank you, officer. We're heading for the Cleddau Bridge and then it's only a couple of miles and with streetlights most of the way.'

'That's alright then. Just take care and don't forget, get that light fixed. Goodnight madam.' He returns to his car and the alien flashing lights disappear as quickly as they arrived.

'Phew, that was close, Old Girl. C'mon, let's get home.' Her Ladyship relaxes as the friendly lights of the Cleddau Bridge in the distance welcome us.

'Not long now, Old Girl, I'll be glad to tuck you up in your garage and get to bed. What a day... a frantic one don't you think? Tomorrow I will clean you up, fix that light and give you an oil change and a new filter. Think about it, Old Girl, your first filter change in 78 years. Anyway, once that's done you'll be fit and ready to attempt the JOGLE.'

I can't think of anything worse.

Chapter Two

She is about to turn us north when she lets out an almighty yelp, slams on my brakes and leaps out. Mister Thompson is quite taken aback.

Llangwm to Nantwich

'Right, Old Girl, let's check the emergency spares and supplies. Hmmm, fire extinguisher – yup. Ethanol repellent – yes, that's there and I think there's enough. Spare fan belt – good, spark plugs – yesss.' I do wish she'd shut up.

'Contact set – it's there. Spare filter and oil – mmm, that's fine. Can of gin and tonic?' What? That's hardly emergency supplies. 'Never know when I'm going to need that, Old Girl.'

It was quite late when Her Ladyship ticked off that final item on her check list last night. I now have every single part of my anatomy loaded up with spare parts, tool kits, and everything else that Her Ladyship could conjure up and find a space for. She had a triumphant look on her face as she assured me that we were now one hundred percent fit and ready for the off and that she would see me bright and early. The thought of seeing Madam up before dawn made me chuckle. As she was shutting my garage door, her phone rang.

'Hello? Who's that? Oh hello… yes I'm dropping him up to you first thing. He's looking forward to it. What? Heart attack? In hospital?' I could see by the look on her face that Her Ladyship had absolutely no sympathy for whoever had suffered the heart attack.

'Do you know anywhere else I might dump… I mean take him? Oh. Not at this short notice. Right okay.' She snarled as she hung up. 'Bloody woman. How dare she! How dare she have a heart attack! The place I was taking Dog suddenly can't have him. The kennel owner's had a heart attack. How bloody inconsiderate of her. There's no way I can sort something out now. I suppose he'll have to come with us.' I think I was as thrilled as she was. This news meant that I had to be completely unloaded and everything rearranged so that we could accommodate The Asthmatic Barking Dog on the back seat.

The garage doors fly open. It's still dark.

'Goooood Morning Old Girl! Ready for the off then?' She seems unhealthily hearty. That won't last. 'Let's get you warmed up while Dog and I have breakfast.' She rolls me out onto the drive and starts my engine. Then she disappears indoors, The Asthmatic Barking dog happily trotting along behind her. I think he's rather pleased to be coming along. I wish I could show the same enthusiasm.

Ten minutes pass and I watch the house as lights gradually go out. Her Ladyship reappears with The Asthmatic Barking Dog. I wonder if he realises that by coming along, he is going to be stuck inside me just about all day for the next ten days. 'In you get Dog, that's it.

A small crowd has gathered at the bottom of the drive, waving flags and holding a sign that says "Good Luck Miss Daisy". I can't think why I might need luck. I'll just do what I am told. It's you-know-who that is going to need the luck.

Her Ladyship stands in front of me and waves at the crowd. To my horror she decides to make a speech.

'Friends, in a moment Miss Daisy and I will embark on an eight day adventure into the unknown. We leave from here to arrive in John O'Groats by lunchtime on Saturday and then start on the massive run all the way down to the tip of Cornwall. We expect to reach there next Wednesday as long as this old thing behaves herself.' Her Ladyship stretches herself to her full height, and looks skywards.

'It's a far greater thing that we…' A voice from the rear of the group interrupts her.

'Oh do get on with it. It's flipping cold and I want my breakfast.'

'Oh, yes, right, oaky.' She turns to me. 'May God bless you and all who drive in you. And let's hope that the snow they've forecast for mid-Wales today isn't too bad.' You are not the only one who hopes that, Your Ladyship. She clambers into my driver's seat and starts down the drive, waving madly at our well-wishers, who've already started to wander away. She swings me towards Haverfordwest and we're off amid some half hearted cries of 'Good luck!'

Her Ladyship taps some instructions into her satellite navigation Thingy. I don't know why she bothers, she'll completely ignore it. Having said that, I think she rather likes the Thingy's voice talking to her. I can't help wondering why she just doesn't buy a wireless set. Not that she'd be able to hear it over the sound of my engine.

Twenty minutes later we repeat the action because Madam has forgotten her handbag. This time the spectators have all gone.

'We need to be in Llandeilo by ten o'clock, Old Girl. You're going to be on the television and we're meeting up with the others who are coming on the run. We've a couple of hours, do you think you can make it?' Don't ask me, you planned this trip.

We roll into Llandeilo ahead of time. 'Gosh, Old Girl, well done. New engine eh? Perhaps we really should attempt this trip non-stop.' Don't worry, she won't, she values her beauty sleep too much. Not that 'beauty' is much in evidence nowadays.

We don't have to wait long for the others to arrive. There are four of them. I don't know the others, but I am very relieved to see that The Nice Mister Arthur is among them. He was a godsend when we went round Spain last year. I lost count of how many times he had to sort me out then. Perhaps we'll stand a chance of making it now.

'Okay, where's the TV crew then?' The Nice Mister Arthur strolls over.

'They said ten o'clock,' Her Ladyship replies, checking her makeup. 'They said they'll need us for about thirty minutes here and then they'll follow us a bit of the way north.'

'Well, as long as it is only thirty minutes, the forecast's not good and we need to make it to Cheshire today.' The Nice Mister Arthur turns and spots an estate car pulling into the car park. 'Is that them?'

The car pulls alongside us and one man gets out, I think he must be the reporter. The other man stays in the car to fiddle with his equipment.

'Are you really serious about taking these old things all the way to John O'Groats then Land's End and back?' I bristle at that remark, as do my Austin Seven relatives. Her Ladyship seems offended too.

'We'll do our best,' she replies curtly. The second man is now setting up his camera.

'I'll talk to you first and then to a couple of the others? After that, we'll do some action filming as you head towards Builth?'

'Hang on, Frank, can I just get a few close-ups of the interior and the engine before we start?'

'Yup, okay. I'll have a chat with some of the others while you do that?' He turns to Her Ladyship. 'Perhaps you could introduce me?'

'Delighted to.' Her Ladyship wanders off with The Man Called

Frank while the cameraman begins to film his close-ups of me. Headlights, radiator, wheels, windscreen wiper; I sense that The Asthmatic Barking Dog is taking an interest in the cameraman. I wouldn't open my door if I were you, Mister Cameraman. Oh dear, he has. A deep rumble emanates from my rear seat. The rumble morphs into a long, low, deep growl.

'Hello Doggy... doggy, doggy, doggy.' There is a distinct nervousness in that cameraman's voice. 'Hello Doggy, nice doggy, you will let me take a few shots won't you?' Oh dear, that really wasn't the right thing to say.

'Grrrrrrrrr... arf, arf, arf, arf.' The cameraman quickly withdraws himself from my interior, but not before The Asthmatic Barking Dog manages to clamp his teeth firmly around a furry protuberance sticking out from the front of his equipment. A tug of war ensues as the cameraman attempts to pull it free from my interior with The Asthmatic Barking Dog stretching every sinew of his body to hang on to his furry prize. With a supreme effort and much grunting he manages to haul the camera back inside with a progressively angry cameraman also clinging on for dear life.

'Dog! Put that down, NOW, give it back. You bad dog.' Her Ladyship has returned, looking very angry. But as I have previously learnt, she has absolutely no influence over The Asthmatic Barking Dog when he's having fun.

'Let go! Drop it!' She grabs the camera as well and with the cameraman manages finally to haul the camera out with The Asthmatic Barking Dog hanging determinedly from the furry protrusion. Madam manages to separate The Asthmatic Barking Dog reluctantly from his new found furry friend. Pushing him back onto the rear seat and slamming the door, she turns to the cameraman, who is checking his equipment.

'I'm so sorry, are you alright? Has he damaged your microphone?' Her Ladyship seems very concerned.

'Yes, I'm fine, but I'm not so sure about the camera.'

The Man Called Frank has rejoined us by now. 'You should keep your dog under more control,' he says sharply to Her Ladyship.

'I do. But when someone thrusts his equipment into the car when I'm not there, it's little wonder that he should get protective and make a grab for it.' By now the others have joined us, intrigued and amused by the events that have been unfolding.

'It's alright,' says the cameraman. 'It's fine. The battery pack had come loose. Can we get on now?'

'Yes, let's,' said The Man Called Frank. 'We need to get this piece back to base and you need to make it through to Cheshire.'

Her Ladyship gathers herself and glances in my wing mirror to check how she's looking. And that's pretty awful if you ask me, and her hair is all over the place. She makes her best effort to improve her appearance... not very successfully I'm afraid.

'I think we'll have you standing here by the bonnet. There, yes that's fine.' He turns to the man with the camera. 'Are we rolling?' The man nods.

'Can you tell me, first of all, why on earth you would want to drive these beautiful old cars on a gruelling trip like this?' Her Ladyship ponders the question for a moment.

'I'd like to say because it's there. But it's more than that, it's a challenge. Anyway, I've never been to Scotland before.' I don't think that was the answer he wanted.

'But you have no heaters and these cars don't look that comfortable. And surely at eighty-odd years old, you're asking for a load of mechanical breakdowns.'

'So we wrap ourselves up well, carry plenty of spare parts and a tool kit. Tell you what though...' she leans towards The Man Called Frank. 'The chaps on these runs just love it when the cars break down. But I think perhaps it's the good old British spirit of adventure, the Dunkirk spirit if you like.' The Man Called Frank glances at the cameraman who looks back and raises his eyebrows. Her Ladyship ploughs on.

'You climb into the car, start the engine, sit back and think of the Empire.' What on earth is she on about now? The reporter seems to have lost faith in the dippy old woman that he is facing and is about to stop her. But she's in full flow.

'Every time we take these cars out, we really never know whether they will get us home at the end of the day. This time it isn't a short run, but eight days of solid driving, doing around two hundred and fifty miles every day. That's the excitement of it all, especially when you consider that I suffer from haemorrhoids. They're murder at the best of times.' The Man Called Frank glances at his colleague with a look that asks, where the hell are we going with this now? He turns back to Her Ladyship.

'Umm, yes, well, umm… What will you do if you break down permanently?'

'We call the rescue service and they'll take us home.' The Man Called Frank is shaking his head now. He's terrified that Madam will raise another issue relating to her health. She has not delivered anything he wanted.

'Thank you, I think we'll talk to some of the others now.' He nods at the man with the camera and they go off in search of a more sensible interviewee.

'That wasn't too bad, was it Old Girl?' Oh if only I could speak to her. She grabs a cloth and idly wipes down my bodywork. She's obviously hoping the cameraman will want to come back and get some shots of her driving. Somehow, after his experience with The Asthmatic Barking Dog, I don't think he'll be too keen. I'm right, he chooses to climb into one of my other relatives, switches on his camera and they head off for a short run on their own. Her Ladyship's nose is firmly out of joint. She harrumphs and puts the cloth away.

It isn't long before the relative returns with a satisfied and very happy cameraman. He gets out and chats to his colleague.

'Alright?'

'Yup, excellent… On top of that, no dog trying to eat my camera in that one.' Both men come over to us.

'Okay, thank you, we're happy. What we want to do now is get you all driving off together. So we'll follow you for a while and pass you every now and again taking shots, both from the Volvo and from the roadside. Okay?'

'That's fine,' says Her Ladyship. She turns to the others. 'Are we ready for the off?' I realise with some concern that we are going to be leading everyone else.

'Next stop Builth, Old Girl, and some lunch I think.' She starts me up and we're off with the news car in hot pursuit. At the first opportunity they pull out and slowly drive past us with the cameraman poking his equipment out of the window. As they come level with us, Her Ladyship preens herself and turns her head slightly towards the camera and smiles. In so doing, she not only ruins the shot, she's rendered it impossible to spot the turning we should be taking. My relatives obediently follow us like a load of chicks following their mother hen down the wrong road.

'Where's that blooming turning, Old Girl? We should have reached it by now. Oh blast it! I switched the Sat-nav off when we "reached our destination" in Llandeilo. Hang on.' She stretches over to switch Thingy on again and swerves across the road, blocking the path of the news car as it tries to pass us again. The news car blares its horn, Her Ladyship swerves me back to the proper side of the road and it pulls past and drives on, doubtless to stop and take a few roadside shots of us. In another life I think I could have been a TV news car.

'Make a U turn if possible and turn right after five hundred yards.' Oh, Thingy has started working again then.

'What? No. We've gone too far, Old Girl, we have to turn round.' At that, Her Ladyship swings me into a parking area, drives us through and turns right out of the exit, back the way we came. We are met with a series of bemused looks from the others as they do the same.

'Sorree,' she shouts at them as we head back down the road. 'There it is, Old Girl. That's the turning we should have taken.' She turns me up the new road and we are on the correct route to Builth Wells again. My relatives all follow but there's no sign of the news car.

As we arrive in Builth Wells the sky has gone very grey and it's definitely getting colder. We find a car park and Her Ladyship clambers out and stretches herself.

'Good God, Old Girl, only another two thousand miles to go and I'm as stiff as a board already.' Her mobile phone rings.

'Hello. Oh hello, did you get enough shots then? What do you mean where the hell are we? We're in Builth. Where are you? Where? How did you get there?' Very slowly it dawns on her that we had taken that U turn just moments after the news car had passed us.

'Oh sorry, my fault. We realised we were on the wrong road and turned back. I said I was sorry. There's no need to take that manner with me. Well, if that's how you feel…' She hangs up and puts the phone away.

'Stupid man. Come on, Dog, let's take you for a walk.' She opens the door to let him jump out. 'Hang on a sec, I think you'd better have your lead on.' She attaches it to his collar a split second before he spots the cat. He's away like a lion making its final charge at a herd of wildebeest. Her Ladyship struggles to stop the lead extension running out and there's a long painful sound of a ratchet followed by a clunk as she manages to stop it. The jerk causes her to fall forwards, still gripping the lead. The Asthmatic Barking Dog, with all four feet off the ground, is spun around in mid-charge and lands firmly back on the ground, but now he's no longer looking at a cat, but at a prostrate owner. He shakes his head, confused, wondering what happened to the cat. At the other end of the lead, Her Ladyship gathers herself together and clambers back onto her feet. Then, like an angler who has just caught an enormous salmon, she gradually hauls The Asthmatic Barking Dog in.

'Listen, Dog. If you do that again I will leave you in Scotland and you won't like that. I remember you wincing when there was a man playing bagpipes on the TV. So take that as a warning. Do that again and I'll find a school for pipers and leave you there. Now get on with your business.' As if nothing whatever had happened, The Asthmatic Barking Dog trots around looking for somewhere to lift his leg and we all know where that's going to be. That's it, my wheel.

With The Asthmatic Barking Dog back on my rear seat, Madam prepares to trot off for some lunch with the others, who have been thoroughly entertained by her exploits. As she leaves, some children come over to take a look at all the Austin Sevens. Her Ladyship spots them.

'Don't touch anything,' she shouts to them. 'You can look, but don't touch anything.'

'Silly old cow,' says one of the boys. 'Wow, these are old, aren't they? Hey look, this one's got a dog in it.' The children gather round me and peer in. The Asthmatic Barking Dog is pleased to see this group of young human beings. He's wagging his tail. One of them opens the door and stretches over to stroke him. The Asthmatic Barking Dog is delighted.

'I said don't touch.' Her Ladyship's back. She slams the door shut and the children run off. 'Leave these cars and my dog alone,' she commands and stomps off in the knowledge that she's now at the back of the queue for lunch.

As soon as she's gone the children return and The Asthmatic Barking Dog, pleased to see kindred spirits, wags his tail again.

'I know how we can get our own back,' says one particularly grubby child.

'How?' His friends are almost in unison and at that he produces a drawing pin from his pocket. He removes a small piece of gum that he's been chewing, puts it on the back of the pin and sticks it to my driving seat.

'That'll teach her a lesson. Silly old cow.' Satisfied that the pin is securely in place, he shuts my door. They wander off to look at the other cars and then disappear.

Her Ladyship and the others return and find an elderly and rather frail old gentleman admiring us.

'I say,' he says to Her Ladyship as she opens my door. 'What wonderful old cars they are. I learnt to drive in one like that.' Her Ladyship is full of bonhomie. Obviously she's had a good lunch.

'Did you indeed,' she smiles in response. 'They are wonderful aren't they? I've had this one for eight years and we've been on a lot of adventures together. We've done France twice, Spain…'

'By Jove, have you indeed,' the man interrupts her. 'And the trips have been trouble free?' Her Ladyship chuckles.

'Well not exactly. This old girl likes to remind me who's in charge of the success or lack of success of our progress. She makes her point quite regularly.'

'I'm sorry, I haven't introduced myself. My name's Archibald Thompson, I live in Welshpool. I've been visiting a relation and I'm waiting for the bus to take me back home. It goes right past my front door, very convenient I must say. I don't drive anymore. But if I did, I'd dearly love to have one of these again.

'Hello Mister Thompson, I'm delighted to meet you as well. Did you say that you're off to Welshpool?'

'Yes, I did.'

'Well we're going that way. I'd be delighted to offer you a lift. It'll save you from having to wait for the bus.' She looks up as a snowflake lands on my bonnet. It is followed by another, and then another. 'Oh dear, they forecast this didn't they? You don't want to be waiting at a cold bus stop. Mind you, we don't have a heater so I can't guarantee that you'll exactly be warm in this old thing.'

'I'm sure that I'll be fine, and thank you for the offer. I'd be delighted to accept.' Her Ladyship opens the passenger door to let Mister Thompson struggle into my passenger seat. The Asthmatic Barking Dog sniffs a cautious welcome. Her Ladyship goes over to The Nice Mister Arthur who is also settling down ready for our next hop.

'I've offered this gentleman a lift home. He lives in Welshpool. I'd like to take him straight to his home and make sure he's safe inside. Would you guys like to head on to the overnight stop and I'll meet you there later?'

'You've pulled, haven't you?' The Nice Mister Arthur gives Her Ladyship a big grin.

'Certainly not, he's in his eighties. I just thought it would be a nice gesture and it will give me someone to talk to on this next hop.'

'Judging by this weather we'd better get a move on. We need to be in Cheshire before nightfall.' Her Ladyship nods and returns to me. She opens the driver's door and plonks her backside firmly on the seat. I wait for a reaction… nothing. She manoeuvres her position to ensure that she's comfortable and starts my engine. Still no reaction. One by one we pull forwards and head for the car park entrance. Still nothing… no reaction whatsoever. Can she have removed the pin when she got in?

We reach the entrance and Madam looks for the sign that will point us towards Llandrindod Wells and with a grunt of satisfaction she spots it. She is about to turn us north when she lets out an almighty yelp, slams on my brakes and leaps out. Mister Thompson is quite taken aback and The Nice Mister Arthur nearly drives into my rear end. I was expecting this, but I don't understand why it has taken Her Ladyship quite so long to feel it. The others following all stop and get out to watch Her Ladyship doing what might be very loosely described as a Tarantella.

A peal of childish laughter emanates from behind some trees and Her Ladyship, collecting herself, spins around to see where the laughter is coming from.

'You little toads. How dare you? You could have caused an accident!' The children scatter and Her Ladyship starts to calm down, but continues rubbing her bottom. The Nice Mister Arthur enquires of Her Ladyship's condition.

I'm alright now. The little devils had stuck a drawing pin to my seat. It doesn't half hurt, but I'll be fine. Let's get a move on.

'Little swine,' she says to our new passenger. 'Not funny, not funny at all.' Mister Thompson grunts softly in agreement.

'Here we go and let's hope the snow doesn't get any worse than this.' I couldn't agree more. At my time of life, I shouldn't be doing snow. Her Ladyship swings me out onto the road. The others follow and as we climb out of Builth Wells the snow gets worse.

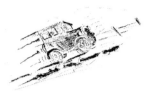

Half an hour passes and we are now ploughing through a heavy snow storm. I am covered in the stuff and Her Ladyship has switched on my headlights and windscreen wiper. A fat lot of good that's achieved as there's a two inch covering of snow on each lamp and there is only a very small section of my windscreen cleared as the wiper, nearly in vain, manages to slowly manoeuvre itself to and fro to maintain a triangular peephole. Her Ladyship is leaning forwards, squinting through the peephole looking for the road. Our passenger seems to have gone very quiet.

Eventually she spots a sign indicating that we are approaching a parking area. 'I'm going to pull in here to clear the screen,' she says to our passenger. 'Ah, there it is.' She yanks my steering wheel over and we swing into the parking area, whacking my nearside wheel into a deep pothole which had been hidden by the snow.

'Shit!' Her Ladyship exclaims and then, remembering that she has an elderly passenger, 'I'm so sorry for the language but that caught me unawares.' We slow gently to a standstill.

'Don't worry,' says The Quiet Mister Thompson. 'I've heard worse expletives than that in my time.' The others all pull in behind with minor snowdrifts collected on their windscreens too. Some of them don't have working windscreen wipers at all so I dread to think how their drivers were able to see.

'I'd better get out and clear our screen. You stay in the car, it's very cold out.' Her Ladyship clambers out and cleans my windscreen and lights.

'Had to stop,' she shouts to the others. 'I couldn't see a thing. I didn't half whack my wheels when I pulled in. Blooming pothole.'

The Nice Mister Arthur takes a look at my front end.

'Looks okay to me.' He wobbles both of my front wheels. 'No, they're fine. We'd better get a move on. We don't know how far this snow stretches north, or if it's settled.'

'Thank goodness for that,' she says. 'I didn't fancy sitting here to wait for the rescue service. Anyway, I'll drop my passenger off in Welshpool and see you guys later.' Her Ladyship gets back in, starts me up and rolls anxiously forwards, peering back along the road to see if anyone is coming.

'Can't see a blooming thing,' she says to The Quiet Mister Thompson, who doesn't reply. 'Oh well, here goes.' She pulls us back onto the road and we head north again.

Twenty tense minutes pass and the snow starts to ease up. 'That's better. It looks as though we'll have a clear road to Welshpool now.' Her Ladyship decides to engage Mister Thompson in conversation. 'So tell me, when did you have your little Austin?' Mister Thompson lets out a deep sigh.

'Whoops, sorry, I didn't realise you'd dozed off. We'll soon get you home.' Her Ladyship decides that perhaps silence is the best option for a change.

The snow has completely cleared by the time we arrive in Welshpool. Even the sun is trying to poke its face out from behind a cloud.

'Here we are then. Now where do I need to drop you off?'

Silence.

'Hello, Mister Thompson? We're here now... back in Welshpool. Can you tell me where to go?'

More silence. Her Ladyship nudges The Quiet Mister Thompson's arm. He slumps forwards against my windscreen. The colour fades from Her Ladyship's face.

'Oh my God. He's dead. This is all I need.' That comment was rather thoughtless, I felt. No concern for our passenger. She pulls us over to the side of the road and nudges him again.

'Oh shit, damn, bloody, bugger, cuss, we've killed him, Old Girl.' Don't try to blame me, Your Ladyship, I didn't invite him along. Her Ladyship gets out and the others drive past, hooting their horns and waving. Her Ladyship starts to run after them waving back.

'No, stop, stop, stop! My passenger has kicked the bucket... he's dead! Come back!' My relatives disappear into the distance. 'Now what are we going to do, Old Girl?' Don't ask me, I am merely a pawn on the chessboard of this trip and, if you remember, you did tell the others to carry on after Welshpool and that you'd catch them up this evening.

Her Ladyship peers at my passenger again, possibly hoping that she has been dreaming and Mister Thompson isn't dead after all. She gives him another nudge. There's still no response. She looks around to see if she can flag down some help and sees a sign indicating that a hospital is nearby. She quickly gets back into my driving seat and rolls her rear end around. Obviously the effect of the drawing pin is still causing discomfort.

'Hospital sign... over there. And it's got an A&E. Come on, Old Girl, let's take him there. They can deal with him. I just hope we don't have to hang around to talk to the police. That will really put the kybosh on our trip today.' We drive off, following the signs to the hospital. Madam swings me into the ambulance parking area.

'Oi, you can't park there. Can't you read? Ambulances only.' The newcomer taps vigorously at the sign. The car park's over there.

'But I need help. My passenger has dropped dead. I need help.

I don't want to drive to Scotland with a dead body sitting next to me. He'll get smelly after a few days.' By now more people have wandered out of the Accident and Emergency door to see what is going on. 'Oh, can you help me? I think my passenger's dead. I gave him a lift from Builth and about half way here, just after the snow, he didn't speak to me anymore. He's quite old and this car doesn't have a heater. Has he frozen to death?'

'Don't worry. We'll take over now. Is that dog dangerous? What's his name?'

'Oscar... why do you want to know the dog's name?'

'Not the dog. What's the man's name?'

'Oh, Archibald, Archibald Thompson. Is he dead?'

By now, The Asthmatic Barking Dog has woken up. He's absolutely fascinated by the attention our passenger is getting. A trolley arrives and the medical people start to ease Mister Thompson out of his seat and put him on the trolley. Her Ladyship is pacing up and down and occasionally rubbing her backside.

'Hello Archibald, Archibald, can you hear me? Has anyone checked his pulse? Are we certain he's dead?' The man who spoke feels Mister Thompson's neck. 'There's a weak one. Come on, let's get him inside.' The medical people disappear through some doors with Mister Thompson.

'I said... you can't park here.' It was the man who confronted us when we arrived.

'What? Oh... I'm sorry. I am so, so sorry.' Oh dear, Her Ladyship is angry now and sarcasm is becoming evident. She walks over to the man, who is about five inches shorter than her, and she looks down at him.

'I am so, so sorry. I've only had what I thought was a man dying in my car for the last twenty miles and for all I know it may still end up with him dying and I am only doing what any good citizen would do by delivering the said dead or not so dead body to a hospital.

And,' she leans even closer to him. What a shame she had garlic bread with her lunch. The little man winces. 'And all you can bloody do is tap at a sign and tell me I can't park here. Well, I have news for you, you Little Hitler. I am bloody well going to leave this car here while I go in through that door there and find out how that man is.' At that she spins on her heel and heads inside. Do you know, there are the odd occasions when I rather admire this woman.

It's dusk when we pull into our overnight stop close to Nantwich. The others all come out to meet us.

'What the hell happened to you? It doesn't take three hours to drop someone off at their home. Did you pull in the end?' The Nice Mister Arthur looks knowingly at Her Ladyship.

'Of course not. He's an octogenarian. Even so, you'll never believe what happened during those three hours.' Her Ladyship starts to remove the straps that hold her suitcase to my luggage rack. She stops to rub her bottom. 'Well, you know when I pulled over and you all drove past?'

'Yes, you waved at us.'

'I didn't wave at you, I was trying to stop you. My passenger had slumped in his seat. I thought he was dead. I tried to wave you down. What could I do? Anyway I found the local hospital and delivered him to the A&E department. Then I had this row with a security man.'

'What happened to the man?'

'Well, he was shorter than me and I was able to intimidate him... officious little devil.'

'Not him, what happened to the man who was dead?'

'Don't be obtuse. The man who I thought was dead wasn't actually dead. As it turned out he was in a diabetic coma.'

'So what happened then?'

'Well this blooming Little Hitler…'

'No, not him. What happened to the man who you thought was dead but wasn't?'

'Oh, him. They managed to bring him round with a glucose injection. They told me if I'd been much longer getting him to the hospital, he might have died. Then something happened which seemed really odd.

'What was that then?'

'You remember when I sat on that drawing pin the kids had stuck to my seat at Builth Wells?' Everyone nods. They must be wondering where on earth Her Ladyship's ravings are going now.

'Well, I was still suffering the discomfort from that drawing pin and had been rubbing my backside, I suppose rather too much. They asked me if I was alright. I told them that I was fine, and that I'd just had a little prick in my bottom. Then they all started laughing, one of them so much that she nearly fell over and had to grab a colleague for support. And then one man, I think he was a doctor, commented that I shouldn't be doing things like that at my age. I mean, what's so funny about that? Now you're all laughing as well. Will you please tell me what is so funny?'

Chapter Three

Duncan merely gives a wave, tosses his bag over his shoulder and wanders off. I'd like to say he's singing "I belong to Glasgow", but I think he's just chuckling to himself.

Nantwich to ~~Stonehouse~~ Helensburgh

'Good Morning, Old Girl. Sleep well? Morning Dog. Let's get you out to stretch your legs.' Her Ladyship is bright and breezy. She must have slept well in her comfortable farmhouse B&B. Not me, I spent the night in a biting north easterly wind being stared at by a cow chewing the cud barely two feet in front of my radiator and The Asthmatic Barking Dog snoring away on my back seat. Imagine the noise, scrunching in front and zizzing behind, occasionally interrupted by either a gulp followed by a smacking of lips or a deep rumble followed by a breaking of wind. I mean, how could I sleep through all that?

'Had a fabulous breakfast, Old Girl. A really comfy bed as well.' She slips the lead over The Asthmatic Barking Dog's head so that he can hop out and do his morning's business, but this time he's distracted by all the new smells. She hooks the extendable lead onto my wing mirror and tidies my rear seat and the bed on which The Asthmatic Barking Dog had been sleeping.

'You're a typical bloke Dog, aren't you? Only a bloke would leave his bed in this mess.' The Asthmatic Barking Dog gives Her Ladyship a look that says "What? What d'ya want now?"

'Come on, time for your breakfast.' Her Ladyship puts his two bowls down and the look changes to "Food! Gimme, gimmee, gimmee!" Into the first she empties a tin of dog meat and goes to pour in some biscuits. But she doesn't get a chance. He's dived in and is tucking in so voraciously you'd think he hadn't eaten for weeks. She shrugs her shoulders and puts away the biscuits, and then fills his water bowl, which he ignores until he's cleared the contents of the first bowl.

'I'll give you a proper walk when we have our coffee stop.' Moments later he's eaten, done his business and is back on my rear seat settling down for another snooze. Her Ladyship gets into my driving seat and takes some notes.

'Golly gosh, Old Girl, we did over two hundred miles yesterday. Not bad eh? We've got to do that again today, and by lunchtime we should be in Scotland. Apparently, it's also possible that we may see the Olympic torch. It's supposed to be crossing the Scottish border at about the same time as us. That's exciting isn't it?'

Well actually no. Why would I be excited by a bunch of people in what look like shell suits carrying a flaming torch?

The others have come out by now and are loading up their luggage. They had originally planned to camp in the farmer's field but had changed their minds after experiencing the cold winds. As a result, all were full of bonhomie after a good and hearty breakfast.

'What route are we taking today then?' The Nice Mister Arthur wanders over to see how Her Ladyship is getting on.

'It's rather a lot of motorway, I'm afraid,' replies Her Ladyship. 'All the way up the M6, then the M74. We're stopping just short of Glasgow, some place called Stonehouse. It's another farmhouse and they have a field you can camp in. The forecast is better for today and tonight. They say it should get quite warm now. Who knows, I might take the Old Girl's hood down later on. I thought we'd stop for lunch at a motorway services. Is that okay with you?'

'Yes. Let's get as many miles done as we can. But remember,' The Nice Mister Arthur wags his finger at Her Ladyship. 'Whatever you do, do not, I repeat, do not go into Glasgow. If you do, you'll get swallowed up by their road system and find yourself driving out the other side before you know it. Okay?' Her Ladyship looks almost offended.

'You think I'm incapable of navigating myself to our next stop off, don't you?'

'I happen to think of the time you led us all up the garden path and down again when we went to Santiago de Compostela and then…'

'Oh that time,' she interrupts him. 'Well I think that's a bit unfair. I'd just put the wrong settings into the Satellite Thingy and it didn't want to take us on a motorway. You can hardly blame me for that little delay caused by scattering numerous chickens as we crossed a plethora of farm yards.'

'That little delay lasted five hours actually and it was dark when we reached our destination. All for avoiding a one mile stretch of motorway.'

'Yes, well. Anyway, I've got it sorted now. I've decided that today we'll manage without the Satellite Thingy. We'll be fine, I'm sure.' There was a degree of doubt in Her Ladyship's voice.

'Well, as long as you understand that we won't be coming after you if you get lost on this bit of the journey. Shall we go then?' He turns and heads back to his car.

'Come on, Old Girl, let's be off.' She starts me up, we pull out of the farmyard and head north towards the M6.

I'm very impressed at the progress we've made. We are just a few miles short of the Scottish border now. We had a little break for coffee after three hours of driving. Her Ladyship needed some caffeine, The Asthmatic Barking Dog needed his walk and I needed a little rest. But I have to say that I am feeling good. I don't know what The Nice Doctor John did to my engine, but gosh every move seems so easy.

'Are we all ready for the off then?' The Nice Mister Arthur looked enquiringly at everyone, hoping that they were all ready. But as his eyes turned towards Her Ladyship, he knew he'd be disappointed.

'I'll catch you up. I need the loo.' As soon as the others were gone she turned to me. 'Let's give them a couple of minutes, Old Girl, and we'll not only catch them up with your new engine, we'll pass them. What do you think of that then?'

What could I think? She just wanted to show off, again. We caught the others up, quite easily actually, and Her Ladyship delighted in passing them one by one, waving regally with no regard for the long queue of vehicles stuck behind us as we crept past them all at 45 miles an hour. My engine may have given me a new lease of life, but my gears are still the same and as Her Ladyship would say, 'Scotland is uphill, Old Girl,' so we aren't really going any faster than before. It's just easier to get there.

So here I am now, sitting in the warm sunshine, while Her Ladyship is enjoying her lunch. I should be enjoying the peace and quiet, but I know that it won't last long. I'm right. Here she comes.

'Hello, Old Girl. Miss me?'

No, actually, I have been enjoying the view, but all good things must come to an end. Her Ladyship flips open my bonnet and checks my engine.

'Oh, look at that, Old Girl! Still spotless. No oil leaking anywhere. Let's see now, let's check your levels.' She plunges her hand in to my nether regions and withdraws my dipstick.

'Perfect, still full. Now your water.' She unscrews my radiator cap.

'Hmmm, you need a drop of that.' She replenishes it as The Nice Mister Arthur strolls over.

'Everything all right? Silly question really, judging by the way you raced past us back there.' There was a hint of sarcasm in his voice. 'How's that fan assembly now?'

'Dead quiet, I think we've sorted it.' Her Ladyship closes my bonnet.

'That's good. Now don't forget what I said this morning. Whatever you do, don't get yourself drawn into Glasgow. We need to get off the motorway at Stonehouse and give Glasgow a wide berth. Okay?'

'Yes, I'm fine with that, turn off at Stonehouse. Let's go then. You take the lead for a while, I'll plonk myself in at your rear.' She climbs into my driver's seat, wiggles her bottom and smiles happily. No drawing pins this time and it seems that her bottom is better. I allow my engine to burst into life.

'Isn't it a glorious day, Old Girl? It's lovely and warm. Tell you what, let's take your hood down.' Her Ladyship gets out, removes my side screens, folds my hood back and tucks it away. As she is doing this we are approached by a tall, rather lanky apparition with a bony face. He is quite young, wearing a roll-neck sweater of no particular colour, a kilt and a pair of long woollen socks inside some warm walking boots. Between the top of the socks and the bottom of the kilt I spy a pair of knock knees with rather a lot of hair growing out of them. He has a ragged rucksack with a faded 'Ban the Bomb' sign painted on it. I might be wrong, but this might be a native of Scotland.

'Ah dornt suppose ye ur plannin' tae cross th' border intae Scootlund ur ye?' Her Ladyship turns towards the newcomer and looks him up and down with a degree of distaste.

'I beg your pardon?'

'I said, ah dornt suppose you're plannin' tae cross the border intae Scootlund ur ye?' Her Ladyship looks bewildered.

'I'm sorry, but – Do – You – Speak – English?' The newcomer bristles.

'Ay coorse I speak English, hen. Scootlund,' he points up the motorway. 'Scootlund, are ye headin' to Scootlund?'

'Oh Scotland, why didn't you say so in the first place? Yes, I'm going to Scotland. Indeed all the way to John O'Groats, why do you ask?'

'Och stoatin. Would ye be guid enough tae gi' us a lift then?' Her Ladyship stares at him while she tries to tune in to what he is saying. A smile indicates that she has understood, well she assumes she has understood.

'You want a lift over the border to Scotland?' The newcomer nods. 'Ah, I understand now, of – course – you – can – have – a – lift – over – the – border.' She speaks this very slowly. It reminds me of when we were in Spain and she insisted on speaking very slowly and succinctly to anyone she met with a foreign accent.

'That's kind o' ye, hen.' He opens the passenger door and swings his rucksack in onto my rear seat. The Asthmatic Barking Dog lets out a yelp, not happy about the sudden jolt out of his slumbers. 'Whoaps, sorry Dug.' He pulls the bag back out, obviously fearing that The Asthmatic Barking Dog might decide to make a meal of its contents. He climbs into the seat and stuffs the bag firmly into my footwell.

'Right, let's go then. You aren't going to be cold are you? It's a bit breezy in this car with the hood down.' Her Ladyship, glancing at a pair of hairy knees, engages my second gear. Going into first would have taken her hand dangerously close to those knees. We head off down the slip road to join the motorway north. She keeps glancing back at the hairy items perched between kilt and socks as the swirling air in my driving compartment flicks the hem up and down. She is so blooming obvious. I know what she's hoping. Our new hitchhiker pushes his hands forward to hold his kilt down and protect his vanity. Madam, though, just can't take her eyes off those knees.

'Are you sure you're alright?'

'Och aye. I'm fine, dinnee worry hen. A wee draught won't do me any harm. And afore ye ask, the answer is nae. It's all in perfect workin' order.'

'I don't know what you mean. What's in working order?'

The Scotsman looks at her quizzically.

'I'm sorry but ye Sassenachs always ask th' sam question ta a man in a kilt. "Is there anything worn under you kilt" an' I answer "Nay it's all in perfect workin' order." Mah nam is Duncan by the way.'

'How do you do, Duncan, I'm pleased to meet you. I think you're the first Scotsman to have ridden in this old girl since I got her. Mind you this is all a first for me. I've never been to Scotland before. I'm only in your country for a few days before I head back down on the other side of this road, heading for Cornwall.'

'Och, the old John O'Groats to Land's End run is it, hen?' Madam nods.

'Yes indeed. Mind you, that's if we make it. Where are you from then?

'Och I'm from Glasgae, Dennistoun actually. I's a stoatin place.'

'I'm sure it is.' There is a sincere doubt in Her Ladyship's voice. I think because she hasn't a clue what stoatin means. Mind you, I don't either.

'I'm not going quite as far as Glasgow actually, not today. I'm planning on staying at a place near Stonehouse. But I can drop you off somewhere convenient I'm sure. Oh look, that looks like the border.'

'Och it is, hen. Nearly home then. We'll soon be breathin' braw Scottish air. 'An not that mingin stuff I've had to breathe in Englain.'

'Yes, well.' Her Ladyship has obviously chosen not to go down that conversational route, and changes the subject.

'Tell me then, what do I need to do to ensure a safe trip through Scotland? I haven't brought my passport.'

Duncan ponders this question very carefully and a light flickers in his eyes.

'Ye need a haggis, hen. It's better than a passport. It'll gie ye anywhaur an' it has lots ay uses.' Her Ladyship glances at him. She doesn't believe him. I don't believe him either, but I bet she'll buy one in the end. Just to be certain.

'You're pulling my leg, aren't you?' Duncan sits expressionless staring at the approaching Scottish border. He says nothing.

'You are not pulling my leg. Are you really serious? Are you suggesting that if I get hold of a haggis it will be my passport through Scotland as I head to John O'Groats and back down over this border?'

'That's reit, hen, it'll be yer perfect Scottish accessory, and it'll be yer perfect passport fur a smooth trip.' He looks at Her Ladyship and there is still a significant degree of doubt in her posture. 'Look, hen, it's nae jist fur eatin', it has lots of uses. A pillaw tae sleep on, a wedge tae hold somethin' in place, a weapon. Look, in th' early days, in naval exercises aroond Nelson's time, th' haggis was used in place ay th' canon ball in order tae test th' accuracy of th' gunners without inflicting damage tae ships or personnel. A weel placed shot could also benefit th' receivin' ship wi' an extra scran ur two; particularly if caught whole by a crew member. However, a shot fired through riggin' took a while tae clear up an' presented a slippery hazard when spreid ower a wet deck.'

'I haven't a clue what you are talking about. But you are serious, aren't you? You're saying that if I get hold of a haggis it really will ease my path through Scotland?' She still seems doubtful. 'But before I drop you off, perhaps you would be kind enough to direct me to a suitable purveyor of this gastronomic delicacy.'

'Ah ken jist th' place, hen. An' ye'll not need tae drive intae Glasgee to get it.'

'No, let's not drive anywhere near Glasgow. I've been told that getting onto the Glasgow roads is a nightmare and I would get lost.'

'Ye'll be fine, hen, promise.'

Our friend Duncan is apparently half asleep as we approach the turn off for Stonehouse. Her Ladyship starts to swing me up the slip road when he wakes up.

'Nae, hen, not here, yee nid to go a bit further up th' motorway.'

'But I have to turn off here. The Sat-Nav says it leads to where I'm staying.'

'Turn that thing off, I ken where we're goin'. It's nae far, hen, it'll only be abit twenty minutes out yer way.'

'As long as you're sure.' Her Ladyship hesitates, then turns off the Sat-Nav Thingy. She turns me back onto the motorway again.

As we progress closer to Glasgow, the traffic starts to build up as more roads start to join the motorway.

'How far now?' Her Ladyship is becoming prickly. Her irritation exacerbated by the anxiety that she is on a road that she shouldn't be on, and she is getting worried.

'Next junction, hen, it's just up there.' Her Ladyship lets out a long breath of relief. The Asthmatic Barking Dog is eagerly poking his head over the side hoping that we are going to stop soon. We reach the junction and she swings me up the slip road.

'When you get to the roondaboot, hen, tak' a left an' then follow th' road.' Her Ladyship obeys and we find ourselves driving through what looks remarkably like Glasgow suburbs. The truth of the matter slowly dawns on Her Ladyship.

'This is Glasgow isn't it? I told you I didn't want to go into Glasgow. How on earth am I going to find Stonehouse?'

'Och donna worry hen. Ye jist go back th' way ye came after ye've dropped me off. Now turn reit at those lights, than tak' a first left an' we'll be thaur.'

Her Ladyship follows his instructions and we eventually pull up in a rather tired looking street. Duncan grabs his bag and hops out.

'Thank ye, hen. You're very kin'. I'll be off noo.'

'But, but… I thought you were taking me to a place where I could buy a haggis.' Oh dear. She is not a happy bunny.

'Och aye, ye'll get one at that corner shop ower thaur. Cheerio th' noo.'

Oh dear, here we go. Five, four, three, two, one…'

'WHAT? What the hell? You've brought me all the way into Glasgow when I could have picked up one of these blooming things from a corner shop? I don't bloody believe it.'

Duncan merely gives a wave, tosses his bag over his shoulder and wanders off. I'd like to say he's singing "I belong to Glasgow", but I think he's just chuckling to himself. Her Ladyship harrumphs and pulls me forward to park by the door of the corner shop.

'Flipping con-man.' She gets out and grabs her bag. 'Won't be a minute Dog. I've got to get one of these haggises now. I'll get you an extra-nice tin of dog food for your supper as well. At least you didn't wind me up.' She heads into the shop and moments later returns with a tin of dog food and something that looks like a very large and very fat sausage.

'Right, Old Girl and Dog, this is a haggis. And the nice man in the shop told me that I could have bought one anywhere. C'mon, Dog. You look like you need a pee.' The Asthmatic Barking Dog hops out as soon as Her Ladyship has slipped on his lead and lifts his leg. He must have been bursting. He hops back in. Her Ladyship clambers in and settles herself as well.

'Let's fire up the Sat-Nav and find a way to Stonehouse.' She starts me up and we head off up the street.

'Ah, there's a junction right ahead and a sign to the M8 motorway. Thank heavens for that. We'll be back in Stonehouse before you can say Blue Moon, Old Girl.'

Blue – Moon – Old – Girl? Nope! We're still in Glasgow.

We've been going for nearly an hour and I've lost count of the number of times Her Ladyship has taken a turning. But we are now on a motorway. I'm a bit worried, because the sun is getting lower in the sky and we are driving towards it. So while we may be on a motorway, I have a funny feeling that it's either the wrong motorway or we are going down the right motorway, but in the wrong direction. We are not using the satellite Thingy. It threw a wobbly in the outskirts of Glasgow, something about us being in Marseilles. But hey ho, Her Ladyship seems confident that we are still heading in the right direction. The Asthmatic Barking Dog is fast asleep.

'I'm surprised we haven't found the turn off yet, Old Girl. Ah, there's a sign to Dumbarton, I'm sure we're going the right way.'

Oh dear, after the pride comes the fall. Her Ladyship starts to slow down, never a good idea on a motorway.

'Or is it? I think I'll pull over and check the map.' She swings me onto the hard shoulder and hauls out her map. But The Asthmatic Barking Dog has other ideas. He wants to take a walk.

'Hang on, Dog. I'll put your lead on.' Her Ladyship gets out, attaches the lead to his collar and both stroll off up the hard shoulder, the dog taking a lot of sniffs at this new country. It's rather obvious that he doesn't much approve of the place, because he's lifting his leg at every opportunity. Now bored with this little leg stretch, Her Ladyship turns back towards me and The Asthmatic Barking Dog reluctantly follows.

'There we are Dog. Get in.'

A car pulls up behind us. One of those ones with flashing blue lights on top. Here we go again. A rather large policeman gets out of the car, puts his hat on and approaches us.

'Good afternoon, Madam, are we having a problem?' He has the Scottish accent, but he is much easier to understand than Duncan. The Asthmatic Barking Dog emits a long, low, deep growl. He really does have a thing about men in uniform. Postmen are his favourite.

'We, as you say Constable, are not having a problem. I, however, am having a problem. I've been led astray by one of your countrymen, a man who dumped me in the middle of Glasgow when I wanted to go to my B&B in Stonehouse. And now I am lost, having just passed a sign that said Dumbarton.'

'You've stopped on the hard shoulder, Madam.'

Her Ladyship turns slightly to observe the traffic charging in both directions on the motorway. Why do I get the feeling that she's in one of her sarcastic moods?

'So?'

'You are only supposed to stop on the hard shoulder in an emergency. Failure to observe this could result in a one hundred pound fine.'

Oh dear he's pulling out his little note book.

'You don't understand, Officer. This is an emergency. I've been led astray by one of your fellow countrymen and now I am lost.' Her Ladyship lets out a pathetic sigh. The policeman shows not the slightest sign of concern. He opens the notebook and licks the tip of his pencil. Why is it that policemen always lick the tips of their pencils? I mean, the germs. I have noticed that The Asthmatic

Barking Dog licks the tip of his thingy, but at least that isn't as unhygienic as a pencil. Well I don't think it is.

'Can you describe him, Madam?'

'Oh yes, I can. He was about five feet ten inches, I'd say in his twenties. He wore a kilt, he had a beard, auburn coloured hair and hairy knees.'

'Hmm, well that's whittled down the number of potential suspects to about two million. Can you tell me anything more about him?'

'Oh yes, he told me that there was nothing worn under his kilt. And it was all in working order. Oh yes, his name was Duncan.'

'That brings it to about a million then. Where is he now?'

'I dropped him off in Glasgow about an hour ago.' The policeman seems bewildered, it's as though nothing that Madam has said has helped him one little bit. He tries another question.

'Was that before or after he led you astray?'

'After of course, I wouldn't have been in Glasgow would I? I would have been in Stonehouse, parked up and having a rest.' A spark of understanding passes the police officer's face.

'Let me get this correct now. He didn't actually take advantage of you, bu… '

Her Ladyship interrupts.

'Yes, he did take advantage of me. He made me drive him into Glasgow when I wanted to go to Stonehouse, to my B&B.'

'Please don't interrupt me. He didn't assault you in any way. His leading you astray was simply because, one way or another, he persuaded you to drive him into Glasgow. And now you are here on the M8 hard shoulder because you are lost.'

'Yes, that's what I said.'

The policeman lets out a long slow breath, closes his notebook and puts it back in his pocket.

'Okay,' he looks at his watch. 'Stonehouse is rather a long way and I wouldn't encourage you to go all that way back. You'll hit the

Glasgow rush hour. That's not a good idea. Come off at junction thirty and take the A82 to Dumbarton. You'll find somewhere nice to stay near Helensburgh. It's only about twenty five miles and whatever you do, don't turn off that road until you find the turning for Helensburgh. Looking at this old jalopy...' Old Jalopy indeed. I am beginning to go off this man. '...am I right in assuming that you're heading for John O'Groats?'

'That's right. How did you know that? I hope to get there the day after tomorrow.'

The policeman smiles slightly. 'I know, Madam, because earlier today I pulled over another old car like this and they were heading to John O'Groats as well. All I can say is good luck. I hope you both make it.

He turns to go but as Her Ladyship clambers back into my driving seat, he turns back. 'Oh by the way, next time you get lost and stop on the hard shoulder, don't use the opportunity to take your dog for a walk. Good afternoon, Madam.'

Her Ladyship's face goes bright pink and her mobile phone starts to ring. She gropes around looking for it.

'Are you going to answer that, Madam?'

'Yes, I am. Is there anything wrong with doing that?'

'You can only use a mobile telephone in a car if it is stationary, with the engine switched off and the keys out of the ignition. Unless I am very much mistaken, your key is still located in the ignition.' Her Ladyship pulls the key out.

'Is that alright, Constable, may I answer my phone now?' The policeman doesn't answer, he just shrugs his shoulders, turns on his heel and gets back in his car. Her Ladyship is well and truly "banged to rights" I think. She finds her phone.

'Hello? Who's that? What? A free holiday if I dial oh nine. What? Who's there? Answer me, hello? Press what? Speak to me. Hello?' She hangs up. 'God knows what that was all about.'

The phone rings again.

'Hello? Now look, if you are calling me again about a free holiday… what? You're already there. Where's there? Oh you're in Stonehouse? Already? Me? I haven't a clue where I am. Actually Arthur, that's not true. I'm on a motorway, heading towards Dumbarton I think he said, heading west and if I'm very much mistaken you are to my east. What? What did you say? No, I'm on the other side of Glasgow. What? Yes, that's right, Glasgow. I was led astray by a mad Scotsman, and then nearly arrested by a not so mad Scottish policeman, but I have got my haggis now, so all will be well. I said haggis. Well the mad Scotsman said I had to carry a haggis as it would ease my path through Scotland. I can't imagine why a haggis will make my life easier. Umm no. I think I'll find somewhere along here to stay the night. It's too far to go back to Stonehouse and it will be dark by the time I get there. I'll catch up with you in Inverness tomorrow, via Fort William. Yes, that's right. Will you give my apologies to the B&B? Byzee bye.'

She clicks the phone off.

'Come on, Old Girl, let's get going to Helensburgh then. I'm whacked and Dog is as well. We'll work out a new route to Inverness tomorrow morning.' She starts me up and taps the screen of the Sat-Nav thingy.

'Oh great, guess what Old Girl. We're still in Marseilles. I'm fed up with this blooming thing. It would be easier to navigate using the stars. Right, it's exit time for you!' She rips the Thingy off my windscreen, and flings it out into the grass.

We roll back onto the road and continue our journey westward.

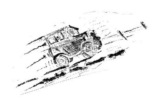

It hasn't taken us long to find the road to Helensburgh. Her Ladyship seems positively relieved and she soon spots a house offering bed and breakfast. We pull up. Her Ladyship gets out and knocks on the door. A little old lady answers.

'Hello, can I help you?'

'Yes, I do hope so, do you have a room for the night? I'm afraid we got rather lost looking for Stonehouse and now we're here on the wrong side of Glasgow. I was led astray by…' Her Ladyship stops, obviously deciding that it really isn't worth going on about being led astray by one of her countrymen.

'Och, I'm sorry my dear, we're fully booked up for tonight. I cannot help you I'm afraid.' Her Ladyship is taken aback. She thought that finding a bed and breakfast would be the easiest thing to achieve after getting out of Glasgow.

'Oh dear. Umm well, can you recommend somewhere else I might get to stay?'

'Och, bless you, hen. You won't find anywhere round here to stay, not tonight. The torch is coming through tomorrow morning and every room in the area has been booked for weeks.'

'Torch? What, the Olympic torch?'

'Yes, hen, the Olympic torch. It's passing through tomorrow morning. We've been booked up for weeks.'

Her Ladyship is not pleased.

'What? Are you telling me that just because a flame, a torch and an entourage of hangers-on are coming through here, every room in the place is booked up?'

'Aye, hen. It's terribly exciting, isn't it?'

Somehow I fear that Her Ladyship doesn't agree. 'Och, is that your car then?'

'Yes it is. We're on our way to John O'Groats to take part in a run to Land's End.' The little old lady walks out to take a closer look at me.

'In this old thing? You're driving all that way? In this?'

'Yes we are. I'm very tired and hungry and desperate to find a place where I can have some supper and get to bed. I have a very long drive to Inverness tomorrow.'

'I'm so sorry, hen,' she reaches in to stroke The Asthmatic Barking Dog, who enjoys this attention, and she notices some of the camping kit. 'Is that a tent I can see, hen?'

'Yes it is. Why?'

'Och, you're very welcome to camp in the field just there. Indeed I'd be very happy to do you some supper and a breakfast. Would that help?'

In Her Ladyship's case, camping for a night is one of the last things she'd want to contemplate. She'd only packed the tent for a dire emergency and I have a feeling that it is dawning on her that this is such an emergency.

'Umm, yes, actually, thank you. Yes, thank you very much. Can I park and set up just over there?'

'Aye, that'll be fine. When you've done, come on in and I'll do you some supper. It's the least we can do. Anyway, my husband Hamilton would love to talk to you about th' car and th' trip you are doing. Ye can bring yon dog in with you as well. We canna leave him out in th' cold.'

'That's very kind of you. I'll join you in about half an hour.' Her Ladyship gets in, starts me up and moves me the few yards to where the little old lady had indicated. She gets her camping equipment out and starts to put up the tent.

'I hope I can remember how to put this thing up, Old Girl. It shouldn't take long. You stay there Dog, while I do this.'

Her Ladyship starts to put the tent up, and realising that there are some bits left over, she starts to pull it down again.

'Where do these bits go then? Where are the destructions?' She finds a large piece of paper with drawings on it. 'Oh, so that's how it's done.'

She tries again and this time there are no bits left over. She pumps up the inflatable bed and shoves it into the tent along with all the bits and bobs she feels are essential for camping. Finally.

'And here we are, Old Girl. This is more important than the bed, actually, my brand spanking new portable toilet.' The Asthmatic Barking Dog and I watch with interest as she pulls what looks like a fold-up fishing stool out of a box, the only difference being that it has a white lavatory seat fitted to it.

'Right, we need to fit this plastic bag in here and clip it in place. There we are, all done. The most compact portable toilet on the market.' Madam proudly places her new acquisition into the tent. 'No more squatting out in the cold, Old Girl. Now Dog, it's time you went for a little walk before we go in for supper.'

They wander off towards the road with The Asthmatic Barking Dog's nose hovering barely an inch from the ground.

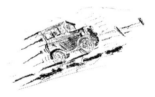

Several hours have passed and Her Ladyship totters out of the house with The Asthmatic Barking Dog in tow. She seems very happy. Mind you, so is the man who is coming out with her. He must be the old lady's husband, Hamilton.

'Thank you so, so much. That wasz a really lovely supper, and what wasz I thinking about? Oh yes, tha' whiskey was really, really nishe. I think I might be a bit tiddly.

'Aye, hen, it's a good one. Now will you be all right? Do you need a torch?'

'No Ham, Hamm, Hamil, Hamilton, itsh'll, I mean I'll be fine I have all the mod conzz I need. Even a lava, lava, loo, I mean a toilet, a portable toilet. S'like an en suite room. D'you want to have a look?'

'Och no. Mebbee not. But I'd like to tak' a look at yur car. If I'm not mistaken, i's an Austin Seven is'ne?'

'Yes, she's called Misth... Misth Dai... Misth Daisy. We've been together for the last, ooh, shix, sheven, no, eight, eight years. We've been everywhere togeth, together.'

'Och she's very nice. I had one of these back in the nineteen sixties, when I was a student in Edinburgh. I played rugby for my college and we used to get six of us in to get to away matches.'

As soon as she hears the word rugby, Her Ladyship loses any interest she might have had in what Mr Hamilton has to say. She's standing beside my radiator, swaying gently in the breeze, anxious, I am thinking, to change her position from vertical to horizontal.

'Och aye, they were the days. We'd get tanked up on beer after the match and me' old Austin, I called her Malmuira, would stagger back to our digs. Och so much weight in her. She collapsed in the end... rear springs. I'll bid ye goodnight hen. Sleep well. Breakfast will be at eight.' He wanders back towards the house, while Her Ladyship endeavours to get unsteadily down onto all fours and crawl in to the tent. She turns to look at me.

'Good night Old Girl. Sshleep well. I know I will. In you get Dog, on your bed and don't you blooming shnore.'

It's a very strange sight watching the silhouette of Her Ladyship's form getting undressed, the image projected onto the side of the tent being made larger by the light from the torch which doesn't seem to stay where it should be, as the silhouette keeps disappearing, immediately followed by an unrepeatable word. There are several grunts and ouches before finally she clambers into her sleeping bag. She struggles with the zip.

'Bloody thing. It'sh not long enough. Why ijz it, that they think everyone ijz only five foot six in the camping world? Shtupid blooming thing.' The lamp goes out.

Five, maybe six seconds pass and the light goes on again, and, oh yes, there goes the zip.

'God it'sh cold. I need my jumper.' She struggles putting it on in the enclosed space and the silhouette endeavours to get itself back into the sleeping bag. The zip is pulled up again. Again not for long

'Oh blooming Henry, my jumper'sh all ruffled up now.' The zip opens once more and I am watching the silhouette bouncing up and down on the air bed. It settles down. Ziiiiiip.

'G'night Dog.' The torch goes out, followed by a series of grunts. Two minutes pass this time and it comes on again and an even more frustrated voice emerges from the gloom.

'Blasht it, pillow's too low now. I need something to raise my head. But what?' There is the sound of a scrabbling around, then the Ziiiiiiip.

'I know what I can use.' I see her silhouette making for the entrance. Then after a much longer Ziiiiiiiiiiiip, Madam emerges from the tent and clambers to her feet. She stretches and walks over to me.

Hello, Old Girl, shtill awake? You need your beau- beaut- beauty shleep you know. It'sh a long trip tomor- tomorr- tomorrow. Now where'sh that Haggish? Here it ish. Right perhaps now I'll get to shleep. She grabs her purchase of a few hours ago and totters back to her tent. Two brisk zipping sounds follow and the torch goes out. Sweet dreams, Your Ladyship.

I'm awoken a few hours later when the torch goes on again. The Asthmatic Barking Dog stops snoring, suggesting that Her Ladyship has woken him up.

'Sorry Dog. Need a pee.'

I'm intrigued. Ziiiip. The silhouette slowly rises from the horizontal and then swings its legs round suggesting that Madam is in a sitting position on the side of the inflatable bed.

'Right, you and I need to get acquainted.' I think she is addressing the portable toilet. One of Her Ladyship's problems is that she cannot stand upright in her tent, so I witness her stooped silhouette half crawl and half walk to the side.

'I think you need to come into the middle, I can't pee with my back stooped over.' I see a silhouette of the famous fishing stool as the gargantuan form of Her Ladyship lowers itself onto it. All she needs now is a fishing rod. There's the sound of running waters.

'Well, that's brill. No problem at all. Now where's the loo paper.' Madam's silhouette twists round in search of the roll. 'Ah.'

The silhouette twists back. There is a sudden CRACK, followed by a GLOOP! Oh dear, I think it's collapsed with Her Ladyship still sitting on it. The silhouette certainly suggests that she's now sitting on the ground and splashing around.

'Bloody useless thing. It's not supposed to do that. Oh blast it, there's pee everywhere.' I see the shadow of loo paper being whipped off its roll with amazing vigour as she endeavours to mop the area up. Eventually, after much movement, the tent entrance unzips and first the broken toilet, then lumps of soggy toilet paper and finally a damp towel fly out onto the grass. The tent zips up again and the silhouette manoeuvres itself back onto the air bed.

'Last time I bloody camp. Bloody useless toilet. Cost me fifteen pounds as well. What time is it?' The torch goes out.

Chapter Four

I think we'll park up here to enjoy the scenery and take a little rest Old Girl.
Isn't this view spectacular? I wonder if we'll see the Loch Ness Monster.

~~Stonehouse~~ Helensburgh to Inverness

Unsurprisingly, Her Ladyship was up bright and early. She'd had a bad night after that little accident with the portable toilet. I kept hearing mumbles of 'damned sharks,' 'fifteen bloody pounds,' 'blooming waste of money.' As she emerges from the tent she isn't in the best of moods. I don't even get the usual 'Good Morning, Old Girl, sleep well?' Instead I get a look and a harrumph and a 'Never again. Not in a million years.'

She grabs a clean towel and a change of clothes, walks across to the B&B and gingerly knocks on the door. The Asthmatic Barking Dog emerges at the entrance of the tent, observes Her Ladyship for a while and then wanders out to examine the bits and pieces that were cast out of the tent during the night. He sniffs them and then lifts his leg on them to add to the pungency that's already there. Then, after such a vigorous burst of exercise, he decides that's enough excitement for now and returns to the tent to turn in again. The little old lady appears at the door of the B&B.

'Och, hello my dear.' She steps a pace backwards as she notices the smell of stale pee that pervades Her Ladyship's environs. 'Oh my, did you have an accident?'

'Not exactly, but the blooming portable toilet collapsed on me and has splashed everywhere. I don't suppose I could have a shower before breakfast?'

'Of course you can my dear, there's a shower along the passage there. I think it's free. Mr Anderson was using it but I think he's out now.' She steps well out of the way to allow Her Ladyship to pass, then grabs an air freshener and follows Madam down the passage spraying it left, right and centre.

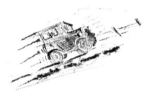

A very different and more ebullient Madam emerges after her shower and a hearty breakfast. She strolls over to me.

'Good Morning, Old Girl. Lovely breakfast again. I'm ready for the day now. But first I'm throwing all this stuff away, the loo and the tent. It all stinks and I don't want a smelly tent in tow. C'mon Dog. Out. Time for your walk and then some breakfast for you, I think.'

The Asthmatic Barking Dog emerges happily from the tent with his look that suggests he knows the meaning of the word breakfast. She slips his lead on and they walk off up the road together, The Asthmatic Barking Dog's nose firmly to the ground. They are not gone very long and as they return, Her Ladyship seems to be in a hurry.

'We'd better get going Old Girl, we've bumped into some people walking into town. They told me that the torch will be arriving soon and we certainly don't want to be held up by that. We could get stuck behind it for hours if we aren't careful.' She opens a tin of dog food. 'Get that down you, Dog, and hurry. I've got a map if we get stuck. That reminds me, I must recharge the Sat-nav. Ah, no, I forgot. We don't have the Sat-Nav anymore do we?'

No we don't, do we? You might remember that you lost your

temper with it yesterday when it told you we were in Marseilles again and it made a permanent exit from the car.

'Och, ye'll be on your way then?' It's Mr Hamilton, the gentleman who helped Her Ladyship back to her tent last night and, judging by his bright red nose, the same gentleman who plied his fine Scottish malt on her as well. Her Ladyship is irritated by this interruption.

'Yes we are. I want to get away before we're held up by the torch parade. We need to meet up with the others in Inverness tonight and it's a long way.'

'Which way are ye goin'?'

'I thought I'd head for Fort William and then carry on up the main road by Loch Linnhe, and follow that road all the way up past Loch Ness to Inverness. Who knows, we may even spot the monster.' Mr Hamilton raises an eyebrow, suggesting he is dealing with a Sassenach idiot.

'Yes well... if ye' follow the road in tae town ye'll get stuck behind yon parade. Where's yur map? I'll show ye' how ye' can miss 'em.' Her Ladyship pulls out the map.

'Now, ye' see that road there?' Her Ladyship nods. 'Well tak' that one before getting in tae town and simply follow it all the way to the main road there. Dinna tak any turning, just follow this road.' He hits the map with his forefinger to emphasise his point. 'But when ye get to the main road, ye must be very careful. It's a blind turn and ye canna' see the traffic coming from yur left or yur right.'

'Oh that seems to knock a few miles off the trip as well. I didn't see that one. Thank you very much. I'll go that way.'

'Are ye sure ye dinna want a dram afore ye go, hen?'

'That's very kind, but I think I'm going to need a clear head for this bit of the journey. Oh gosh, I nearly forgot. How much do I owe for the supper, camping and breakfast?'

'Och, ye needn't worry about that, hen,' Hamilton says with a broad grin. 'Yur company last night was payment enough.' Her

Ladyship looks bewildered. I have a feeling that she cannot remember what she did or said last night. Judging by the entertainment I had after she encamped, I think it better that she doesn't remember.

'I'm very grateful, that's very kind of you, thank you. Well, Old Girl, here we go, we've a long run ahead and we need to miss this blasted Olympic parade.' She climbs into my driving seat and starts me up.

'Och, hen. What aboot yur camping equipment?' Mr Hamilton has just spotted the pungent tent and the associated disaster.

'Oh, would you mind throwing it all away? After my experience last night I have a feeling I will never climb into a tent again. Right, Old Girl, Inverness, here we come.'

We pull away from Mister Hamilton as he turns to tidy up Her Ladyship's mess. He takes one look, then steps back holding his nose. I have a feeling that we'll need a few rain showers before that stuff finds its way into a tip. We turn out onto the road.

'Let's keep an eye out for this turning, Old Girl. We don't want to miss it.' As she says this, we shoot past the said turning, which looks no more than a dirt track. Her Ladyship does a three-point-turn. On a main road, I'll add. There are cars jamming their brakes and beeping their horns and drivers shaking their fists at us. Don't blame me, it's my driver's fault!

We swing up the side road. It's one of those with pot holes to the left and right and a large tuft of grass up the middle so high it tickles my sump.

'Gosh Old Girl, aren't these roads terrible? I'll write to the

Scottish Minister of Transport.' She starts to dictate the letter, shouting it out to anyone who would care to listen. Fortunately for us, and with the exception of The Asthmatic Barking Dog, there's no one to hear.

'Dear Sir, I wish to complain in the strongest possible terms about the state of Scottish roads. Umm...'

The Asthmatic Barking Dog, who had been enjoying the scenery, decides that perhaps this is the right time for a snooze. Already bored with composing her letter, Her Ladyship tries another route to self-entertainment.

'What's that song, Old Girl?'

Don't ask me. I might be a fount of motoring information but I am certainly not an expert on songs.

'I know the one, The Bonnie Banks of Loch Lomond.' She starts to sing at the top of her voice. *'By yon bonnie banks and by yon bonny braes, where the sun shines bright on Loch Lomond; where me an' my true love will never meet again* – Oh look there's the junction – *On the bonnie, bonnie banks o' Loch Lomond* – We'll be driving along those banks later today, Old Girl, or is it Loch Ness? It doesn't matter. It'll be a loch of some sort. I wonder why they don't call it a lake.'

Do I care? No!

'Ooooh ye'll tak' the high road an' I'll tak' the low road – Can't see a thing, Old Girl. Can you?' We have reached the junction and Mr Hamilton was right, we cannot see a thing. There is one of those mirrors on the other side of the road but it has a slogan painted on it about 'Home Rule for Scotland' and is partly covered over by undergrowth.

'Well that's a lot of use, isn't it, Old Girl?' Her Ladyship leans forward as if believing that by leaning forward the state of the whole road and traffic conditions will be revealed. Of course it isn't, our view is completely blocked, both ways in fact.

'This is useless, Old Girl. We'll have to creep forwards and hope that no-one is coming.' She slowly releases my clutch and we edge out into the road. Nothing happens. Even so, we still can't see anything.

'*An I'll be in Scotland afore ye!* Here goes, Old Girl, here goes! *For me an' my true love will never meet again…*' She slams her foot on the accelerator and we shoot out over the white line to turn right just as one police motorbike swerves round the front of us and another swerves behind us. I hear the squealing of tyres and the blasting of a tumult of car horns. I also hear an intake of breath as Her Ladyship closes her eyes, imagining no doubt, that this will prevent anyone from bumping into us.

We stop and Her Ladyship gathers herself enough to pull on my handbrake and switch off the engine. She sits absolutely still, her fingers gripping my steering wheel and her head tapping my horn button. I find myself unwillingly letting out regular short beeps. At least she's kept the rhythm of that blooming song.

The cacophony of horns and squealing of tyres dies down and Her Ladyship slowly releases her grip on my steering wheel. She clambers out to see what havoc has been wrought. The two police motorbikes that swerved past us are lying on each side of the road. Fortunately, their riders appear to be vertical and breathing. The next two police motorbikes had been able to stop, but the large four-by-four behind them had swerved to avoid hitting them and had run into a wall. All four doors are now open and people are piling out as fast as they can.

'Whoops,' is all that comes from Her Ladyship's mouth as she surveys the unfolding scene of chaos. 'Oh blooming, blasted whoops!' She climbs out, sits on my running board and watches. Smoke starts to pour out of the open doors of the four-by-four. 'Oh whoops, whoops, whoops. We didn't cause this, did we, Old Girl? We took every precaution…'

We? I like that, I had nothing to do with this. I was just doing what I was told.

'They must have been going very fast. Why didn't we hear them coming?'

Perhaps because you were singing at the top of your voice?

The people who had piled out of the car are now attempting to reach in and grab something, but the smoke is getting worse and they cannot find what they want. I wonder what they are after. The two police men who had swerved their bikes to avoid me are now walking back towards their colleagues. They completely ignore us apart from a brief glance and what I could only describe as a snarl.

People are now piling out of all the other vehicles that are part of this convoy. All seem to be watching the activity surrounding the crashed car with great interest. A man with a fire extinguisher steps determinedly towards the smoking car and plays the foam into the rear compartment. The smoke dies down and disperses. Someone else reaches in and pulls out something that looks like a miner's lamp. It is covered in foam.

'It's gone out,' someone else shouts. 'It's bloody gone out! Who's responsible for this?' Gradually all eyes turn towards us. Her Ladyship stands nervously and walks apprehensively round to the other side of me, hoping, I presume, that I will offer her some protection. She feels she has to say something. I wish she wouldn't.

'Hello. Have you a problem?'

The man who had been shouting now bristles, and charges towards us like a wild animal, only to be restrained at the last minute by one of the policemen.

'Have we a problem? Have we a problem? Of course we have a bloody problem, woman. You've achieved with that old banger what millions of pounds of expenditure have so far avoided. You've succeeded in putting out the Olympic flame, you stupid, bloody, idiot p-p-p-person.'

After that, I'm on Her Ladyship's side. How dare he? Old banger indeed. I can't help it if one of these overpriced cars can't stop properly. He's quite a little man. He's too fat for the London 2012 sweat shirt that he's wearing, which sort of rolls up over his stomach and stretches so much that the Olympic rings look more like horizontal rugby balls. He's now gone bright purple and his beard, which covers his receding chin, seems to change colour too, but this time to a slate grey. I hope he isn't going to have a 'corona' as Her Ladyship calls it. He's trying to break free from the policeman again. 'I'm going to bloody kill you...' Another policeman joins his colleague, obviously concerned that this man might actually mean what he says. Her Ladyship decides that the best form of defence is attack, especially with me as a barricade.

'Don't you call me a stupid bloody idiot, you silly little man. Umm, um, um...' She grasps around for some inspiration and spies a road sign telling people to slow down for a blind turning. 'You were, you were going too fast. Yes. You were all speeding. You were all going far too fast for your own safety and the road conditions. Anyway, who gives a damn for some silly little flame? I've got a box of matches in the car. You can use that to relight the damned thing.'

The man struggles to break free again. He's still hell bent on murder, I fear. How will I get home if he kills her? Another man steps forward, one of those people with an intense air of authority and a quiet determined voice. Unlike Her Ladyship's impending killer he's tall, slim, clean-shaven and with an air of having absolutely everything under control. He comes over to Her Ladyship who is genuinely angry now. He disarms her with a warm smile and turns to the assembled crowd.

'Is anyone hurt?' Mumbles from the crowd emerge, suggesting that everyone is fine.

'Apart from the car carrying the flame, is anything damaged?' Her Ladyship opens her mouth briefly, but decides that silence is the best way forward at this stage. The entourage look around at each other. There is much murmuring then a mass of shaking of heads and a chorus of mumbles suggesting not.

'Good. Can that car still be driven?' A group of people go to examine the car impaled on the wall. A voice shouts out.

'It's driveable… I think.'

'Good. Now this is what we'll do. We'll carry on to our next town. Luss, isn't it? And we'll phone ahead for an identical replacement car to carry the flame to meet us en route. The thing is, ladies and gentlemen, I think perhaps we were travelling a bit too fast, maybe not speeding, but this road and that turning suggests that we should have approached at a much slower speed. What's more important is that we really do not want the media getting hold of this and we must thank our lucky stars that they aren't with us at the moment. They are all waiting at Luss. Let's get ourselves sorted out and carry on. Who's got the spare flame?' A voice from the rear announces that all is fine and the spare flame is okay.

'There we are then. This story stays right here and it doesn't go anywhere else. Okay?' Everyone murmurs agreement. The silly little man is being helped into a car, still muttering protests, turning now and again to point at Her Ladyship and mouthing threats. The man with the air of authority turns to us.

'Are you all right, Madam?'

'Yes, thank you, well I think so.' Her Ladyship replies. 'But, but, but that horrible little man…'

'You do agree that it's best that this story doesn't get out to the media. You don't want to find yourself spread all over the world's press with the story that your driving this old car across the path of the Olympic Torch relay caused a major incident, do you? I can see the Red Top headline, "Old Banger Bangs Out Olympic Flame." We really don't want that to happen, do we? You'd be hounded by them for weeks and I can assure you, you really don't want that. Is your car all right?'

'Yes, I think so. We're just a bit shaken. But that awful little man, he wanted to attack me.'

'You leave him to me. In this instance, I think it's better that we let this particular sleeping dog lie don't you?' He gestures towards The Asthmatic Barking Dog, doing just that. 'Just like him.'

'Yes, I suppose you're right, Mister? Mister?'

'You'll forgive me for not introducing myself, the least known and all that…'

'Yes… I suppose… well, okay.'

'Thank you, Madam. Can I ask where you were going?'

'Oh, John O'Groats actually. We're going to attempt the run to Land's End.' The man smiles.

'Well, I wish you the best of luck. I hope you make it. But might I suggest that you wait here a while and let us pass through and get well out of the way? We don't want you to have another accident, do we?' Her Ladyship, obviously flattered by this man's kind manner acquiesces. The two police motorbike outriders haul their machines up from the road, engines start up, the battered car pulls away from the wall and the vehicles all gather together to leave. We watch the entourage slowly pull away past us and head north. The damaged four-by-four has developed a very loud and annoying squeak which occurs with every wheel rotation.

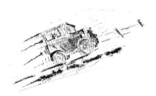

We have done well, we are now only a few miles short of Fort William. Her Ladyship has recovered from the Olympic flame experience and keeps humming that flipping song.

'Look, Old Girl, there's a parking area over there. I think we'll stop and I'll give Dog a bit of a walk.' We pull across the road and Her Ladyship parks me up beside some other cars. It's a sort of picnic area with tables and benches, a café and a couple of coaches parked beside it.

'Come on Dog… walkies!' Asthmatic Barking Dog opens one eyelid very slowly. This is followed shortly by the other one.

'C'mon Dog, do you want to go for a walk or don't you?' She reaches for his lead while he very slowly gets to his feet and looks around to take in this new scenery. There are some people picnicking while others walk in and out of the woodland behind us. A few children are messing around in a play area next to the café. The Asthmatic Barking Dog decides a walk might be rather a good idea. Before Her Ladyship can slip the lead over his head, he leaps past her and out onto the grass, sniffs briefly at it and trots off into the woodland.

'Come back you stupid animal!' No response. 'Come back this instant. DOG! Come. Here!' She's put on her authoritarian voice, but still no response. There are far more interesting things to do, sniffing and examining, than listening to you-know-who howling on. Her Ladyship marches off in the direction of the wood, hoping, I presume, to intercept The Asthmatic Barking Dog. He, I think, plans on enjoying his freedom for as long as it takes Her Ladyship to catch up. For me it is a chance for some peace and quiet.

A large and rather gaudy coach pulls in to the car park. A gabble of tourists pile out. Is that the right word for a coach full of tourists? A gabble? Judging by the way they can't stop talking, I think gabble is most appropriate.

'Gee Aylmer,' cries one rather rotund woman with platinum blonde hair that is completely inappropriate for her age in my opinion. 'Just you look at that cute liddle automobile.' I am not sure I like being called a cute liddle automobile. She walks towards me. She's larger than I first thought. She's wearing some loud aqua blue shorts that even Her Ladyship would turn her nose up at, revealing incredibly large thighs supporting a plethora of varicose veins. Her upper half sports a salmon pink T shirt over which she has an open Hawaiian shirt also in aqua with a bright yellow and orange floral pattern. On her head is a beige floppy hat. She also has a sort of pouch hanging from her neck, which settles itself comfortably between her breasts, one of which seems to point north and the other south. This truly is a sight to behold and it's walking towards me.

Aylmer is still struggling down the coach steps. He is a tall thin man also wearing shorts but his are a bright orange, blue and red tartan. He wears a Hawaiian shirt that matches that of his wife and on his head is a baseball cap announcing that the wearer is something to do with New York Yankees, whatever or wherever that is. Both Aylmer and his spouse are wearing brilliantly white trainers.

'Goddammit, Dolores, I don' wanna stand and stare at some old British automobile, I need the john. C'mon let's get into the diner.'

'But Aylmer, it's just so cute. How old do you think it is? D'you think it was once driven by Robert the Bruce?'

'Jeez Dolores, you don't half talk rubbish. Robert the Bruce was a king. He wouldn't have had a goddam liddle thing like this. He'd a' driven a Rolls or a Cadillac.'

What on earth are they talking about?

'Yeah, you could be right.' She sighs, obviously quite disappointed that I hadn't been transport for a king. No king for me madam, I'm stuck with Her Ladyship.

'Oh Aylmer, before we go into the diner, will you take a photo of me? Ma'll love to see a picture of me sitting in a liddle Scotch automobile.'

'The word's Scottish, hen,' shouts a voice from a nearby bench. 'Scotch is wha' we drunk!'

And madam, I'm neither Scotch nor Scottish. I'm British and proud of it.

'Oh all right, honey,' he opens my door. What are you doing now? 'In you get.' Dolores attempts to wedge herself in into my driving seat but it's a very tight squeeze and I feel my offside sink several inches towards the ground.

'Ain't you goin' to put your legs in and sit looking out the windshield honey?'

'I don't think I can Aylmer. It's very tight in here. It doesn't help that the steering is on the wrong side either.'

All I can say is Her Ladyship can manage quite well. She may have a rather gargantuan form but it's nothing compared to yours. And as a matter of information, my steering is on the correct side.

'Just sit there honey, I'll try to get the hood and trunk in the picture as well.'

I'm confused. The hood's up for all to see, you don't need to move round to my front to get it in the picture.

'Big smile honey… there you are. Now can I go to the john?'

'Hang on, Aylmer. I can't get out.' Aylmer drops his camera and it bangs against another one hanging from a strap around his neck.

'Here, grab my hands.' Dolores obeys and Aylmer endeavours to haul her back off my seat and onto her feet again.

'Gee, Aylmer; these Scotch people must be much smaller than us to get in and out of these liddle automobiles.'

'We're SCOTTISH,' the voice a few benches away cries out in exasperation.

'Breathe in honey. Push your legs down.' Both heave, Aylmer pulling and Dolores pushing and she finally pops out like a cork from a bottle.

'Thank you honey. I thought I was going to be stuck in this thing permanently.'

'That's all right Dolores, now can I get to the goddam john?'

'Of course you can Aylmer,' she turns to take a final look inside me. 'Wait a minute, what's this?' She produces the haggis that Her Ladyship had stowed away under my driver's seat. Aylmer's shoulders drop as he turns back.

'I don't know honey, I haven't a clue. Can we go now?' Dolores takes a sniff at it.

'It smells of meat, Aylmer.'

'Honey, I need to get to the john.'

'Can I help you?' It's Her Ladyship returning with The Asthmatic Barking Dog. Rescued – just in time. Noticing that she's about to confront strange foreign people, she stretches herself a couple of inches taller so she can look down on both of them.

'Good afternoon, ma'am. I'm Aylmer T. Schwartz Junior and this is my wife Dolores.'

'Charmed,' she replies in a manner befitting a real Her Ladyship and holding out her hand in a manner that suggests Aylmer should kiss it. He starts to bow, but on losing his balance corrects himself. 'How can I help you?' Oh it's posh voice time as well.

'Well ma'am, we were admiring this liddle automobile, is it yours?'

'Indeed it is. Why do you ask?' She almost whistles the 'wh' of the word 'why.' Oh the pretentiousness of the woman.

'Well ma'am, Dolores here wondered why the steering wheel was on the wrong side.'

'But it's not. It's on the correct side. We British drive on the left. Haven't you noticed?'

'Yes ma'am, but that's the wrong side of the highway.'

'No it isn't. We drive on the left side of the road. That's because in the old days when we rode horses, we had our sword arm free should we be attacked by someone coming towards us. That meant we didn't have to stretch a sword across the horse's neck and possibly injure it in a fight. When the motor car arrived, we continued to drive on the left. It made complete sense.'

Aylmer looked thoughtful.

'That's why the left side of the road is the correct side for us. You are doubtless wondering why you Americans drive on the right. Well I can tell you. It was a sign to anyone else on the road that you were travelling in peace. Simple really. You drive on the right side and we drive on the correct side. It couldn't be simpler.'

Both Aylmer and Dolores look confused.

'Ah, I see you have my haggis. What are you doing with it?' It's that "what whistle" again. I'm impressed.

'Well ma'am, we were wondering what it's for.' Dolores decides that she should return the haggis to me. She then decides that perhaps a curtsey is appropriate. She too nearly loses her balance.

'For eating, of course. At least that's what I've been told, never eaten one myself though. I also learnt as I crossed the border that by travelling with a haggis in Scotland I'm assured of a safe journey. Don't you have one?

'Gee, no ma'am, no one told us.'

'Well I think it would be a good idea if you acquired one for yourselves and perhaps you should tell the other members of your group. Now if you will excuse me, I must get my dog back into the car and continue my journey. I bid you good bye.' She holds out her hand again and Aylmer takes it lightly, but cannot quite make the attempt to kiss it. Dolores attempts another curtsey and fails. Without a further word, Her Ladyship brushes past them to help The Asthmatic Barking Dog back onto my seat as Aylmer T. Schwartz Junior and his good lady head for the café.

'Goddamit honey, that's why we've had these disasters on this trip. We'd better buy a haggis at the first opportunity.' Dolores waddles along beside him.

'Do you think we should buy two, honey? One for each of us?

'Good idea Dolores. Now where is that goddam john?

'Right, Old Girl, let's get off to Fort William. I did think of lunching here, but in a café full of tourists, I think not. Let's go.' She starts my engine and we continue north.

We appear to have gone straight past Fort William. 'Blinking place is full of damned tourists, Old Girl. I really can't face any more with their "What a cute little car, is it yours?" Aylmer T. Schwartz and Dolores were plenty enough for one day don't you think?'

So we've reached Loch Ness. Madam decided on a quick lunch at a petrol station, and even then people were coming up to us making remarks about me and expressing surprise that I am capable of making it all the way to Land's End. I am pleased to say that Her Ladyship supported me by telling them that there was no doubt whatsoever that we will both reach our destination in five days time, because we are British.

'Here we are then, Old Girl, that's Loch Ness. Only about thirty miles to Inverness and we're making good time. I think we'll find a nice spot to park up to enjoy the scenery and take a little rest. I wonder if we'll see the Loch Ness Monster. Isn't this view spectacular?'

If you say so, Your Ladyship, but shouldn't you be watching the road?

'There we are. Here's a nice place to stop. Right beside the loch and look, there aren't any tourists. The place seems deserted. She pushes her hand out to advise those behind that she's turning right and we slow down to take the turning. As we start to turn, the car behind us blows his horn.

'Haven't you got any bloody indicators?' Shouts that driver as he swerves to avoid us. Her Ladyship shouts back.

'Yes I have, actually, but if you'd studied your Highway Code you'd know that a right hand sticking horizontally out of a car window means that I'm turning right. Or are you blind?' But the car has gone too far down the road for its driver to hear her, perhaps fortunately. I am glad Her Ladyship has stopped, because I'm not feeling a hundred percent.

'Let's have a rest here, Old Girl. Let's just enjoy that view.' She shuffles her bottom to get more comfortable. I wonder if the discomfort she took in her bottom from that drawing pin has finally eased. It appears so, because I can hear her rhythmic breathing, suggesting that she has drifted off into the land of nod. The Asthmatic Barking Dog gets up and starts to try and dig a hole in my rear seat.

'Cut that out, Dog. Lie down.' The Asthmatic Barking Dog is taken aback, responding with an "uuh?" He too thought Madam was asleep. He shrugs and flops down as heavily as he can and like Her Ladyship dozes off to sleep. I find the quiet snores quite soporific myself. I look along the loch. There are a few boats plying the waters but they are a long way out and hardly seem to be moving. I imagine they must be fishing. It's quite cloudy and the air is very still.

I've heard stories of the Loch Ness monster over the years and I have also heard that it is probably a myth and doesn't exist. Oh gosh, I'm feeling tired as well. I wonder what the monster looks like. The skies seem to be getting darker, the clouds heavier. There is a ray of sunlight now, it's cutting through a small gap in the clouds and it's painting the otherwise grey water surface with a shaft of yellow misty light. The water is beginning to get choppy, too. The little boats are moving away from the centre. What's happening?

The water is getting rougher. I suppose there must be a storm brewing, yet there doesn't seem to be any wind. That's really strange. Fortunately we are a good mile from all this and it's still calm just here. I feel as though I am almost in another world watching what is happening. I can see white foam where the shaft of sunlight hits the water. I wouldn't like to be on a boat over there. The loch is starting to churn, as if it were boiling.

Suddenly an enormous eel-like creature breaks through the water, its head rises up and it starts to swim down the loch towards us. It's still nearly a mile away, but it seems as though it is a hundred yards long. Its body curves up and down as it swims towards me but its head stays aloft some twenty feet above the surface of the water. It's hard to describe, but if you think of a snake moving over the ground it sways its body left and right so it can move along. This creature does the same thing vertically, yet its head and eyes seem focussed on us. This can't be the Loch Ness monster, can it?

It's barely a quarter of a mile away now and it has turned in our direction. We need to get away. Come on Your Ladyship and Dog, wake up. We have to get away!

The monster reaches the shore barely a hundred feet from us. Madam and The Asthmatic Barking Dog are fast asleep. WAKE UP! The monster starts to rise up, higher and higher and opens its mouth to reveal sharp fangs. It pulls its head back, ready to make an attack. For heaven's sake woman, start me up and drive me away before it's too late! The monster sways its head preparing to strike at us. It's attacking. Your Ladyship! Please, wake up!

'Wake up, Old Girl, what on earth is the matter with you? Why won't you start?' It's Her Ladyship and she's awake.

'Come on, Old Girl, start your engine. It's time to move further up the loch towards Inverness. We'll probably have another stop further along because I fancy a cuppa.' She pulls the starter button again. I don't fancy starting. 'What on earth is the matter with you? I've never known you shake so much when I've tried to start you before.'

I cast my eyes across the loch. All is calm, no heavy clouds, no shaft of yellow sunlight, the little boats are bobbing on the water and it's very calm. Have I been dreaming? No, it was more like a nightmare. It was horrible. I finally allow my engine to start. It still doesn't feel right.

'I'm not absolutely convinced your engine is okay, Old Girl. There's a nasty vibration I haven't noticed before.' She fiddles with my spark advance and retard control.

'That's better, if we retard your spark a bit you seem happier. We'll keep it there. Come on then. Let's go.' She engages reverse to pull us back from the shore and turns me to face north. We pull away and I notice a series of small pools of water stretching from the shore to almost where we had been parked. No, surely not. It can't have been.

Something is definitely not right with me. That blooming haggis isn't doing anything to ease my passage but Her Ladyship's adjustments seem to have improved things.

'Not far now, Old Girl. We've reached the end of the Loch. Let's pull in off into Drumnadrochit. I expect I can find a cuppa here. Oh look, there's a ferry approaching. I expect they'll have a cafe at the terminal. Tell you what, we'll take your hood down when we get there. All ready for a nice drive for the last hour.' We pull into the village. The weather seems to have improved as well, it's now a lovely afternoon.

We arrive at the ferry terminal and Madam parks me with a good view of the loch. We appear to be in a place called Nessie World, I think it's a bit "touristy." Her Ladyship is looking around and taking in the scene. Judging by the look on her face I am not sure she will stop here for long.

'Rather a lot of grockels, Old Girl.' She starts to fold my hood down. 'Not sure it's the place for us. I'll have a quick pee and buy a cuppa and we'll be on our way to the B&B. I'm determined not to get lost this time.' She turns to The Asthmatic Barking Dog and attaches the safety lead she uses to stop him from jumping out when the hood is down. 'I'll let you have a quick leg stretch here when I get back and we should still have some daylight when we get to our destination for you to have a nice long walk.' She heads into the terminal building.

It doesn't take long for Her Ladyship's so-called grockels to come over to look at me.

'That's an old car isn't it Daddy?' A man and his young daughter are looking into my interior.

'Can I get in?'

'No Suzie, not with that ice cream. You might drop some of it on the floor and the owner would not be very pleased if you do that.

'Oh please?'

'I said no. I know you. You'll drop it.' A voice calls out from the far side of the car park. The father turns.

'Geoffrey, c'mon. It's time we got on the ferry.' The girl called Suzie moves like greased lightning. My driver's door is open and she's clambering inside. You better watch that blooming ice cream young lady. Oh pook, she's dropped it. The man called Geoffrey turns back to catch the sight of the ice cream landing on my carpet.

'Suzie, I told you no, and now look what you've done.' Suzie's lower lip starts to tremble.

'Waaaaa. I've dropped my ice cream. Waaaa.' She stoops to pick it up, but the man called Geoffrey grabs her, pulls her off my seat, slams my door and heads towards the ferry. The sound of Suzie's wailing fades into the distance. Her Ladyship is going to be absolutely delighted. Someone else approaches, a young man this time. He wanders around me, examining my contents with rather too much interest if you ask me. The Asthmatic Barking Dog wakes up and takes a dislike to this new visitor as he starts to rummage through my glove pocket.

'Grrrrrrrrr.' The Asthmatic Barking dog issues a warning. 'Grrrrrrrrrrrrrr.' The man ignores him and keeps rummaging. Then, with a triumphant look on his face he finds Her Ladyship's emergency purse.

'Yesss.'

Arf, arf, arf, Grrrrrrr. Arf, arf.' The Asthmatic Barking Dog is straining at the safety lead now, but the man, knowing that he's at a safe distance, turns and walks away, examining the contents of the purse. The Asthmatic Barking Dog tries to jump out, but can't.

'Hey you? Fellow! You there!' It's Her Ladyship returning, now half walking and half running. 'What are you doing? What have you got there?' She reaches me and takes a quick look.

'He's got my emergency purse.' Then at the top of her voice, 'STOP THAT MAN!' Her voice reverberates across the loch and everyone turns to see what is going on. People picnicking, people watching the ferry arrive, people getting out of their cars, all turn their attention to Her Ladyship. This is so embarrassing.

She turns to The Asthmatic Barking Dog. 'Why didn't you stop him?' Dog looks bemused and, I think, hurt. She opens the door and unclips his lead. 'Go on Dog – kill!' With one leap, he's out of the car and off after his prey. Finally, after three days shut up in me, he is going to have some fun. The man's walk speeds up to a half hearted run. He knows that Her Ladyship won't catch up, but it's just possible that The Asthmatic Barking Dog might. However, it's looking as though the dog is already getting bored. He's slowing down. There are too many nice smells to distract him.

Her Ladyship decides that The Asthmatic Barking Dog needs some help. Her eyes search around inside me as if looking for something, anything that might stall this thief's progress.

'Ah! That'll do.' She reaches down and grabs the haggis. Straightening up and flicking the haggis from hand to hand, she focuses her eyes on her target. The haggis settles in her right hand and she slowly swings her arm back. Almost in slow motion I can see her right arm propel the haggis with all her might towards the thief. With him as an exception, all eyes watch the haggis flying through the air towards its target.

'Floomp.' The haggis smacks the thief firmly on the back of his head. He stumbles and falls down. There is a round of applause. An elderly man wearing a smart striped blazer and a boater rises to his feet.

'I say, well thrown madam. English cricket could do with your talents.' Her Ladyship is obviously delighted at this compliment.

'I was champion shot put at school, actually,' she shouts back as she reaches her semi-conscious prey. 'That is mine, I believe.' She wrenches her purse from his hand. 'And that.' She grabs the haggis which has settled beside the body. The Asthmatic Barking Dog decides that this prone figure is in need of his attention too, so he wanders up and down sniffing various parts of his anatomy. He concludes that there is little deserving his interest, so he lifts his leg against the man's backside.

'Come on Dog. It's time to move on.' The applause has died now and others have wandered across to take a look at the result of Her Ladyship's labours. She opens my door for The Asthmatic Barking Dog to hop in, secures his lead, and gets in herself. She examines the haggis.

'I believe that it is customary to address a haggis. Well all I can say is well done and thank you. That man Duncan was right, you certainly do help to ease my passage through Scotland. Come on,

Old Girl, time to get to our B&B.' She stows the haggis under her seat and her purse in the glove pocket.

'What on earth is that?' She eyes up a large soggy ice cream on the carpet. It's slowly spreading outwards as it melts.

'BLOODY GROCKELS!' She screams at the top of her voice as she leaps out. 'Rags, water, where is it Dog?' She points The Asthmatic Barking Dog at the mess which he gleefully inhales. Grabbing his water supply, she splashes it onto the little that remains and starts to mop it up. 'Bloody people, why don't they just leave you alone, Old Girl?' She tosses the rags into a bin and gets back in. She starts me up and we pull away.

Her Ladyship steers me close to the thief, who is now sitting up, rubbing his head and examining his damp trousers. He looks up.

'You assaulted me, you Old Bag,' he shouts after us. 'I'll report you to the police. You can't go around knocking people out. I'll press charges.'

'Oh go away, you silly little man. Grow up and remember, no-one crosses Miss Daisy, Dog and me.' At that she presses down my accelerator pedal and we continue north up the road towards Inverness.

We arrive at our overnight port of call as the sun is settling low in the western sky. The Nice Mister Arthur and the others have already arrived and have pitched their tents in a neighbouring field.

'You made it then,' The Nice Mister Arthur says as he comes over. Did you have a good drive?'

'Well,' says Her Ladyship. You might prefer to call it eventful.'

'Eventful? How do you mean?'

'Put it like this. First of all I managed to put out the Olympic flame. Then it all went downhill after that.' Her Ladyship puts my hood back up, plonks some dog food and a bowl of water down on my rear seat and extracts her overnight case.

'But I'll tell you one thing. Everyone should carry a haggis in their car. They can be very, very useful.' The Nice Mister Arthur looks at her quizzically. Surely he knows by now that it is not safe to let Her Ladyship out on her own.

'I'll take you for a walk later Dog,' she cries over her shoulder as she walks in to the B&B to check in. The Nice Mister Arthur wanders back to the others shaking his head.

Chapter Five

'Dog! For heaven's sake will you get out from under the car? What on
earth have you found?'

Inverness to Inverness – Via John O'Groats

'Slept like a log, Old Girl.' Her Ladyship slips the lead over The Asthmatic Barking Dog's head to ready him for his morning amble. It's not a walk, it is the act of thoroughly inspecting every blade of grass in front of his nose and lifting his leg against any of them that might have been sprayed by another of his species. I have little doubt that The Asthmatic Barking Dog intends making his mark at every opportunity in Scotland.

'How did you sleep then?'

Well actually, Your Ladyship, not at all well. Whatever you fed The Asthmatic Barking Dog last night caused him to sleep restlessly and break wind rather a lot. Why am I bothering to answer you? You never listen.

'C'mon Dog, let's stretch our legs, then you can have breakfast.'

She's barely walked out of the drive when a police car slowly passes the entrance. There's a little squeal of brakes and it reverses, stopping by the gate so its occupants can see me parked up and preparing myself for another day's outing in Bonnie Scotland. He reverses a bit more and turns into the drive, stopping in front of me. The two officers get out and walk around me, apparently examining every part of me. They come around to face me again. One turns to his colleague.

'I think this was the one tha' was reported yesterday, Hamish. That number rings a bell.' He reaches for his radio.

'Five Three Seven – Sierra India?' A crackly voice replies.

'Go ahead Five Three Seven.'

'Was'ne a report of an incident yesterday at the Nessie World Pleasure Park involving an elderly woman and a vintage car?'

'Aye that's correct,' came back the crackly voice. 'Hang on I'll check the detail for ye.' The two policemen look at each other, then at me and then the view. The Nice Mister Arthur and his friends, who were camping across the road, are packing up and readying themselves to head north as well, but a police car parked in front of me distracts them from their tasks.

'Five Three Seven?'

'Aye, go ahead.'

'Yes, I have the detail here. It involved Jimmy McTavish, probably doin' his usual wander roond a car park to see if he could tak anythin' from cars. It was he that reported that he had bin attacked by a haggis!' Both policemen raise their eyebrows.

'Did ye say a haggis?'

'Aye, a haggis. He reported that, to quote – "I was mindin' me own business walkin' across the car park at Nessie World when this crazy woman hurled a haggis at me, hittin' me – whack, on the back of me heed. An' she set her blinkin' hound on me." We sent a car to Nessie World and asked for witnesses. An elderly gentleman came forward to tell us that he saw the whole thing. Our Jimmy had reached in and taken a purse from the old car. The female owner on approaching the vehicle saw what he was up to, challenged him and as he started to run away, she hurled a haggis and knocked him over. He added that it was the best throw he'd seen in ages. Anyway, why d'ye ask?'

'We think we've foond the vehicle. It's an old 'un all right. A very old 'un. D'ye have a registration number?' The cheek! Very old 'un indeed.

'Nay, but McTavish said that he thought the first two letters were U-D. Have ye got tha'? U-D?'

'Aye I think this is the one. I canna see a haggis though. D'ye want us to bring the woman in?'

'I'll leave that to ye. Have a little chat with her first and then decide what ye want to do.'

'Och aye, Two Four oot.' He clicks the radio off. The other policeman can hardly control his laughter.

'Weel Hamish, I've dealt with some odd cases over the years, but assault wi' a haggis taks the biscuit. Shall we go an' have a chat with the people at the B&B?'

'Aye, let's do that. Perhaps this dangerous elderly haggis hurler is in residence.' They both start laughing and wander towards the house. They press the doorbell and a woman comes to the door.

'Och, gid mornin' to yerselves officers. Can I help ye?'

'Aye if ye can M'aam. The owner of yon vehicle, is she stayin' with ye?'

'Aye she is, but she's not here at the moment. I think she's walkin' her dog. Why d'ye ask?'

'Well, we've had a report aboot a woman assaulting a man at Nessie World wi' a haggis.'

'A haggis d'ye say?'

'Aye.'

'Weel, she does have a haggis. She asked me to put it in ma refrigerator yesterday, when she arrived. It did look the worse for wear. Are ye saying she attacked someone wi' it.'

'Aye we are.'

'Is she dangerous?'

'We dinna think so. But she might be a tad eccentric.'

'Aye she is tha'. I saw her talkin' to yon car this morning.' I'm suddenly offended. I'd been enjoying this conversation until now.

There is nothing wrong with Her Ladyship and I having a chat, even if she never listens to a word I say.

'She's not in th' hoose then?'

'Och no, I said she's taken her dog for a walk. She won't be long.' At this point, Her Ladyship trots into the drive with a very happy Asthmatic Barking Dog in tow. She spots the police car and then the two policemen. She strides towards me and lets The Asthmatic Barking Dog hop onto my rear seat. He turns to stare at the policemen and I sense rather than hear the familiar deep rumble. It's the uniforms that get to him. Mind you, Her Ladyship also has a thing about men in uniform. I wonder if The Asthmatic Barking Dog is aware of that and, let's face it, she belongs to him before anyone else. So I suppose he's warning people in uniform off. That's my theory.

'Good morning Officers, can I help you?' The two policemen turn to face Her Ladyship. One grabs for his baton, then realises he left it in his car. Without taking his eyes off Her Ladyship he gropes his belt for something else that might make a suitable substitute, I presume just in case Madam-the-Suspected-Arch-Criminal runs amok. The other policeman speaks:

'Aye yes madam, perhaps you can. Were you at the Nessie World pleasure park yesterday evening?'

'Yes indeed I was. I needed a leg stretch, a pee and a cup of tea. Why?'

'Did you by any chance have a confrontation with a young man while you were there?'

'Indeed I did. Yes. He had stolen my emergency purse from the glove pocket of my motor car. So I set the dog on him and when Dog lost interest in him, preferring to examine a half eaten burger, I hurled a haggis at him. The thief that is, not the dog. My hurling of the haggis just happened to whack this thief on his head and knock him over. It was a bit like playing Boules, except in this case the jack was a thief. I was able to get my purse and a slightly bruised haggis back and we continued on our way here. Simple justice and the stolen goods returned to their rightful owner. Is there a problem with that?'

'Well aye, there is madam. The man ye knocked over with the haggis has made a complaint against ye.'

'Made a complaint? Made a complaint? This little man reaches into my car, helps himself to my money and trots off without so much as a how d'you do and HE complains about ME?'

Oh dear, here she goes again.

'You people weren't around – nothing new about that. So I did my best to stop the little bastard myself. I couldn't run after him, not at my age. The dog lost interest in chasing him. He's no spring chicken either. So I reverted to Taking Reasonable Means – I think you chaps call it – to stop him. It just so happened that my aim was pretty good and I felled the little toad.' I think the policemen are considering whether or not they should defend their fellow countryman.

'Aye, well, yes. We'll be arresting him. But we shuid be charging ye fur assault.' He looks at his colleague who nods. He turns back to Her Ladyship. 'Might I ask, where ye goin'?'

'Me? I'm off to John O'Groats and then I come back here tonight, before heading to Land's End. Why?'

'Ye mean in yon old car?'

'Yes in "Yon old car" why?'

'Och nothin', I just hope ye'll make it.' He pauses and takes out his notebook. 'We're not goin' to press charges on this occasion, but we'll have yur nam and address and keep it on file, just in case we come across ye agin afore ye leave Scotland. If you please, Madam?' Her Ladyship decides not to push matters further and starts to give him her details. While they are doing that his colleague, the one called Hamish takes another look at me. He wanders over and slowly walks around me. I bet he's looking for something wrong.

'… Pembrokeshire, Is there anything else you need to know?'

'D'ye have a mobile phone number, just in case we need to contact ye afore ye git home.'

'Yes, but I can never remember it.' She whips her phone out of her pocket and punches the buttons. 'Here you are. It's that one, the oh, seven, eight…'

'Thank ye madam.' Her Ladyship turns her attention to his colleague. 'I say, hello. Be careful. For some strange reason the dog doesn't like men in uniform.'

'Grrrr, wheeze arf, arf, wheeze arf.' PC Hamish takes three quick steps back, catches his boot on a decorative stone surrounding a pond and lands, bottom first in it. Her Ladyship and his colleague come over, grab his hands and haul him out.

'Are you all right?' Her Ladyship wonders whether she should wipe the pond weed off his backside, but decides to err on the side of caution.

'I did warn you. The old dog is very protective you know.'

'Aye Madam,' PC Hamish replies with a degree of injured pride. 'I'll be fine thank ye'.'

'Can we go now? It's one hundred and twenty miles to John O'Groats and I want to get back here before dark. It's the headlights. You see. They were fine in the 1930s but in this day and age they are not very good. It's like following two orange balls up the road in the dark.'

'Aye, ye are free to go Madam. Have a good trip.'

'Thank you, officer," she looks over to the landlady who has obviously followed every ounce of the conversation so that she can tell her husband all about it. 'Oh Mrs McDonald? Can I have my haggis please? After yesterday, I'm sure I'm going to need it.' Mrs McDonald seems surprised. She disappears indoors and returns almost immediately with the slightly battered haggis.

'Thank you. I'll see you later.' Mrs McDonald gives a half hearted wave and goes back into the house. The bolts on the door slam shut one by one, rather loudly if you ask me.

As the police car reverses out of the drive The Nice Mister Arthur comes over.

'What was that all about then?'

'Nothing much,' Her Ladyship replies casually. 'Didn't I tell you yesterday? I lobbed my haggis at some chap who tried to steal my emergency purse when I stopped for a break yesterday afternoon. Now he wants to press charges. But I have a feeling that he is well known to Scotland's Finest, but they've let me go. I just hope that nothing else untoward is going to happen before I leave Scotland. Come on, let's go and find John O'Groats.'

It's taken us four hours to get to John O'Groats. The roads were pretty rough, but they were clear of too much traffic. In fact as we got closer, most of the cars coming towards us were my relatives who were already on their way to Land's End. The Nice Mister Arthur was following us.

'So this is John O'Groats, Old Girl. Not much of a place is it? It's rather dead isn't it? I wonder where the starting line is. Shouldn't there be a reception committee?' We drive around what appears to be a small, rather grey, village.

'Hmmph, it reminds me of a tiny version of Halifax. All grey and the only colours are the yellow no parking lines down the side of the road. Hang on a minute. What's that over there?' She's spotted what looks like some sort of colourful tower. She swings me towards it and as we pull around the side of a building there, in front of us, is an array of relatives of all shapes and sizes all lined up, many with open bonnets, their drivers peering in and fiddling in their nether regions. Others are having plaques attached to their radiators declaring that they are taking part in a run from one end of the country to the other. She parks me up and the Nice Mister Arthur parks behind.

'Here we are then, Old Girl. Gosh, there are the others who came up to Scotland from South Wales the other way. All seven of us. All here at the same time. Hello everyone. Now that's a turn up for the books, all arriving at John O'Groats together.' The contingent from South Wales comes over.

'Have you checked in yet?' They all nod and murmur their yeses. 'Well I better check in too. Are we all going the same way?' This is followed by a shaking of heads.

'We thought we'd head down the west coast,' says one.

'We're going down the A9 and then joining the motorways, so we can get there quickly,' says another.

A third voice adds, 'Oh we don't want to go near the motorway. We're sticking to the normal roads.'

'So,' says Her Ladyship thoughtfully. 'It's a sort of race then is it? A chance to see which the quickest route is?' She's desperate to push me to my limits isn't she?

'No.' The Nice Mister Arthur interjects. 'This isn't a race. It's an endurance run. Her Ladyship looks rather displeased at that answer.

'Oh, okay. But I bet I get there before the rest of you. C'mon Dog, Walkies.' The Asthmatic Barking Dog, having endured four hours without a break, leaps out and lifts his leg against my wheel and rather than wait for his lead, trots off.

'Come back here Dog!' The Asthmatic Barking Dog decides to ignore that command, much as he does all her other commands. 'I

said – Come Here – spelt C-O-M-E H-E-R-E. Come Here Dog!'
No response whatsoever from The Asthmatic Barking Dog, but Her
Ladyship has achieved the full attention of not just the South Wales
contingent, but all the other drivers and officials.

The Asthmatic Barking Dog has spotted another of his species,
one not dissimilar to him in looks. They happily trot towards one
another. I've watched this ritual so many times before. First they
take a good sniff at each other's rear ends, and then having satisfied
themselves that the smell is pleasing, they sniff at each other's
muzzles then walk around each other to return to smelling each
other's nether regions again. This is generally followed by a series
of leg lifting, fortunately this time on another relative's wheel. I can
imagine their conversation.

'All right, Mate?' Sniff, sniff.

'All right, Mate? Where's yours?' Sniff, sniff – leg lift against a
wheel.

'That's mine over there. The big woman. Where's yours?'
Another leg lifts against the same wheel.

'That's him over there, the one fishing. Seen off any cats
recently?'

'Nah, too much like hard work. Mind you, my woman sent me
after a thief yesterday.'

'Did you manage to nip him?' The stranger lifts his leg again.

'Couldn't be bothered. There was a nice half beef burger on the
ground. That was much more interesting, so I stopped to give that
some attention instead.'

'Did he get away?

'What the burger?' Leg lift.

'No, the thief, did he get away?'

'Nah. My woman hurled a haggis at him instead. Knocked him
out.'

'Wow. Didn't you prefer to eat the haggis?' Leg lift, but this time the leg's owner realises that he has no pee left. He examines his rear end to check it's okay.

'You've got to be joking. Humans eat that sort of thing. Uh oh, my woman's coming over and she doesn't look that happy. Got to go. Good to meet you, Mate.'

'Good to meet you too, Mate.'

The Asthmatic Barking Dog debates briefly whether to trot off again, or wait for Her Ladyship and accept her wrath. Remarkably he opts for the latter. She grabs his collar, then doesn't say a word. That's not like her. She slips his lead over his head and they walk off, no doubt to check in for the JOGLE. I can only assume that she doesn't want to make a scene in front of everyone.

Looking around, my relatives appear to be really fed up. I'm not surprised. A near thousand mile run ahead of us over just four days, carrying a multitude of backsides, coupled with the present brief pause in this most depressing of places, it's enough to persuade us to drive over Beachy Head. But that's at yet another end of this island isn't it? Ah, here comes Her Ladyship returning with The Asthmatic Barking Dog and a pack of instructions. Wait a minute, Oh Wrinkled One, I know you are going senile, but that is the wrong Miss Daisy. Oh for heaven's sake, she's going to need a carer before long. She opens the relative's door,

'Come on, Dog, what's the matter with you? Get in.' The Asthmatic Barking Dog looks from her to this other relative and then to me.

'Get in I said. You've been really badly behaved this morning, now, hup, get in.' The Asthmatic Barking Dog still refuses.

'Have I got to lift you in? Oh come here.' She grabs The Asthmatic Barking Dog and pushes him onto the rear seat.

'Where's your blanket then? What have you done with it?' The Asthmatic Barking Dog just looks out at me in a pathetic manner, appealing for my help. I can't do anything. Her Ladyship rummages through the luggage wedged between the rear and front seats of the other relative.

'What the hell do you think you're doing with that filthy creature in my car? Get it out.' She hasn't previously noticed this gentleman who has come up behind her. Now she has. She looks at him with total disdain.

'Not that it's any business of yours, but my filthy creature as you call him, seems to have lost his blanket. A blanket, which I should add, I always place across the rear seat of MY car, so that MY dog can be more comfortable. What have you done with it?' Her Ladyship almost spits out her reply.

'Your car? You stupid woman. This is my car.'

'How dare you call me stupid!' Her Ladyship stands suddenly upright, cracking the back of her head on the hood frame.

'You must be stupid not to know your own car. I know mine. I have owned this car for over fifty years. I could tell it was mine with a blindfold on. Now get that filthy creature out of it.' Rubbing her head, Her Ladyship steps back to examine the relative she'd just been battling with. She takes a closer look at it.

'No. It's mine,' she says. 'Look, I can prove this is my car. UD 5956, that's the registration number and I always keep my emergency purse in the left hand glove pocket. It was stolen yesterday, by some little thief, but I got it back. Knocked him out with a haggis, actually. But if you want proof, I'll show you.'

'The number of this car, my car is YA 3942. Look!' A crowd starts to gather. People love a good row don't they?

'Frightened of me being right about my own car?' Her Ladyship thrusts her hand into the glove pocket to reach for the purse I know isn't there. The look on her face turns to panic as she discovers the truth. She turns angrily to the man.

'What have you done with it? What have you done with my purse?'

'Do you know, I've met some really stupid people in my day, but you take the biscuit. If you'd care to come to the front and look at the registration number, you will see that this is not your car.' Her Ladyship, still angry that her purse appears to be missing, walks to join him. 'There.' They've gathered quite an audience by now, everyone wondering what will happen next.

'Hmmph. Well, that's that then,' is all she can say. She doesn't like being proved wrong and being made to look a bit of a fool as well always annoys her. She looks around, her eyes searching for me. Finally she spots me.

'Now, will you kindly remove that filthy creature from my car and go.'

'There is no reason to take that attitude. Our cars do look alike don't they? Come on Dog. We know when we're not wanted.' And she flounces over to me, The Asthmatic Barking Dog trotting along as if nothing had happened.

'In you get, Dog.' He leaps happily in onto my rear seat while she looks over at the man settling himself back in his car and readying himself for the off. 'Bloody man. He didn't have to make such an issue of it, did he? So what? So it turns out to be his car and not mine. Anyway, Old Girl, you're much nicer that that pile of junk.' She starts me up.

'Hang on a minute, Old Girl. I've got an idea to get my own back for his rudeness. Stupid indeed. Let's go and join the starting queue.' She manoeuvres me to a position just behind the gentleman sitting in my look-alike. She grabs the by now weather-beaten haggis, gets out, holds it behind her back, puts on a suitably contrite face and walks over.

'I say, look I am sorry about that confusion earlier. I was really convinced that this was my car. They do look alike don't they?' Is she going to offer him that haggis as a peace offering? Surely not.

'I really don't want to discuss it any further. Just move on will you?' The man is still annoyed with her.

'It was really silly of me.' I wonder what she is up to. She wanders round to the back of his car. 'I say, I do like your number plates.' She squats down and deftly rams the haggis firmly onto his exhaust pipe and quickly gets to her feet again. Well "quickly" and "gets" aren't quite the words I would use. Grabbing his spare wheel and clambering would be a better description.

'Where did you get them from?'

'Would you please go away.'

'I am only trying to apologise.' Her Ladyship turns on her heel and returns to me with a triumphant grin on her face. She clambers in. Do you know, I do like that word clamber. It's so perfect when describing Her Ladyship's body movements. She starts me up.

'See you at Land's End – if, of course, you make it – which I doubt.' The man pulls at his starter button. A continued Wurrrr-urrrr-urrr emanates from his starter motor, but with no sign of life.

Her Ladyship edges me past and after establishing a suitable distance between us she bursts out laughing. 'Well, Old Girl, that was inspired, wasn't it? It'll never start with that haggis up his exhaust. My mother told me that she used to shove potatoes on people's exhausts when she was young. Eventually the engine would go bang and propel the potato away. He'll never guess to look at his.'

We nose in near the front of the queue of cars waiting to be started.

'Right, have you got your paperwork and fitted your plaque?' One of the scrutineers wanders over. 'You're all leaving at one minute intervals. We don't want to make this a race now do we?' Her ladyship has barely stopped laughing, and she still has a big grin on her face as she peers over to where the man is examining his spark plugs. The scrutineer follows her gaze.

'Oh poor chap. He's driven all the way from London. The last thing he needs now is a break down.'

'Mmmm yes,' Her Ladyship replies, stifling a giggle. 'Can we go now?'

'Yes.'

'Thank you. Bye.' She lets out the clutch and we are off on our long journey south. As we swing round out of sight of the other relatives she pulls me over.

'Hang on, Old Girl, I want to see what happens.' She gets out and peers round the corner of a building. I can hear the wurr-urr-urr again. A pause and the noise starts again. Then there's an almighty bang and I spot something flying through the air and into the sea. I presume that was her haggis. Her Ladyship returns, very pleased with herself.

'Oh that was brilliant wasn't it, Old Girl? I'll have to get myself another haggis now. But that was worth every penny. As Duncan would say "aye hen, it will ease your path through Scootland." Come on then, let's get back to Inverness. Actually I'm a bit hungry. We need to think about somewhere to stop for lunch. Are you hungry Dog?'

We've been travelling a couple of hours and Her Ladyship is happily humming tunelessly to herself. The Asthmatic Barking Dog is fast asleep on my rear seat. Madam's enjoyment has been occasionally interrupted by remarks like 'Bloody roads. You'd think these damned people would do something to improve them wouldn't you, Old Girl?' Or 'God almighty, look at that pot hole!' Then, after a 4x4 roared past blaring his horn, 'Oh I'm sorry. Not going fast enough for you, am I?'

'Let's find somewhere for lunch, Old Girl? There's a village up ahead. I'm sure they've got a pub or a café. Hopefully there'll be a shop too. I can buy another haggis. Ah there we are. What a strange name for a village, Golspie. Sounds like someone's coughed up some phlegm.' She mimics a Scottish accent, 'Och I've had a Golspie!'

We pull into a small car park beside the pub and Her Ladyship clambers out. There's a menu by the door and she goes over to inspect it. She returns, obviously pleased with herself and still feeling triumphant after that nasty trick she played on that man. She can be so childish at times. I feel rather sorry for him. Well not so much him, but my look-a-like relative.

'C'mon Dog, you're allowed in the bar. Let's go. I'm not that hungry, so you can share with me.' This time she puts the lead on The Asthmatic Barking Dog before letting him out of the car. They stroll off into the pub together. I settle to enjoy the view and it isn't long before some of my relatives drive past, heading south.

I might have expected it would happen, but here comes my relative driven by that rude gentleman. He spots me and pulls in beside me.

'In the pub, is she?' He says to himself. 'I can't let this opportunity pass me by.' He gets out of his car and strokes his chin. 'So what are we going to do with you to slow you down a bit? He opens my bonnet and peers inside.

'Ah, I know. If your belligerent owner knows anything about cars she will spot this, not immediately, but after a little while, and it'll certainly slow her down.' He removes two of my spark plug leads and swaps them over. 'I wonder how long before she figures it out. See you in Land's End – I don't think! Well at least, not straight away.' He starts to get back into my relative.

'Actually, I've got an even better, idea,' he gets out again. He rummages through his luggage. 'Ah, here they are.' He produces a couple of kippers. 'These were for breakfast tomorrow but this is a far better use for them. He produces a coil of wire, lies down on the ground, and attaches the kippers to my exhaust. I glance at my relative which in turn gives me a knowing look as if to suggest that we are both dealing with children.

'Right madam,' he says. Let's see how you handle that. He hops into his car, starts the engine and drives off.

Her ladyship returns with The Asthmatic Barking Dog. She's in a good mood, obviously well fed and in her hand a brand new haggis. This bonhomie won't last long, I fear.

'Right, Old Girl,' she says as she shuts my door. 'Inverness, here we come. Ignition, retard spark, choke, full throttle and – Wurr-urr-urr-urr, cough cough splutter.

'That's odd, what's the matter with you? You started perfectly in John O'Groats. Try again.' Wurr-urr-urr cough, cough, splutter, cough. I start but with difficulty. Her Ladyship tries to rev my engine, but it really doesn't want to respond. She switches me off again and gets out. She opens my bonnet.

'Now, Old Thing, what could be wrong?' She peers around inside my engine compartment. 'You were fine getting here. So what has happened to upset you now?' At this point a relative drives past blowing its horn with its passengers waving. Her Ladyship wipes her hands on an old rag and waves back. She peers after the departing relative for rather too long. I think something's dawned on her. She turns back to me.

'Sabotage. That's it. That bloody man driving your look-a-like Old Girl. He came here while we were at lunch, didn't he?' Do you know, there are times when I really do wish I could communicate with you, Your Ladyship.

'So what could he do to mess you up and move on quickly? Plugs – they're tight. Plug leads tight too. Distributer leads, they're tight too. Hang on, what's this? Oh, very clever, brilliant. He's swapped the leads over. That's why you're struggling. Thank God the Nice Doctor John numbered them. That blooming man has swapped leads one and three over.' She swaps the leads back again and clambers back in. She pulls my starter and I'm happy again.

'This is war, Old Girl. Wait until we see him again. I'll sort him out for once and for all.'

'Hello Mrs McDonald. All back safe and sound.' Her Ladyship parks me up by the house. 'No real problems, except from another driver who was a complete pain in the proverbial. Here, can you put my haggis back in your fridge please?' Mrs McDonald examines the haggis with some bemusement.

'Och, this one's new. Did ye lose the other?'

'Not exactly, Mrs McDonald.' A broad grin spreads over Her Ladyship's face. 'Not exactly, another competitor shot it into the North Sea.' Mrs McDonald takes a long look at Her Ladyship, decides to say nothing and turns back towards the house, gripping the haggis rather tightly. It's almost as if she is expecting the need to protect herself from you-know-who with it.

'Och, by the by,' Mrs McDonald turns at the door. 'Sergeant Drummond, one of the policemen who was here this mornin' called to ask if ye'd pop doon to the station when ye get a chance.'

'Oh, right. I'll do that right now. I have a long day tomorrow. We want to reach the Scottish border. Can you tell me where the police station is please?'

'Och, it's quite easy. Get back onto the A9. Go a couple of miles south and ye'll see the signs for the police.'

'Thank you Mrs McDonald. See you later. Look after that haggis now.' Mrs McDonald looks closely at the rugby ball shaped delicacy. I think she's expecting it to hatch. Her Ladyship clambers back onto my driving seat. The Asthmatic Barking Dog looks confused. He was expecting a leg stretch. Her Ladyship starts me up and we head slowly down the drive.

As we pull into the car park, Her Ladyship spots Sergeant Drummond walking into the police station.

'Hello, Sergeant!' She deftly swerves me into a parking space both in front of the sergeant and the entrance. 'I think you want to see me.' The sergeant turns.

'Och, ye came then?'

'Yes indeed. What's the problem?'

'Nay, it's not a problem really, but we'd be obliged if you could look at some photographs and identify the man who stole yur purse.'

'I'd be delighted Sergeant, lead the way.'

'Are ye goin' tae leave yon car there?' Her Ladyship bristles slightly. I'm not surprised as the sergeant's tone is akin to one of those traffic wardens she loves to hate.

'I thought so,' she mutters through gritted teeth. 'Are you saying you'd like me to park it somewhere else?'

'Weel, yon parking space is really for the Chief Constable.' Sergeant Drummond looks around as if his boss is about to appear.

'Seriously Sergeant, it's gone six. Your Chief Constable will be at home sipping his first dram of whiskey for the evening. Let's go and get this identification done. We won't be long will we?' The sergeant shrugs his shoulders.

'Aye, an' that's where I should be too. Come on then.' They disappear inside the police station, the sergeant pausing at the door and peering around the car park, just to be sure that the boss really isn't there.

They are barely gone before they are back again.

'Thank ye, Madam. We thought we had the right man and ye've confirmed it. Since ye managed to get yur property back. I don't think we'll be chargin' him but we will give him a caution. We won't be troubling ye again.' He turns to shake Her Ladyship's hand, but her mind is already on something else and her eyes are riveted on the road.

'There he is!' She exclaims jabbing her finger towards the entrance. 'There look, the old car, there, there, there. The one that looks like mine. It's him. It's the man who sabotaged my car!' Sergeant Drummond's shoulders visibly drop and his face suggests that his day is far from over. He can see that dram waiting for him about to disappear over the horizon. Her Ladyship turns to him.

'Come on, let's get after him.'

'Will ye excuse me if I've missed something, but what has yon car got to do with the attempted theft of yur purse?'

'Absolutely nothing, Sergeant, absolutely nothing. You've not kept up with me, have you?' Her Ladyship clambers onto my front seat. 'That's the man who sabotaged my car earlier today and I need to have words with him.'

'Whoa now, by what do ye mean sabotaged?'

'He swapped my plug leads around while I was having lunch with my dog.' The Asthmatic Barking Dog sits up from his slumbers with a look that says, 'Don't involve me in this.'

'So get in, won't you? We have to apprehend him.'

'Slow down, Madam, let me get this straight. Ye were taking lunch with yon dog, an' yon man there who has just driven past swapped around the plug leads on the car. Do ye always eat meals with yur dog?'

'What's that got to do with it? The pub where we stopped for lunch allows dogs into the bar, so I took him in with me.' The Asthmatic Barking Dog is looking straight at the Sergeant and I think he's nodding in agreement. 'I gave him some of my chicken curry and chips and he's been breaking wind all afternoon.' The Asthmatic Barking Dog glances guiltily at Her Ladyship, settles himself down again, breaking wind at the same time. A flicker of light appears in the sergeant's eyes. I think he's spotted a way out and maybe, just maybe, he isn't going to say goodbye to that dram.

'Nay madam. Swapping sparking plug leads is'ne an offence here in Scotland. Be on yur way will ye? An' I'd advise ye to go now. It's gettin' dark and your headlights don't look as though they will help ye find yur way back to yur accommodation.'

Her Ladyship starts me up and looks almost accusingly at the sergeant, failing to understand why the attempted sabotage of me wasn't considered a heinous crime in his country.

'Can't stop… got to get after him. Come on, Old Girl, let's go.' And we are off. For heaven's sake, oh Wrinkled One, don't speed out of here or you'll have the whole of Inverness's finest chasing after us. I manage a glance at the sergeant as we reach the exit. He stares briefly after us, shrugs his shoulders and goes back into the police station. He must have decided to leave this well alone and if we do speed, cause a breach of the peace, or in any other way break the law, it will be another policeman's problem, because he is off home. At that we are gone, following my relative's trail. The sergeant was right, it is getting quite dark and my relative must have gone past several minutes ago. So how on earth Her Ladyship expects to catch up with him, I do not know.

At every junction, we stop. Her Ladyship peers in all directions in the vain hope that she will see her prey, but without luck. She takes a wild guess as to which turning to take and we shoot off down a new strange road somewhere in Inverness.

We must have taken five turnings and we're travelling along a fairly quiet street when I spot two yellow, dim lights approaching us. Her Ladyship spots them too.

'There he is, Old Girl. That's him. Let's stop him. I need to have a word with that man.' To my horror, she swings me across the road right in front of my relative to block his path. The driver slams on his brakes and they come to a standstill less than a foot from my side. Her Ladyship leaps out of me, no clamber this time, and she's marching around me to confront the driver. He's out of his seat too.

'What the hell do you think you were doing?' demands an unfamiliar voice from behind the headlights. 'You could have killed us both.'

'What was I doing? What was I DOING?' Her ladyship has her pecker up I fear. 'What was I doing? It was you, you who tried to sabotage my car back there in some village with an unmentionable name on the road to John O'Groats. So don't blooming question what I was doing.' The man steps forward, we can see him now in the reflection of my relative's headlights. He looks nothing like the man who had fiddled with my plug leads. This one is much younger. Her Ladyship realises this as well.

'Ah, umm, yes, ho hum. You're not the man I'm after are you? 'No?'

'No. The man I'm after sabotaged this car. He's not you.' I could see her crumbling, desperately trying to think of an excuse as to why she nearly drove this relative off the road. 'Mistaken identity, I am afraid. Ummm, are you all right? Is your car all right?'

'No thanks to you, the answer is in the affirmative to both those questions. I should really call the police after you shot across this road in front of me like that.'

'No! No, don't do that. I've just come from them telling them about how my car was sabotaged by someone in a car like mine, and like yours. Then I saw him driving past the police station, but the sergeant didn't understand. I tried to explain the seriousness of the crime, but he wasn't interested and told me to go back to my accommodation. I thought you were him.'

'Who?'

'Him, of course. The man who sabotaged me.' Her Ladyship is quite flustered now and this man could have her locked up.

'Look, I'm tired and looking for my hotel. Why don't you get back to yours before you cause any more incidents?' Her Ladyship almost curtseys in gratitude and clambers back into me.

'Thank you, and good luck on your run to Land's End.' She starts me up and after a few manoeuvres points me in the direction of our accommodation.

'Phew, Old Girl,' Her Ladyship says as we pull back into the B&B. 'That was a close one.' She switches off my engine and clambers out. 'C'mon Dog. Time to stretch your legs before some supper and bed.' The Asthmatic Barking Dog jumps out. He presses nose to ground and goes off in search of somewhere to lift his leg. The Nice Mister Arthur wanders over from the campsite on the other side of the road.

'You're a bit late getting here. Everything all right? Her Ladyship half turns towards him, yet still keeping an eye on Asthmatic Barking Dog. She's not put his lead on.

'Yes, fine. I was here a while ago, but the landlady told me the police sergeant wanted to see me. So I've been down to the police station doing an identification from some photographs. Then I saw the man who I thought had sabotaged my car. He was driving past.'

'Did you manage to identify him?'

'What? No, how could I? He was a couple of hundred yards away, across the car park.'

'What, the sergeant with the photographs?'

'No not him. The man. He was in a car that looks like Miss Daisy driving past the police station.'

'Let me get this straight. The sergeant was in a car driving past and asked you to do an identikit, yes?'

'No, he was beside me and we'd done the identification. I saw this car and I thought it was the one being driven by the man who sabotaged Miss Daisy by swapping her plug leads. But it wasn't him.' The Nice Mister Arthur decides not to take this conversation any further. He shakes his head sadly and wanders over the road back to the campsite.

Mrs McDonald appears in the doorway. She doesn't come right out. She grips the door firmly. Perhaps that's because she wants to be able to slam it in Her Ladyship's face if it turns out she really is a dangerous criminal.

'Ah hope that everything was fine with the police.' Her voice sounded quite nervous. The Asthmatic Barking Dog has just returned and he's trying to crawl underneath me. I have a feeling I know why.

'Hello, Mrs McDonald. Yes, all is absolutely fine. What are you doing Dog? Get out from under there.' She turns her attention back to Mrs McDonald. 'They just wanted me to look at some mug shots to identify the man who took my purse yesterday. Then as I was leaving, I spotted the man who... umm.' Her Ladyship decides not to go down this route again. She'd already confused The Nice Mister Arthur.

Mrs McDonald gives Her Ladyship a sidelong look.

'Dog! For heaven's sake will you get out from under the car? What on earth have you found?' The Asthmatic Barking Dog wedges himself further underneath. Her Ladyship bends down, grabs his haunches and tries to pull him out.

'Come on Dog, we don't have time for this now.' Her Ladyship pulls at him with all her strength and manages to pull him free. She attaches his lead.

'There we are. Let's go for that walk'. She pauses briefly and sniffs the air.

'Can you smell kippers, Mrs McDonald?'

Chapter Six

'Where the hell did you come from?' Her Ladyship enquires.
'Och, I've bin here all along.' No you haven't, you materialised right
beside me. I saw you. Well I didn't see you until you were here.

Inverness to ~~Gretna~~ Moffat

'Sorry Mrs McDonald,' Her Ladyship is coming down the steps of her B&B and shouting over her shoulder. 'I can't stop for breakfast. My over-sleeping has made me late.' She almost runs across to me and shoves her hand luggage into the area between my front and rear seats. She glances across the road to the now abandoned camp site. Oscar The Asthmatic Barking Dog decides it must be time to get up. He stretches himself and wags his tail with an enthusiastic "good morning." Her Ladyship completely ignores him, so he settles back down again with a look that says, "You're not my friend anymore!"

'Right, Old Girl, let's quickly check your oil and water, today has not started well. You know what I'm like without breakfast.' Yes I do. Please let today be, well, just normal so that we can make it to the Scottish border free of incidents, arrests and pyrotechnics. Mrs McDonald appears at the door clasping Her Ladyship's haggis. She watches Madam conversing with me and decides to go back indoors again.

'Hamish, she's talkin' to yon car again.' Her voice rolls out of the door, but Her Ladyship doesn't notice. A moment or two later she turns towards the door as though something in her memory tells her that someone was there. She shrugs and turns her attention back to me.

123

'Oil's fine. My goodness, Old Girl, you haven't needed a drop since we left Pembrokeshire. Now your water, let's check that.' She unscrews my radiator cap.

'We need a drop in here. Are you overheating a bit? These Scottish roads are enough to try the patience of a saint.' Mrs McDonald comes nervously through the door once more. This time she is gripping the haggis as if to defend herself with it.

'Oh hello again Mrs McDonald. I thought you were already there. But when I looked up, there you were, gone.'

'Aye well,' Mrs McDonald shuffles her feet as if reluctant to get any closer.

'Ah, you've got my haggis,' Her Ladyship remarks. 'I hope it behaved itself in your fridge during the night.' Mrs McDonald takes a couple of nervous steps forwards, then steps back again as Her Ladyship decides to walk over to her. Holding out her hand, Her Ladyship says, 'Thank you Mrs McDonald. I hope I don't need this today.'

'Need it? What d'ye mean, ye hopes ye dinna need it today?'

'It's just that the haggis, well, that man I told you about, you know, that Duncan from Glasgow said... well he said it would ease my path through Scotland.' Her Ladyship chooses not to explain any further. She's realised that Mrs McDonald already thinks she is off her trolley. She sniffs at the air and changes the subject.

'Can you smell kippers, Mrs McDonald?'

'What?' Mrs McDonald's voice is quite shrill and The Asthmatic Barking Dog wakes up with a start.

'I said, can you smell kippers? Because I'm sure I can.'

'Och, weel, I did serve Mr and Mrs Smith kippers fur breakfast...'

'Oh did you? But the smell seems to get stronger when I go near the car. Oh, never mind, I think we should be getting on our way. My haggis please?' Mrs McDonald drops the haggis into Her Ladyship's hand and retreats to the safety of the porch. 'Thank you.' Her Ladyship returns to me and stuffs the haggis down behind her seat.

'C'mon Dog. We'd better at least give you a quick walk before we set off.' The Asthmatic Barking Dog, now bored with events, is reluctant to get out. Then he smells the kippers, leaps eagerly out and once again shoves his nose under my rear end.

'What on earth is the matter with you?' Her Ladyship pulls him free and attaches his lead. 'Come on, let's go. We're late, the others have already gone and we need to catch them up.' Mrs McDonald scurries back into her house and once again I hear the familiar slam of the door and the three bolts being rammed home.

'Nice to meet you too, Mrs McDonald,' Her Ladyship cries at the closed door. Come on Dog, we've got two hundred and fifty miles to cover today.'

'I don't believe this, Old Girl. I thought that today at least wouldn't offer up the problems we had yesterday and the day before. At this rate I'll develop an allergy to Scotland. I mean, why can't he just pick them up in their boxes rather than a bunch at a time?'

Perhaps I should avail you, dear reader, of our situation. We are sitting in the village, or is it a town? I don't know to be honest, except it's called Grantown on Spey and we're on a road we shouldn't be on. We cannot move forwards because a van delivering bananas seems to have shed its load in the road. How it shed that load, I haven't a clue, but the driver appears to be in no hurry to clear them away, so is removing the said bananas a bunch at a time and placing them carefully back into his van.

'Oh for God's sake, what is the matter with the man?' Her Ladyship's blood pressure is rising... again! 'At this rate he'll take all bloody day. Get a bloody move on will you? I have to get to Gretna.' The man must have heard Her Ladyship because he stops, stretches his back and peers at the traffic jam of vehicles all waiting for him to finish. I can only believe that the drivers are as irritated as Her Ladyship.

In front of us is a rather smart Land Rover and behind us are several other cars. I imagine this must be a big traffic jam for this part of Scotland.

You may be wondering why we are on this road rather than the main one we are supposed to be on? The answer lies with Her Ladyship. No surprise there then. She took a wrong turning out of Inverness and it took her ten miles to realise that she had. Matters haven't been helped by that strange noise coming from my engine, the one that Her Ladyship noticed before we left Pembrokeshire. She hasn't worried that much about it but it seems permanent and more persistent now. I wish she'd do something about it. It's really annoying me.

'I think we're lost, Old Girl,' she'd said after pulling into a lay by. 'The map said we should take the A9. So how the hell did we get onto the A96? It's all your fault.' She always blames me.

'We should be going south, not east,' she said. 'Look, the sun's straight ahead of us. Hang on, we're coming into somewhere... what's it called? Nairn? There must be a way of turning south there. Let's take a look at the map. Yes, here we are, if that's Nairn over there, we can take the road here,' she stabs at the map with her finger... 'to Grantown on Spey, then we can find our way back to the A9 and south from there.' This all took place an hour and a half ago and now we are stuck in Grantown on Spey unable to move any further.

The delivery man glancing at the smart Land Rover suddenly

touches his cap and with an unforeseen vigour he starts to load his van up with the remaining bananas.

'That's more like it, but I wonder why he suddenly decided to get a move on?' He kicks the last few bananas out of the way, gestures to us that we can move past now and bows low as the Land Rover starts to move forwards.

'Sarky devil,' mutters Her Ladyship as she starts my engine again and we move forwards too. 'This little man holds us up for God knows how long and then bows low as we go past, the cheek of him. Right, Old Girl, I think we need to stay on this road now. The turning to the road that will take us back to the main road can't be far, it shouldn't take long.' Her ladyship manoeuvres me cautiously through the village, her eyes skinned for the turning. I wonder if this sleepy little place has ever seen so many vehicles coming through at the same time. Some pedestrians stop to watch us and wave as we go past.

'What nice people,' says Her Ladyship. 'We don't usually get friendly waves like that. I'm beginning to like Scotland now that we'll be out of it in twenty four hours. Where's this road then? It can't be that one. Tell you what, that Land Rover seems to know where he's going, we'll follow him.' We keep the Land Rover in sight and before you can say engine oil we are through the village, crossing the River Spey and continuing south.

'No, no, no, no, no. It can't be this way. Did you spot the turning, Old Girl? Because I didn't.' She shrugs her shoulders as if resigned to the situation.

'Look, everyone else is following this Land Rover. They're probably local, we must be alright.'

We arrive at a junction, I can see that our road is off to the left but the Land Rover is signalling to turn right.

'I think we should still follow it, Old Girl, don't you? Everyone else is indicating right.' Don't ask me, I am developing worrying feelings about all this. We signal right too and follow the Land Rover.

After about a mile the Land Rover stops in the middle of the road and as we catch up with it we see someone in the passenger seat pick up some binoculars and peer out of the window.

'Oh for heaven's sake, what now? Are we ever going to get to Gretna?' Her Ladyship angrily blows my horn – three short beeps followed by a really long one. The Land Rover fails to react.

'Right that's it. I've had enough of this nonsense.' Switching off my engine, Her Ladyship throws open my door and gets out. The Asthmatic Barking Dog decides that something demanding his attention is required and a walk might be in the offing. I fear that a walk is the last thing in Madam's mind. She is in the mood for a row with the poor driver of that Land Rover who, it seems, has only stopped to enjoy the scenery.

Her Ladyship has barely reached the Land Rover when a number of little red dots appear on her back. Voices shout from behind.

'You! Armed police! Stay where you are, get down on the ground, lie down, and put your hands behind your head!' Her Ladyship spins round to see where the voices have come from. The little red dots now play on her head and chest.

'You've got to be joking,' she shouts back. 'Have you seen the state of this road? It's covered in mud puddles. I will be writing to the Scottish Minister of Transport when I get home.'

'Armed Police,' the voices shout again. 'Stay where you are, get down on the ground, lie down, and put your hands behind your head!' Her Ladyship finally gets a grip on this state of affairs and gingerly lowers herself to the ground. She is still, to my great embarrassment, complaining.

'Oh bloody hell, I'm going to get filthy. Look at this mud.' The Asthmatic Barking Dog, deciding that Her Ladyship perhaps wants to play after all, jumps out through my open door and trots over to her. He starts sniffing and nuzzling at her.

'Push off, Dog,' Her Ladyship mumbles through the muddy puddle that her face is lying in. 'Can't you see I'm in some difficulty?'

A policeman comes over, takes Her Ladyship's arms and handcuffs her. Another man joins them, and both help her to her feet. Oh yes, those puddles are very muddy. She has mud all down the right side of her face and her front.

'Would someone please tell me what the hell is going on?' Hasn't she realised yet?

A Land Rover door opens and a Corgi jumps out. The Asthmatic Barking Dog nonchalantly wanders over and begins his usual bottom sniffing ritual. The Corgi seems appreciative, if a little reserved. I imagine that The Asthmatic Barking Dog will want to have one of his chats

"Hello Mate. You alright?" Sniff, sniff

"Hello. What are you doing here?" The Corgi has a refined sniff.

"Don't know, Mate. My owner makes all the decisions. But she ain't half in a proper mess now. Those men with the guns, are they something to do with you?" Sniff, lick.

"Yes they are actually. They are protecting us from people like her." Sniff.

"That her is my owner and she's going to be impossible after this." The Asthmatic Barking Dog lifts his leg against one of the Land Rover wheels. The Corgi follows suit.

'Excuse me, Madam,' says one of the men, loosening his grip on her. 'You were about to assault Her Majesty. You are under arrest.'

'What on earth are you talking about, Young Man?' Her Ladyship is really rattled. This won't hold well for her when she is hauled up before The Beak. 'I've been stuck behind this Land Rover for miles. I just wanted to get to Gretna before it gets dark and then the bloody thing stops in the middle of the road to enjoy the damned scenery. Then you lot jump out and point your guns at me.'

Another corgi jumps out of the Land Rover and joins the ongoing bottom sniffing and leg lifting activity. Following the corgi, a woman in a headscarf and Barbour jacket steps out. I feel I should bow or curtsey, but I'm a car and cars don't do that sort of thing.

'What's going orn, Stephen?' One of the armed men clicks himself to attention.

'I'm sorry, Maam, but we thought that this woman was about to attack you.' Realisation finally dawns on Her Ladyship and she momentarily goes limp at the knees. The policemen flanking her hold her up to support her.

'Oh my goodness.' Her Ladyship instinctively tries to tidy her hair and brush of the mud, but being handcuffed, she can't. So I brace myself for a deluge of sycophancy instead.

'Your Majesty, Maam. Oh my goodness, oh good grief, oh my God, Maaam, I am so sorry. I never realised it was you. I thought you were one of those farmers who delight in holding up traffic. We get a lot of that in Pembrokeshire. Oh, it's been a terrible mistake, I'm so, so sorry.' Her Ladyship attempts a curtsey, something quite difficult when held firmly by close protection officers.

'We must definitely visit Pembrokeshire, then.' Suddenly everyone's attention is drawn to a yelp from The Asthmatic Barking Dog. One of the corgis is trying to mount him and he looks pleadingly at Her Ladyship.

'Vulcan, do stop that nonsense, it won't get you anywhere.' She turns to Her Ladyship. 'Is that your dorg?'

'Yes Maam, Your Majesty. He's called Oscar but I just call him Dog. He seems to like that.'

'So, how did you end up in the Cairngorms then? Oh Stephen, do take those handcuffs orf. Somehow I don't think this person will cause me harm.' The officer clicks himself to attention once again with a 'Yes Maam' and steps over to release Her Ladyship's hands.

'Well, it was like this, Your Majesty, Maam,' Her Ladyship rubs her wrists and the two police officers continue to watch her suspiciously. 'The truth is, I got lost.'

'You got lorst?'

'Yes, Your Majesty, Maam. I took a wrong turning out of Inverness, headed east instead of south. I got completely lost and then found myself with you, stuck behind those bananas. And that little man, well he was just taking a ridiculous amount of time clearing them away and I got annoyed.

'So did I. It was only when he saw me that he decided to get a move on. But you mentioned Pembrokeshire. What brings you to Scotland?' Her Ladyship brightens up.

'Well, you see, Your Majesty, Maam, I'm attempting the John O'Groats to Land's End run in my little car here to mark the ninetieth anniversary of the Austin Seven.'

'Good heavens, you're nort. Are you? Are you seriously attempting to make it all the way to Land's End? In that?'

Yes indeed, Your Majesty, Maam. Myself and over sixty others.'

Excuse me, your Majesty, but it's me, Miss Daisy, who is attempting the run. All Her Ladyship is doing is planting her fat bottom on my seat and pointing me in the right direction. Of course, you can't hear me can you? How silly of me. But she looks over at me briefly as though she did.

'I used to drive one of those during the war. Do you have to adjust your spark manually?'

'Yes, Your Majesty, Maam. Miss Daisy's a bit of a challenge I'm afraid. She's rather cantankerous at times.' Her Majesty gives a "We are amused" smile on hearing my name. I hope it was a smile of appreciation.

'A bit like the Duke of Edinburgh then?'

'Oh no, Your Majesty, Maam.' She gestures towards me. 'This one's really curmudgeonly, I'm afraid.' Oh thank you very much, Your Ladyship, you've just scuppered any chances I might have for a gong. Her Majesty glances across at the Land Rover.

'I know exactly what you mean.' She says. 'So where are you off to today?'

Well, Your Majesty, Maam, I had hoped to make it to Gretna, but I'm not sure I will now. This old thing isn't good in the dark. The headlights aren't very bright.'

'Stephen, do you think you could rustle up a car to escort this lady and her, umm, car back to the main road so she can continue her journey south?'

'Of course, Maam, I'll see to it straight away.' She turns back to Her Ladyship.

'Well, I trust that from now on you will have a safe and uneventful journey to Land's End.' She sniffs the air. Can anyone else smell kippers?' Her Ladyship involuntarily sniffs her armpit and, satisfied that the smell isn't coming from her, turns to me.

'Yes, Your Majesty, Maam. I noticed it last night and again this morning. I think it might be coming from Miss Daisy.

Her Majesty turns to get back into the Land Rover. 'Willow, Vulcan, get back in the car.' The two corgis obediently do as they are told. The Asthmatic Barking Dog looks crushed. He will never know the high circles he has been moving in.

Her Ladyship attempts another low curtsey and stumbles, grabbing my radiator cap for support. The Land Rover starts up and slowly pulls away.

'It is you, Old Girl. You don't half stink. Where on earth is it coming from?' The Asthmatic Barking Dog takes a last sniff underneath my running board and hops back onto my rear seat.

'Right, you will stay here.' It's PC Stephen. 'I've arranged for a car to come and escort you back onto the main road. He'll be here in about ten minutes. Pull over to let us pass and please wait for the other car to arrive. Don't go anywhere, and I do mean anywhere. Okay?'

'Yes, Officer.' Her Ladyship gets in, starts me up and gently pulls me over to the side of the road. 'How's that? Can you get through?' she asks, meekly.

'Yes, thank you. Now remember what I said, don't move from here. I really don't want to see you again.' He gets back into his car and one by one the cars behind pull past us.

'Well that's a complete pain, Old Girl,' Her Ladyship watches the cortège disappear off into the distance. 'We're going to have to wait here until this other car turns up. I'm sure we could find our own way, don't you think?'

No, actually. Look what your navigation has achieved so far.

'Tell you what, Old Girl, let's have a look and see what this noise you're making is all about.' She opens my bonnet and peers inside. 'Everything looks okay. Let's start you up.' She does so and takes a more careful look at my engine.

'Aha. Well I never would have thought that. It's your fan, Old Girl. The bearing that The Nice Mister Roger put in last week seems to be very dry. I think I'll just give you a squirt of oil for now and see how we go.' She pulls out a tin of Three in One and applies it to the fan assembly. The noise immediately quietens down.

'There, that's better isn't it? A simple solution.' She looks up. 'And here he is.' A car with a blue flashing light pulls up behind us and a policeman gets out. 'It's Sergeant Drummond, Old Girl. Hello Sergeant, how nice to see you again.'

'I wish I could say the same. I thought I'd seen the back of ye yesterday.' He comes over and stands beside Her Ladyship to peer into my engine compartment too.

'What a small world Sergeant.' Her Ladyship sounds nervous. He turns to face her.

'Let me get this straight. Ye were arrested for attempting to assault a member of the royal family? And look at yurself? Yu're in a right mess.'

'It wasn't exactly like that, Sergeant. I didn't realise it was the Queen. I thought it was some blooming farmer taking delight in stopping in the middle of the road to check his land and livestock.'

'Aye, well.' He peers back into my engine compartment. 'D'ye have a problem with this?'

'I did, but it seems fine now. The fan assembly needed a bit of lubrication, that's all. She's as sound as a bell.' Her Ladyship closes my bonnet. Sergeant Drummond sniffs at the air.

'God in heaven, what's that awful smell?'

'You're noticing it too?' He looks at Her Ladyship incredulously. 'It's been getting gradually worse since yesterday. I just can't work out what in this car would smell like rotting kippers.' The sergeant turns to Her Ladyship.

'That's it, rotting kippers. I think I know what yur problem might be.' He gets onto his knees and peers under my rear end. 'As I thought, d'ye have some wire cutters?

'What on earth do you need wire cutters for?'

'To cut the wires holdin' two rotting kippers to yur exhaust. Someone has been playin' a joke on ye.' Her Ladyship rummages through her tool box, produces some cutters and hands them down to the Sergeant.

'What do you mean playing a joke?'

'There ye go, problem solved. Phew, they really stink.' He allows the kippers to fall to the ground. 'I grew up in Fraserburgh, the fishing port, an' as bairns we used to tie fish to people's exhaust pipes as a joke. It would tak' a day or so for them to go off with the heat. Someone's done this to you.'

'And I know which little swine did,' says Her Ladyship. 'I know exactly who did this. I'll get him.'

'Now we dinna want ye to break the law agin do we? At least not in Scotland. Let's get ye on yur way and put ye on the main road south. Will ye follow me?' He gets back into his car and pulls it past us. Her Ladyship clambers back onto my driving seat and starts me up. We follow the police car, which for some reason insists on keeping its blue lights on. This is so embarrassing.

'The absolute bastard,' mutters Her Ladyship as we drive along. 'I'll get him.'

We've reached Hamilton. We had parted company with Sergeant Drummond in a car park just outside Perth. He told us to follow the A9 and roads signed Stirling, Motherwell, Moffat and Gretna and to not get lost again.

'In yur car it'll tak' ye aboot three an' a half hours so you'd best get going.' Her Ladyship, however, decided to stay for lunch and to find somewhere where she could clean herself up a bit.

'I've just eaten my first haggis, Old Girl,' she said when she returned. 'They're quite nice actually, especially with tatties and neeps, smothered in whiskey sauce and washed down with a nice local malt. Tatties and neeps are potatoes and turnips, by the way.' Yes, I do know, Your Ladyship.

'Dog liked the Haggis too. I wonder what's in it.' Do you know, Her Ladyship isn't safe to be out on her own.

There are not many hours of daylight left. I'm not sure we will make it to Gretna, especially as I think Madam will be pulling in to a layby soon. Why? That horrible noise with my fan has started again. You-know-who will eventually get the message.

'That noise has come back, Old Girl.' Yesss I know. 'We'd better pull over when there's a layby. That's another thing I like about Scotland's roads, they seem to have lots of laybys. You never have to go far before you find one.'

That's a turn up for the books. Suddenly she likes Scotland's roads after everything she's said about them. Her Ladyship sniffs.

'Old Girl, can you smell petrol?' Funny you should say that, it's only been smelling like that for the last thirty miles. What is the matter with this woman?

'There's a layby over there. Look… and there's another Austin parked up. Maybe he'll have an idea about a better cure for the fan noise.' We pull in and stop behind my relative. Its owner is lying underneath. Her Ladyship gets out and walks across to him.

'Hello? Trouble?' She asks?

Well that's blooming obvious, why else would he be lying under a jacked-up relative with an open tool box beside him?

'Uh? Hello, yes, I'm leaking oil. I'm just tightening my sump.' Says a voice from beneath my relative.

'Oh dear.' Her Ladyship shuffles her feet on the ground, obviously completely indifferent to the trials of this young man. 'Will it take long? Only I'd appreciate some expert advice about a noise under my bonnet.'

'Yes, I heard it as you drove in. Sounds like your fan assembly.'

'Yes!' cries Her Ladyship in a rather falsetto voice. 'It is! I squirted some Three in One on it this morning and it was fine for a while, but the noise has come back.

'Have you tried pumping some grease into its nipple?'

'Yes, I tried before we left Inverness, but I don't think I had the

136

strength to pump it in properly and I was yanking at the pump as hard as I could.' A snort of laughter emanates from underneath my relative, then the thump of a human head on a chassis.

'Shit and blast.' The man wiggles himself out from underneath my relative rubbing his temple. His face is covered in dirty oil.

'Mammy, how I love ya, how I love ya, my dear old Mammy,' Her Ladyship sings upon seeing him.

'What?'

'Well you do look rather like Al Jolson.'

'Never heard of him, sorry.' He grabs a cloth to wipe his face and hands. 'So let's have a look at your problem. I imagine that's why you pulled over?'

'Well yes, actually. When I saw your Seven and thought you might know how I might more permanently solve Miss Daisy's problem.'

'Daft name for a car, isn't it?' Excuse me, but no, it's not!

'Start her up and let's have another listen.' Her Ladyship complies and the awful grinding and scraping noise ensues.

'Stop the engine, switch it off.' Her Ladyship complies again.

'Look at this. Look at how your fan is wobbling.' He grabs one of my fan blades and wobbles it about. 'There look at that. The bearing has gone. It hasn't been getting any lubrication. That bronze bush is completely shot and look,' he grabs the fan again. 'This is on the verge of chewing up your radiator.'

'That's exactly the same problem I had before I left, but a friend fixed it for me. Is it that bad?'

'Yes, it is that bad. If it had started to chew up your radiator, you would have been looking at a very big bill for a new one. As it stands now, you're looking at less than ten pounds for a new bush and a few minutes to clean out the grease canal in the spigot.' The glazing up of Her Ladyship's eyes as usual suggests she hasn't a clue what he's talking about.

'The simplest solution will be to take off your fan belt. Have you a spanner so I can loosen it?'

'We did that last time, but then I was only driving a few miles. This time it's all the way to Land's End. Won't she overheat?'

'No. Not this time of year, she'll be fine. Just don't sit in traffic jams with the engine running too long.' Her Ladyship passes him a spanner, he loosens the fan belt and removes it. The Asthmatic Barking Dog, having watched these activities with great interest, spots the open car door and hops out. Seeing a rather interesting grass verge he trots over to inspect it.

'There we are,' the man hands the spanner back to Her Ladyship. 'That'll get you to Land's End. But you need to get that sorted properly when you get home.' He peers into my engine compartment again. 'There's an awful smell of petrol in here.'

'She smelt of rotten kippers earlier,' commented Her Ladyship. 'Have I a problem?'

'Perhaps. Let's take a look.' He opens the other side of my bonnet. 'There, look. You've cracked your petrol pipe.' Her Ladyship looks in as well and they both watch as the pipe drip, drip, drips continuously onto the hot exhaust, each drip immediately evaporating in the heat.

'You're lucky you didn't catch fire. We can fix that as well, but only temporarily. Have you some flexible petrol pipe?' Her Ladyship rummages through her tool box. She whips a length of plastic pipe out and thrusts it triumphantly towards him.

'This all right?'

'Perfect. I don't suppose you have some small jubilee clips?'

'No, 'fraid not.'

Don't worry, I have a pair you can have.' He digs deep into his tool box and pulls some clips out. 'I'll cut the broken piece of pipe out and replace it with the flexible hose and you'll be fit and ready to head south again.' Her Ladyship smiles and he sets to work. The

Asthmatic Barking, having satisfied himself that the verge no longer requires his attention, trots back and hops back onto my rear seat, but not before lifting his leg against my rear wheel.

A coach pulls into the layby with rather a lot of smoke coming out of its rear end. It stops ahead of us. The driver hops out and walks around it to the rear. The smoke continues to billow out and the driver just scratches his head. Her Ladyship glances across at the coach and seems to recognise it. It does seem very familiar.

'There you are, all fixed. You're fit to go.' Her Ladyship turns her attention back to the job in hand as the man closes my bonnet.

'Thank you so much, I'm very grateful. Can I pay you something for your trouble?' He looks her up and down, grins and then shakes his head.

'No, no need. Glad to help.'

'That's very kind of you, thank you.' She nods towards the coach, 'I think he's going to need your help too now.'

'No way, I'm getting out of here. Three repairs in the last forty five minutes are enough for me. See ya.'

'Bye… and thank you. Oh, don't forget your tool kit.'

'What?'

'Your tool kit, it's still beside your car. You don't want to go without it.' It's strange but Her Ladyship really does seem to have an obsession with other drivers' tool kits.

'Oh yes, thanks.' He grabs his kit and plonks it firmly on his rear seat. 'See you at Lands End?' He climbs into the driving seat.

'Oh yes, indeed, hopefully. Thank you again.' Her Ladyship's attention turns back to the smoking coach as with a final wave, the man drives off.

'You recognise that coach too, don't you Old Girl? Where have we seen it before?' Her Ladyship busies herself closing up her own toolbox and putting it away, occasionally glancing at this coach which we both know but can't quite place. Passengers begin to leave the coach to see what is going on. Aha, that Hawaiian shirt, now that is familiar. It's Aylmer the American. He looks at the smoke billowing out of the back of the coach and then at the driver scratching his head. Aylmer's face lights up and he goes back into the coach. He returns moments later clasping a haggis.

'Say, Driver,' he says. 'Will this help fix it?' The driver stares with astonishment at the haggis that's being offered to him.

'Wha'? Wha' the hell do ye expect me to do with yon haggis?' Her Ladyship decides that perhaps now is the time to leave, and to leave quickly.

'Sir, we met this lady in an old car the other day.' Her Ladyship starts me up and pulls us quietly forwards. 'And she told us that these haggis things well help ease our path through Scottish land. We've all got them.' He spots us.

'There she is! Hey lady, come over here, tell the driver how to use a haggis to fix this coach.' Her Ladyship has absolutely no intention of stopping.

'Sorree… got to get on. Appointment in Gretna!' She presses her foot on my accelerator and my abiding memory of that coach will forever be of fifty American tourists each proffering a haggis at the driver while he phones for assistance.

'Phew, Old Girl, that could have been a bit awkward. Let's get on to our stop in Gretna.'

It's about two hours since we left that lay by. It's getting misty and rather dark.

'If I am not very much mistaken it's beginning to get foggy, Old

Girl. I think we should start to look for somewhere to stay for the night. We're not going to make it to Gretna, especially if this fog gets worse. There's a sign for somewhere up ahead, let's take it and see if we can find somewhere to stay.' She half turns her head towards The Asthmatic Barking Dog.

'Not sure I can find a place that lets you stay in the room, Dog, but I'll see what I can do.' She swings off the main road.

'I think that sign said Moffat. Golly gosh, this fog is getting worse. Lights on and slow down, I think.' Her Ladyship slows to a crawl and puts my lights on. In front of me are the two familiar yellow balls. Not on the road on this occasion, but attempting to cut through the fog. I am sure my lights were better than this all those years ago. With my lights trying to penetrate the fog, combined with an aura of a full moon trying to penetrate from above, well it makes the whole place really creepy. We pass a street lamp. It casts a brief triangular sodium-coloured beam downward before we plunge into a murky darkness again. Then there's another one and another. Her Ladyship peers over my steering wheel into the yellowy, grey gloom. The Asthmatic Barking Dog? He couldn't care less. He's fast asleep.

'It's getting worse, Old Girl. I really don't know how we're going to find anywhere to stay.' We crawl forwards. Suddenly I see an illuminated number plate in front of me. Fortunately, so does Her Ladyship and she slams on my brakes. We've stopped barely an inch from a lorry.

'Its lights are on, Old Girl, probably somebody around. I'll get out and talk to the driver. Perhaps he'll know where we can go.' She quickly disappears into the fog. I hear her through the thick, black greyness in conversation with somebody and it isn't long before she returns with a triumphant smile on her face.

'I've got good news and I've got bad news Old Girl.' The Asthmatic Barking Dog wakes up, stretches himself and peers at Her

Ladyship getting back in with a look that says "Are we there yet?" Realising we aren't, he settles back down again.

'The bad news is that there's something on in Moffat and the hotels are booked up, but the good news is that if we head up this road for another mile and then turn left down a winding lane and follow that for a while, we'll find a bed and breakfast. Apparently it's the only house down that road and we can't miss it. It's called Schmidt House. Strange name for a B&B, don't you think?' She turns to The Asthmatic Barking Dog. 'And apparently they do allow dogs. That's a stroke of luck isn't it, Old Girl? Right. Check the Speedo and we'll work out that mile.' Her Ladyship's mobile phone rings. She picks it up.

'Hello? Who's that? Hello Arthur… Where am I? I'm in Moffat. You wouldn't believe what's happened today… Well first of all we got lost… What do you mean "Nothing unusual about that"? To cut a long story short, we met the Queen… Yes that's what I said, the Queen… But I was lying in a puddle… What? No, not having a piddle, I was lying in a puddle. The policemen made me do it… No it wasn't some new sort of royal protocol, it was all a big mistake… Look, where are you? At the camp site in Gretna… Yes well, I'm not going to get there tonight. I'm stopping somewhere near Moffat… Yes Moffat. Look, don't wait for me, I'll plod along and hopefully catch you up at Bromsgrove tomorrow evening. Okay? Bye then.' She switches the phone off.

'Right, Old Girl, let's find that B&B.' She starts me up, rolls gently backwards and we creep past the parked lorry. She assumes the position of gripping the steering wheel and peering carefully over the top of it.

It isn't long before we drive through a built-up area. From the windows of the houses lights blaze out horizontally, stretching into the mist but just failing to meet the lights from the houses opposite.

'That must have been Moffat, Old Girl. I imagine we've done

about three quarters of a mile by now. Can't be far.' She continues to peer over my steering wheel, eyes skinned for a possible turning to the left.

'Look, there, there it is. And yes, a sign for the B & B. Schmidt House, that's the one.' Well, there is a sign. It hangs on a couple of chains from what might have been an old gallows. One of the chains is longer than the other so the sign appears to be pointing down a hill.

'Come on, Old Girl, here we go. Blimey, is that or is that not a steep hill?' Perhaps, Your Ladyship, that is why the sign was pointing downwards.

'I think we need to drop a gear or two. This is too steep for your brakes alone.' As we descend this hill, the fog starts to clear.

'Oh it isn't fog, Old Girl, I think it's low cloud and we're underneath it. I can see where we're going now.' She's right. The mist is clearing to reveal a winding lane with untouched grass and weeds growing along the middle of it.

'God knows when someone last drove down this road. The whole place seems deserted.'

We eventually find another gallows with a Schmidt House sign, only this time one chain has broken completely and it hangs precariously in the air. Her Ladyship pulls up and gets out to open the gate.

'I can barely see a thing, Old Girl,' she says on her return. 'Not a light on anywhere, but I think that's the large grey outline of an old house. Come on, let's go and see if anyone's in.'

We roll gingerly down the gravel drive, my wheels scrunching loudly as we crawl slowly up to the house. Her Ladyship pulls up, switches off my lights and carefully applies my hand brake.

'Good grief this place is rather creepy, isn't it Old Girl. Surely they must have heard us coming down their drive, why is there no light on anywhere? Dog, you stay in the car and I'll wander around and take a look-see.' As she gets out and straightens herself, a shaft of moonlight appears from behind a cloud and briefly illuminates a gaunt grey building stretching high above us. Her Ladyship tentatively wanders away from me to take a look around. She rapidly returns.

'C'mon, Old Girl,' she says, quickly getting back in. 'This place gives me the creeps. I think we'll go back to Moffat. I'd rather sleep in you than stay here.' The Asthmatic Barking Dog has sensed the menace as well. He's on his feet now and is looking out through the windscreen. His hackles are up and he gives out a long, low growl.

'Shut up, Dog, you're scaring me.' She starts my engine. He growls again, eerily.

'What on earth is the matter with you?' She switches on my lights.

'AAAARGH! What's that?' There, standing in the dim glow of my headlights as if transfixed like rabbits are a man and a woman, both with very grey complexions in spite of the yellow headlights. They don't move. Her Ladyship switches off my engine but leaves my lights on. 'Just in case, Old Girl,' she whispers as she clambers out.

'Are ye looking fur accommodation?' The man shows absolutely no expression as he says this.

'Aye,' says the woman, again with an expressionless face. 'Are ye looking fur a bed?' The Asthmatic Barking Dog's hackles are still up, but now he can see actual people he decides that watching might be more interesting than growling.

'Umm, well,' says Her Ladyship. The nervousness in her voice is very apparent. 'No, I really don't want to put you to any trouble. I can go somewhere else.' Her voice is getting falsetto now, a sure sign that she is scared.

'Nay woman, ye can bed here.' The man steps forwards, still with an expressionless face. The woman disappears from my lights and we hear a door open. A very dim light cuts out through the remnants of the mist, only to be broken by her silhouette. I am beginning to wonder if this couple are among the living dead. Her Ladyship cautiously gets out.

'Look, it must be out of season for you here. I'll happily go back to Moffat.'

'Nay woman, no need to go elsewhere. Ye can sleep here in our hoose. Shall I tak' yur luggage?'

'Well, umm, yes thank you. A man in the village said that you allow dogs. Is that right?'

'Aye, that's true.' He turns to the woman. 'Isn't it Meg?' The woman is still standing in the light wandering out through the door.

'Aye that's true. We like dogs, don't we Hamish?' Is it me or did that sound menacing? Her Ladyship grabs her handbag and rummages through it. She pulls out her vanity mirror and checks her make up, then she twists the mirror towards Hamish.

'Just wanted to be sure he's not a vampire, Old Girl.' Her Ladyship whispers. 'If he was we wouldn't be able see him in the mirror. Someone once told me that years ago. Or did I see it in an old horror film? Anyway, I never thought it would be useful one day.' She attaches The Asthmatic Barking Dog's lead, but he is reluctant to get out.

'Come on, Dog.' She tugs at his lead and he tentatively steps out onto the gravel. Satisfied that all seems safe, he sniffs around as far as his lead will allow. Her Ladyship removes her case and thrusts it at the man called Hamish with a tremulous 'Thank you.'

'Will ye follow me?' He turns on his heel and moves very slowly towards the house. Her Ladyship and The Asthmatic Barking Dog nervously follow.

'Oh, I forgot to turn off the car's lights.' Her Ladyship comes back to me and reaches in to turn my lights off. 'If I'm not out of that house by nine o'clock tomorrow, call the police.' Oh yes? And how the hell am I supposed to do that?

She turns on her heel and follows the Man Called Hamish inside. I wonder if I'll ever see her again.

Chapter Seven

'Wheear are we goan' Stanley?'
'Nowhere i' particular Branton, we're just goan t'av some fun.'

~~Gretna~~ Moffat to ~~Bromsgrove~~ Rotherham

It's been a rather weird night. In fact it's been rather like a scene out of a 1960s Hammer Horror film. We had a full moon, which occasionally emerged from behind a cloud, casting shafts of silver light and causing the hard-edged shadow of the gaunt Victorian house to slowly move towards me and eventually engulf me. When the full moon disappeared behind the house completely, all I could see was an aura of light that gave the building a menacing halo. Then there were the sound effects. At first the night was completely silent except for the occasional creak of the large fir trees stretching up behind the house as the wind caused them to sway. The trouble was, there wasn't any wind. Then in the distance I heard the spitting and yowling of two cats fighting, accompanied by an hourly chiming of a church clock with what sounded like a cracked bell. Just as I had got used to the cats and the cracked clock and was about to doze off, I was disturbed by the bark of a fox in a neighbouring field. I simply couldn't settle. Then a loud, metallic crash from the rear of the house nearly made me jump out of my tyres.

So I am really pleased and relieved to see the sun start to rise. The question is, will I ever see Her Ladyship and The Asthmatic Barking Dog again? At least it's getting lighter and, looking around, everything appears to be quite normal. To my left is the gravel drive with small conifer trees running along each side. To my right is the house with its high gables and tower-like structure, giving it a menacing aspect that actually isn't quite so menacing in the developing daylight. In front of me is what seems to be a shed and a vegetable garden. There are barely any vegetables growing in it, but it is still spring so I shouldn't expect to see much. No, so long as Her Ladyship and The Asthmatic Barking Dog appear, having breakfasted and are all fit and well, then there is nothing to worry about is there?

The front door flies open and Her Ladyship tumbles out, half dressed, struggling with an unzipped overnight bag and trying to stop clothes falling out. In hot pursuit is The Asthmatic Barking Dog. They both almost fall down the granite steps leading to the drive.

'Come on, Old Girl, let's get the hell out of here.' Her Ladyship starts to pile her luggage in wherever she can find space.

'No time to strap this onto your luggage rack. I don't know how creepy it was out here last night, but it can't have been nearly as creepy as it was in that blooming house. I'm in such a state I've just cleaned my teeth with my haemorrhoid cream. I just thank God I didn't treat my haemorrhoids by rubbing Colgate Spearmint into my bottom. Come on, Dog, you can have a walk and your breakfast when we've got away from this god-forsaken place. I better quickly check your engine, make sure nothing has fallen off.' She hurriedly packs her things away and then opens my bonnet and leans in.

'Are ye sure ye dinna want any breakfast woman?' The man called Hamish has materialised just beside me. 'Meg makes a very fine porridge ye know.'

'Oh-My-God!' Her Ladyship brings her head up so suddenly that she whacks it on the edge of my open bonnet. 'Where the hell did you come from?' She enquires as she rubs her head.

'Och, I've bin here all along.' No you haven't, you materialised right beside me. I saw you. Well I didn't see you until you were here – standing and leering.

'Are ye not havin' breakfast?' Hamish repeats. 'Meg makes a fine porridge'

'No, no thank you. We have to go. Get in, Dog and put your hackles down. I said, get in.' The Asthmatic Barking Dog decides to make a point by lifting his leg on Hamish's trousers before getting onto my back seat. Fortunately he doesn't notice.

'But ye paid fur a bed and some breakfast. If ye dinna have breakfast, then we must refund ye.'

'No, no please don't worry about that.' Her Ladyship shoots into the drivers seat and starts me up. 'We must get off. Long way to go, you know.' She engages gear and lets out my clutch much too quickly and we leap forwards. 'Keep the money, please,' and we are already half way up the drive. With a reasonable distance between us and that strange man, The Asthmatic Barking Dog decides it's okay to have a bark at him.

'Thank goodness we're away from that place, Old Girl,' Her Ladyship says as she shuts the gate behind us and we head back towards Moffat. It was awful... so, so creepy. When we left you, Dog and I followed them in. The woman seemed to have disappeared by the time we reached the lobby. I mean literally disappeared. All the doors leading off the lobby were shut but I hadn't heard any doors actually closing. You remember how silent everything was last night? We would have surely heard a door shut, wouldn't we? So where did she go?' She gives out a little snort. 'They probably slept in coffins in the cellar. There again, wouldn't I have heard the lids creak as they shut them? Coffin lids always creaked in the Vincent Price films. Anyway, I paid the man before going to our room. He asked me when we wanted breakfast and I told him something like eight o'clock, but I'd already decided that we'd hit the road at the first possible opportunity.

'He led us upstairs into that high gabled part of the house. Two bloody floors, he took us up two bloody floors. Don't tell me that there weren't any rooms available on the first floor. I mean, you were the only car there. So why couldn't we have had a room on the first floor? I tell you why, he was leading us to our doom and that was the furthest possible distance from the entrance and therefore from you. It was so creepy, I can't tell you. There were stuffed owls and deer's heads along all the corridors. They cast horrible shadows along the walls. I remarked that it seemed very dark in the corridor.

'"Aye well," he said. "We dinna wan' tae waste electricity do we? Here's yon room." He opened a door… yes it creaked. It was a room right at the back of the house. I heard him switch on a light. There was a fizzing sound and then a faint almost orange beam of light shone… well hardly shone, dribbled out of the doorway would be a better description. "There ye are," he said. "Yon bathroom is at the end of the corridor. I bid ye good night then." And he was gone. Dog and I looked around the room – what we could see of it. To say the furnishings were spartan is putting it mildly. A metal bedstead like we had at school, a bedside table but no bedside light, just the light that hung in the centre of the room – with a large metal bowl sitting on the bedside table. I don't know why there should be a large bowl beside the bed. Possibly something to throw up into when we were scared out of our wits. There was a chair, a matching dressing table and wardrobe which reminded me very much of the utility furniture that was available just after the war. And the place stank of musty mothballs. I was able to lock the door on the inside. I left the key in, in case they tried to unlock it during the night.

'I couldn't sleep. I kept hearing noises in the house. I was sure I could hear someone shuffling up and down the corridor. Dog was unsettled too. He kept waking up and starting to growl. Then, gosh, it must have been about four o'clock, I'd managed to doze off but was woken up by a strange noise outside. I'd had enough. I grabbed the large metal bowl, opened the window and threw the bowl at the noise. It made a hell of a crash, I think I hit some dustbins.' You're telling me, Your Ladyship, it scared me out of my wits.

'As soon as it was dawn I got up, dressed and we sneaked downstairs. Every single stair I put a foot on creaked. That must be how they knew we were up. So without a good night's sleep, I'm absolutely pooped. Oh, look over there, isn't that a café? Let's stop for breakfast.' The Asthmatic Barking Dog snorts in agreement.

'Gosh, Old Girl, we are doing well. Welcome to England and therefore, of course, civilisation. We're coming into Ripon, not bad when you consider we're keeping off the motorways. Let's find somewhere to stop for lunch. I'm sure there'll be a place we can eat round here.' We carry on into town. I'm wondering why Her Ladyship needs to eat a place. But there again, do I care? I have to say, though, there seem to be rather a lot of people about.

Oh look, Old Girl, it's a market day. I must have a look around later. You never know, I might find a bargain. There's a parking space over there beside that pub. C'mon, let's pull in there.' She manoeuvres me through the market goers into the parking space.

'You coming Dog? Fancy a stroll?' The Asthmatic Barking Dog leaps up and hops out and Her Ladyship manages to grab him and put him on his lead before he runs off towards a stall with meat hanging from it.

'Nah then, tha's a naice little cair Lass.' A stranger has stopped beside me and is admiring my lines. Well, that's what I like to think he's doing. 'Aye, a nice little motor indeed.' He's quite stout and I would think about the same age as Her Ladyship, but not nearly as tall as her. He is wearing an old tweed suit, the jacket covering a matching waistcoat with a watch chain attached to one of its buttons. He has bright, ruddy, weather beaten cheeks and a trilby, slightly too small for his head, is precariously balanced on it with long strands of hair hanging down over his left ear. I fancy that this man is bald and that's his dislodged comb-over. Her Ladyship doesn't like men with comb-overs and that is the first thing about him she's spotted. The look of disapproval says everything. In his right hand he's holding a well-used Meerschaum pipe and he's occasionally whacking his other hand with it.

'I beg your pardon?' Somehow I feel the tone of Her Ladyship's voice suggests she doesn't like being called "Lass" by a man with a comb-over. 'What did you say?'

'Ah said, tha's a naice little cair, Lass.' He places his pipe in his mouth and draws on it deeply. A look of annoyance appears on his face and he closely examines the bowl. Her Ladyship stands staring at him while her brain races through her mental dictionary trying to translate what he said. Eventually a flicker of understanding spreads across her face.

'Oh, that's very kind of you to say so. Yes, she is isn't she?' I'm very fond of her.'

'So, wot's tha' doin' 'eear, Lass?' There's another pause, giving him time to pull a cheap lighter out of his jacket pocket which he then prods into the bowl of his pipe. Meanwhile, the cogs of Madam's brain once again endeavour to understand what's been said.

'Oh, here? What am I doing here you mean? Actually I'm on my way to Land's End. I left John O'Groats a couple of days ago and I'm planning to reach Land's End in three more days.' The man looks up from his pipe.

'Eee, Lass, theur does speak posh don' theur? But why aur theur in Ripon?' There's another long pause. To be honest, I haven't a clue what he's saying, but she does. He starts to poke at the pipe again.

'Oh, why am I in Ripon?' She turns to him and speaks very slowly. I – am – here – in – Ripon – to – have – some – lunch. What's this place like?' Her Ladyship gestures towards the pub beside us.

'Oh theur dooan't wan' ta ea' 'thear. Ah'll tek thee somewheear wheear they serve t' perfec' ploughman's wi' Wensleydale and ham. Cum on.' He whacks his pipe against the wall of the pub and a mixture of ash and unburnt tobacco falls out. He unrolls a leather wallet and starts to fill his pipe with tobacco again. He glances up at Her Ladyship. 'Does thee min' uz smokin' ma pipe?'

'Oh good gracious no. I like the smell of a good shag.' He does a double take and peers at Her Ladyship over his pipe. She doesn't react. 'What about my dog? Will they let him in?'

'Aye, Lass, dogs are welcome. Cum on.' Her Ladyship, slightly unsure, obediently follows, leaving me here to admire the market. Why would I be interested in a market? I mean, what use is it to me? I suppose it is something to look at. Usually I am dumped in a car park staring at a concrete wall, or worse still up the bottom of another car. In the distance I spot a couple of lads pointing at me. They walk over.

'Eyup look at t' cair then.' They must have a strange language up in Yorkshire. Like the short, round man, I can barely understand a word they are saying.

'It's owd in' it?'

'Wha' is it? One of the lads comes to examine my radiator.

'It sez Austin on t' front.' His colleague tries my door.

'Ayup, i's not locked.'

'Cum on Stanley, can theur start it? Ah av an ideeur.' The lad called Stanley climbs into my driving seat and starts to fiddle with the wiring behind my dashboard.

'Piece o' piss,' says the lad called Stanley. 'Neya problem. Ah'll 'ave it started i' less than eur minute.' He continues to fiddle with my wires. If only he knew, all he has to do is put a screwdriver in my ignition switch and twist it. I've seen you-know-who do it when she's lost her keys.

'Reet let's try t' starter.' He grabs my knob and pulls it. Nothing, because that was my choke. He grabs another of my knobs. I kick into life. 'Cum on Branton gerr in.'

'Wheear are we goan' Stanley?'

'Nowhere i' particular Branton, we're just goan t'av some fun.' Stanley engages my first gear with an almighty scrunch, lets my clutch out and I leap into the air. 'Jesus Christ, tha' clutch ees reet violent.' Branton feels for a seat belt and, realising that I don't have such modern attachments, grabs my door. Unfortunately, his sleeve catches the door handle and it swings open carrying his upper torso with it, while his lower torso remains on my passenger seat. Branton, still holding on for dear life, manages to swing the door shut again. We head off at a rather unhealthy speed, scattering the last market stragglers in our path. I give a little cough. Branton looks to see what might be wrong and spots my fuel gauge.

'Ayup, we need sum petrol,' says Stanley. 'Let's call i' a' 'tha' owd self service out o' town.' Actually, Young Sir, you-with-the-barely-comprehensible-language, we probably don't need any petrol. Her Ladyship filled up about twenty miles ago. My fuel gauge is simply having a rest. Like me it occasionally decides not to work.

'Aye let's,' says Branton. 'Ah'll grab a few beers int' shop. We'll tak her on a spin then, in't countryside.'

We pull into an old service station. To the side is a workshop with a couple of cars and a pick-up truck parked outside. There is a hammering sound coming from inside suggesting that work is going on. There are just two petrol pumps. They look like they've been there for thirty years. Behind the pumps there is a small office and shop, both are plastered with enamel signs promoting various brands of oil, tyres and sparking plugs. It rather reminds me of the garage that The Nice Mister Weston ran and where Oh David used to take me for a service all those years ago.

Stanley parks me beside one of the pumps. He gets out and looks for my filler cap while Branton ambles into the shop to have a look around. He constantly glances back towards us to see what Stanley is doing. Stanley rams the nozzle into my tank and starts pumping in petrol. Since I'm already full, petrol starts to pour out onto the forecourt and splashes all over Stanley's jeans.

'Ah fook it.' Stanley steps back leaving the nozzle in my tank and tries to wipe the spilt petrol away. He shouts across the forecourt.

'Ayup Branton. C'mon let's go.' Branton runs out of the shop carrying some bottles. There is an elderly attendant in not-so-hot pursuit.

'Eh! Cum bak hur, tha little b…' The elderly attendant pauses to catch his breath. The hammering in the shed stops and another, this time a rather younger man comes out to see what is going on. Branton reaches me, tosses his booty onto my back seat and jumps into the passenger seat. Stanley, meanwhile, has leapt into my driving seat and started my engine. He slams my clutch in, engages a gear, clutch out and we are off. Oh Goody! I'm taking part in a heist! It's like Bonny and Clyde! Come on you guys, let's get the hell out of here before the filth arrives.

The nozzle and hose, which moments ago had been happily thrust into my petrol tank, stretches as we pull away. But my tank doesn't want to let it go. I develop a momentary wheel spin as I feel the hose trying to pull me back. The younger man reaches me as the hose snaps at the pump end, allowing petrol to pour out onto the forecourt.

'Shit!' he cries as he spins around and hits a large red button, I imagine some sort of emergency stop as the jet of petrol shrinks back to a dribble. But it's too late, the forecourt is already awash with petrol. We shoot off with the nozzle still thrust into my tank and a piece of hose happily bouncing along like a long black tail behind us. There's a rather long silence in the car. Branton is the first to speak.

'Wha' are we goan t' do naw Stanley? T' police will be after us an' in a cair lookin' li' this, they won' taek long to find us either.' Stanley looks at this friend.

'Aye tha're reet, Branton. We'll av ta dump it 'n then leg it. Wha' did thee take from t' shop?'

'A few beers, some bottles o' scotch 'an some vodkas, why?'

'Nowt reely. Let's fin' somewheear ta 'ide this car.' Oh, that's a shame. I was beginning to enjoy this. Now you boys just want to give up? We've not had the chase and shoot-out yet.

We drive on in silence, my new rubber tail still in tow. Stanley spots an open gate and swings me through it, parking me close to a dry stone wall. I can still see over the top of it, so I am hardly concealed.

'Cum on Branton, let's see wha' t' owna 'as got int' car.' They start to rummage through Her Ladyship's possessions. I hope they don't find her emergency Gin & Tonic. She'll go mad if they find that. Thinking of Her Ladyship, I wonder if she's missing me yet. She'll be trying to eat her lunch whilst being polite to Mister Comb-over. Branton finds it first.

'Eyup Stanley. Wha's this? As luks li' a rugby league ball, but smaller.' Branton examines Her Ladyship's haggis with great interest.

'No ideeur Branton, can tha' kick un o'a t' tree?' Stanley continues looking through Her Ladyship's possessions and is finding nothing useful. Branton steps back and starts to toss the haggis up, catching it again as if to decide where he's going to kick it.

'Aye, ah think ah can.' He starts to run forwards, tosses the haggis high into the air, swings his leg back to give it a good kick and trips over a tuft of grass. Stanley watches the haggis rise into the air, its climb slowing down until it decides it's not going any higher, whereupon it starts its descent, accelerating downwards directly onto Branton's head. It pauses momentarily as if it's not sure where to go next before rolling onto the ground.

'Bloody 'ell. Tha' bloody 'urt.' Branton climbs to his feet as the distant sound of a police siren sharpens both Stanley and Branton's wits.

'Ayup, tha's police,' shouts Stanley turning to see where the noise is coming from. 'Leev 'a' ball, leave everythin' but t' booze 'n let's get t' hell out o' 'eear.' The boys grab the Vodka, whiskey and beers and run off down the grassy slope towards a wood in the valley, nearly falling over as they run down and leaving me to face the music – typical. That's the sort of thing Her Ladyship would do. Come back! Don't leave me to take the wrap!

It isn't long before the police car arrives. It pulls up on the road outside the gate. Two policemen get out and put their hats on, one with his left hand and the other with his right. It's almost as if they are mirror images of each other. They come through into the field to examine me; neither seems to be in any hurry.

'I've seen sum things in ma time. But using an old wreck like this t' take part in't robbery. Whatever next?' What cheek! How dare he? Policeman One wanders around looking for clues. He spots the haggis lying on the ground. 'Eee George, look at this.' He pulls some medical gloves from his pocket, puts them on and bends down to pick up a now rather beaten up haggis. 'Is this what I think it is?'

'Ah don't know, Radley, what do 'ee think it is?' The policeman called George is distracted by something at my rear end.

'I reckon i's a haggis George. 'You know, from north o' t' border. Does tha think it's somethin' to do with t' robbery at Westside Petrol Station?'

The PC George is staring at my rear end and scratching his head. He can see the length of hose still hanging from my filler pipe and he, too, puts on medical gloves so he can pick it up and examine it.

'Could be, I s'pose, Radley,' says George. 'Ah reckons tha' this bit o' hose comes from Westside Petrol Station too.' Do ye think t' haggis was used as a weapon?'

'Exactly 'ow do ye think they used it?' The PC Radley tosses the haggis up into the air and catches it again. He then gives this question long and careful consideration by staring into the sky.

'Well George, 'e could have threatened Ol' Silas wi' it.'

'Bag it then Radley, it might be evidence. There'll be fingerprints. But t' haggis seems to be a strange weapon t' use. We better tak' this car into t' station. I'll radio in for a trailer. Can ye check the number for t' owner?'

'Aye, c'mon then let's tak' a break until they come. Fancy a coffee? Got a thermos in t' car'

Excuse me, Officers, does this mean I've been arrested? Should you not read me my rights? Where are you, Your Ladyship? You should be here. You are never around when you're needed.

It didn't take long for the police trailer to come out and pick me up and I am now parked in the yard at the police station.

'What the hell have you been up to now, Old Girl? I get back from a very nice lunch with a ruddy-cheeked Yorkshire farmer with a comb-over to find you gone. At first I thought you were being most inconsiderate to run off without me and then I realised that you'd been stolen. It was only when I came to the police to report you missing that I found out you'd been involved in a robbery. I never knew you possessed a criminal instinct. You could get five years for this, but they may knock off a couple of years because of your age. Heh, heh, heh. In you get, Dog. We've got to move on soon.' The Asthmatic Barking Dog, relieved to see his favourite seat again, eagerly jumps in and settles down to rest as one of the policeman who found me, the one called Radley, walks over and joins us.

'Eee, Madam talking to t' car? Is it yours?'

'Oh, hello Officer. Yes this is my car. Is it true that is has been used in a robbery?'

'Aye it 'as bin Madam. A robbery at a petrol station just out a' town. It was dumped just up on the Dales. Apparently two lads took t' car. We know 'em. Can you check it to see if there's owt missing?'

'Yes, of course.' Her Ladyship proceeds to check me through. 'No, I think it's all there. Hang on a minute. No something is missing, my haggis. Yes, my haggis is missing. They've stolen my haggis. I wanted to take that home and eat it after this was all over.'

'We found a haggis in front t' car up ont' Dales. It's int' station, being forensicated at t' moment.'

'Forensicated? What do you mean, forensicated?'

'Checked for prints,' says Radley. 'Tha' knows wha' I mean.'

'Oh yes, will it take long? Only I need to get away as soon as possible. I want to reach Bromsgrove by tonight. I've a B&B booked.'

'Nay, Lass, tha'll not be making it to Bromsgrove today. We need to check t'car over as well. Ye'll be lucky to reach Rotherham.'

'What? You've got to be joking. I was held up yesterday in Scotland, some problem with The Que…' Her Ladyship decides not to go there. Discovering that this woman had interfered with royalty might lead the Yorkshire constabulary into detaining her as well as me.

'Should be done this afternoon. Now we need thee t' maek a statement. If tha'd kindly follow me.' PC Radley turns on his heel and walks back into the police station. Her Ladyship obediently follows.

Moments later a couple of men approach me wearing white zip-up suits, rubber gloves and facemasks. For heaven's sake, anyone would think I'm diseased or something. Noticing The Asthmatic Barking Dog they pause, wondering whether they should proceed with him still in the car. But he's fast asleep. They gingerly unload things from my front half, being careful not to disturb him. But while feigning sleep, he is watching with one eye.

The two men regard The Asthmatic Barking Dog anxiously as they reach down between the rear and front seats to start removing more things, but they are interrupted by that familiar long, low rumble. Hands whip themselves rapidly away from the danger area and the deep rumble stops.

'Go and get t' owner of this jalopy to take tha' dog out t' way.' The speaker's colleague eagerly obliges.

Moments later Her Ladyship returns.

'What's the problem, Officer?'

'Can ye taek dog there out t' car? We need t' check everything.' Her Ladyship's irritated.

'How long are you going to be? I really need to get on. I've given my statement and you've got my fingerprints, although heaven knows why.'

'The sooner t' dog is out t' car, the sooner tha'll go.' Her Ladyship steps forward,

'Come on Dog, let these men get on with their work.'

162

It seems that their forensicating didn't achieve much. Too many different fingerprints. I am not surprised. Almost every time I stop people want to touch me or sit in my driver's seat. Just look at how many people have climbed all over me on this trip alone. Then there must be the 'Dabs' I think they call them from The Nice Doctor John, The Nice Mister Arthur, gosh so many people, too many to count. So the white-suited men have wandered back into the police station.

'Is that it then? Can we go now?' Her Ladyship is walking over to me clutching a plastic bag containing what resembles her haggis. She is accompanied again by PC Radley. 'What the...? They haven't put my stuff back into the car. They've left it all over the place!'

'Eh, well Madam,' PC Radley replies. 'It's easier for you t' pack yur car tha' self. Tha' knows where everythin' goes.' Her Ladyship is rattled and starts to stow everything away again, muttering something about idle brassards, lazy sods, and was that one of her usual 'typical bloody men' comments?

It doesn't her take that long in fact and she only has the emergency supplies she keeps under the driving seat and my side screens left. She stows away the emergency supplies, grabs one of my side screens, stops, looks at her watch and then at the sky.

'It's a nice day,' she turns to the policeman. 'In spite of the delay, I still have a few hours and the sun's shining. I think I'll leave the hood down. She rams the side screens down behind her front seat.

P-Fishshshsh.

'Oh shoot! My emergency can of gin and tonic, I've burst it.' Her Ladyship flings out the screens followed by the fire extinguisher, the bottle of fuel additive, the packet of breathalysers – 'Gosh, I forgot I had those' – and finally she produces the can of gin and tonic with liquid dribbling out.

'Quick, quick, get me a glass! We mustn't waste it.' She pokes out her tongue to try and lick at the fluid running down the side of the tin. PC Radley straightens his back and reaches for his notebook.

'Tha's not goin' t' drink that Madam are thee?' He smells a criminal offence in the offing. Her Ladyship quickly realises the impending error of her ways and pulls the can away from her mouth leaving a vestige of the contents dripping from her chin.

'Whoops. Of course not constable. Barely a drop has passed my lips. Now what am I going to do with this? We don't want to waste it, do we? And it did cost three pounds.' She looks around inside me for inspiration.

'Ah, that'll do.' She grabs an old shopping bag. 'It's only had an oil can in it before.' She carefully pours the contents of the tin into the bag and the new contents of the bag pour out of a little hole at the bottom, onto her feet. She watches the last drips fall away.

'Yes, well, that's that then,' she says sadly, as if a very old friend had passed away and she is watching the ashes being interred. She looks up at PC Radley.

'Can we go now?'

'Ay, tha'll better go afore I tak thee in for drink driving.' Her Ladyship sheepishly packs away the remaining emergency supplies and side-screens and climbs in.

'Phew, what a day. Thank you, Officer, I'd better get going.' She starts me up and with a wave pulls us out of the police station car park and points me on the road towards Bromsgrove.

'Here we are then, Old Girl, we've made it to Rotherham and it's still light. I have to say, I'd hoped we'd have made it to Bromsgrove before dark but we're not going to, are we? I think after all that's happened today we'll have an early night here and hopefully catch the others up tomorrow evening. So all we have to do now is find a bed and breakfast. I'm so exhausted I think all I need is a glass of wine and a sandwich. Come on then, let's go and find somewhere. Fancy a walk, Dog? When we get there?' A groan emanates from my rear seat. The Asthmatic Barking Dog prefers morning walks to evening ones. A small white thing flies out from nowhere and hits my near-side headlight.

'Hell's teeth, Old Girl, did you see that? We'd better pull over.' We glide into a layby. Her Ladyship trips as she gets out and grabs my windscreen support to stop herself falling down. It moves, not just a little, but quite a lot.

'I'm going to need to sort that out before we head off tomorrow, Old Girl. Now let's take a look at that headlight.' She bends over to examine the broken lamp. Her legging-covered bottom stretched tight is all I can see in front of my other headlight. Heaven forfend, what a sight! Her Ladyship straightens herself. Her leggings take a moment to readjust to their new position.

'Bloomin Ada, as they say in this part of the world. It's a golf ball and it's smashed the headlight glass!' The golf ball is still sitting inside my headlight rim, gently rolling to and fro. Her Ladyship is not pleased, not pleased at all.

'Bloody cheek.' She looks around to see where that projectile might have come from.

'There. It must have come from over there! Look, a posh golf club, judging by the castellated club house and flashy cars! I'm not letting this go. I'll need at least a replacement headlight glass. Come on, let's go and demand retribution.' She places the offending golf ball onto my passenger seat, gets back in and starts me up.

'Right, Old Girl, let's find the entrance and have words with an appropriately qualified person.' The Asthmatic Barking Dog has awoken now and is taking a very full interest. That worries me.

There'll be a lot more balls in that place, I imagine. Her Ladyship finds a big gateway and a long drive.

'Here's the entrance, Old Girl, let's go up to that big house up there.' Big house? It looks more like a stately home to me.

Her Ladyship plants me in a parking space with a sign that says "SECRETARY, No Parking." I am not sure I should be here.

'Oi, you can't park that thing thur. Move it.' Her Ladyship ignores the newcomer. Instead she slowly, yet determinedly, climbs out of the driving seat. She leans over, grabs the little white ball, straightens herself up to her full and not inconsiderable height and turns to the man. She gives a little snort, suggesting that she is now ready to indulge in conversation.

'Did you say something?' She asks.

'Yes I did, I told you to move that thur car. T' public car park is over thur.'

'Well I'm not going to move it. My car stays exactly where it is until I get the chance to wring the neck of the person who hit this ball over that wall and smashed my headlight.' She walks to my front.

'There, look.' She gestures at my headlight. The man walks around to take a look. He sucks some air in between his teeth.

'But you can't park thur.' This young man who seemed so arrogant a moment ago is on the defensive now and I'm not surprised. 'This is whur the Club Secretary parks and no one, but no one is allowed to park,' he points to the ground, 'thur.'

'Then you'd better go and find the person who hit this ball into the road.' The man looks anxiously down the drive as if expecting the secretary to arrive any minute. 'Because I am not moving from this spot until the culprit is found and brought before me to pay for a replacement glass and bulb.' Our young man decides he needs some help, preferably from someone important.

'I'll see what I can do.' He runs off into the house and Her Ladyship opens my passenger door.

'Go on Dog, have a little run around, stretch your legs and chase some golf balls.' The Asthmatic Barking Dog jumps out and wanders onto a beautifully manicured lawn. Her Ladyship leans against me and looks around. It's an enormous place and judging by the cars parked in the main car park, one has to be pretty wealthy to be a member here. Across from the car park to our left is a putting green and to our right a notice signifying the first tee. Her Ladyship looks at her watch.

'This won't take long, Old Girl.' She looks up. 'Dog, stop that. Not there.' The Asthmatic Barking Dog has dropped a very large bomb in the middle of the lawn. A wisp of steam rises from it and it wafts in our direction. There is a look of relief on his face. I think he needed that.

'I say, Madam, your dog has defecated on our lawn.' The young man who popped into the house moments ago has returned with someone who looks even more official. Her Ladyship turns slowly to greet this newcomer. She eyes him up and down with a look of disdain. He's tall with immaculately groomed hair and wearing a blazer. His poise and what must be a regimental tie suggests a military man. He looks like one of those men who really enjoys the power of his position in the hierarchy of the golf club. Much like, in fact, the pompous little car park attendant at that hospital in Welshpool.

'So he has, mister... mister?'

'Claybourn, I'm Major Claybourn, the Club Treasurer. Before you go and clear up your dog's mess and move your car, perhaps you'll appraise me of your problem.'

'If... I clear up my dog's mess and move my car remains to be seen. I have diverted here, off my planned route and after driving two hundred miles. I am tired and angry. I want a satisfactory explanation and compensation.' Her Ladyship thrusts the little white golf ball under Major Claybourn's nose.

'Is this one of your balls?' A broad grin spreads across the young man's face. Major Claybourn is rather put out.

'Certainly not. May I examine it please?' Her Ladyship hands the ball to him. 'It is one of the balls that we sell in the shop. But I certainly don't have balls like that.'

'Perhaps you can go and find out whose this ball is, because whoever that is owes me for a new headlight bulb and glass.'

'We have five hundred or so members, Madam, it could belong to any one of them. Your dog is digging up that lawn now, look.' True enough, The Asthmatic Barking Dog, bored with sniffing around and defecating on that immaculately groomed lawn has decided that he'd rather like to know what's underneath it.

'That can be fixed with the use of a foot pressing the earth back into place and some grass seed. You people are rather used to doing that aren't you? To get back to the important point in hand, a ball belonging to one of your members has smashed the rare and valuable headlight glass on this car. What are you going to do about it?' Major Claybourn decides not to protest further. It's obvious that he wants this troublesome woman out of the way before the Club Secretary arrives and finds me in his parking space.

'How much will it cost to replace?' Her Ladyship gives this a little thought. About two seconds thought, in fact.

'One hundred and fifty pounds,' she declares triumphantly. Major Claybourn is momentarily taken aback. He looks across the club car park with its Bentleys, Jaguars and the odd Rolls Royce and mentally calculates what one of those rare and valuable headlamp glasses would cost. Judging by his expression he imagines he has a bargain. I know exactly how much the glass actually costs and he is being ripped off.

'One hundred and fifty pounds it is then. Will you take a club cheque?'

'No, because how do I know you won't cancel the cheque tomorrow morning?'

'One hundred and fifty pounds it is, in cash then.' He turns to his colleague who is still amused by Major Claybourn's balls. 'Simon, would you go to the club bar and ask the steward to let you have one hundred and fifty pounds in cash and leave a note in the till for me when we cash up?' Simon trots away. Both Her Ladyship and Major Claybourn watch The Asthmatic Barking Dog continue his archaeological investigations. Neither says a word.

The young man returns with an envelope containing the money. He hands it to Major Claybourn who in turn hands it to Her Ladyship.

'Thank you,' she says stuffing the envelope into her hand bag. 'Dog, come here. Get in the car.' The Asthmatic Barking Dog, now bored with digging up that lawn trots over and hops in onto my rear seat, just as four men walk across the lawn with their golfing trolleys. I say, you chaps, look where you're going. Too late, one of them treads straight on top of The Asthmatic Barking Dog's bomb. What's worse, he hasn't noticed, in fact no one but me has noticed and they walk right in the main entrance. Her Ladyship clambers back behind my steering wheel.

'You need to think about putting up a mesh screen to stop your little balls flying into the road you know.' She starts me up.

'What about that dog's fouling? Aren't you going to clean it up?'

'I thought one of you would like to do it,' she cries as she drives off, tossing a black plastic pooh bag at them. 'Consider it a penance for breaching public safety rules.' We head down the drive as Major Claybourn hands the pooh bag to the young man, who immediately passes it back to Major Claybourn. We'll never know who eventually picked up The Asthmatic Barking Dog's pooh, if indeed anyone did since a good chunk of it has now spread itself across the front hall of the club house.

'Come on, Old Girl. Let's go and find a bed and breakfast. We've done well out of this. I have a replacement glass among my spares.

It cost twelve pounds. In fact, let's go and find somewhere nice to stay. I'll eat well tonight. We'll sort out the glass and the loose windscreen tomorrow morning, okay?'

Chapter Eight

Xavier gives The Asthmatic Barking Dog a look of horror. 'Oh my heavens, Fiona, she's got a mad dog with her as well. Get it away, get it away!'

~~Bromsgrove~~ Rotherham to ~~Launceston~~ Cheltenham

'Right, Old Girl, let's get you sorted,' Her Ladyship announces as she returns from her morning constitutional with The Asthmatic Barking Dog. He looks pleased with himself, in spite of the fact that he wasn't allowed into Her Ladyship's room for the night. That meant he had to sleep on my back seat. I think his current happy mood comes from the pub kitchen having given Her Ladyship some leftover meat to give him for his breakfast. He watches Her Ladyship expectantly. She puts the extra meat with his food, and places it on the ground with a bowl of water. He buries his nose into his breakfast, almost inhaling it. Well, he hasn't had any real meat for a few days. I'd noticed that he'd been hungrily eying up that blooming haggis, which I am sure is starting to smell.

'Now, Old Girl, let's have a look at you.' She examines my windscreen frame closely. 'Hmm, it's become very loose hasn't it? Now, where's my long screwdriver?' She rummages through her toolbox and produces the said implement and does a little mock sword fight with it. Don't ask me why, but she always does when using that particular screwdriver. Every blooming time, it does get boring.

'Hopefully the nut won't spin around inside,' she says as she screws my windscreen firmly back into place. 'There we are,' she announces as she grabs it and wobbles it. 'All nice and tight now. It must have been those Scottish roads. Let's take a look at that headlight.' She wanders round to face me. 'Crikey, Old Girl, your number plate is coming off as well. You look a proper little wreck. The Asthmatic Barking Dog, having finished his breakfast, trots over to the kitchen waste bins to see if there is anything there he could indulge in. Finding nothing, he trots back, pausing to lift his leg against the wheels of other cars. He sits down to watch Her Ladyship at work.

'There we are, all done. Let's hope nothing else threatens to fall off, Old Girl, but I can't promise to protect you from any more stray golf balls. Come on Dog, in you get.' The Asthmatic Barking Dog complies and prepares to sleep off his breakfast. Her Ladyship puts away her toolkit and clambers onto her driving seat ready for the off. The rear entrance door of the pub flies open and the landlady runs out waving Her Ladyship's haggis at us.

'You forgot t' 'aggis,' she cries as she comes over to us. 'It's beginning to smell a bit tha knows.'

'Oh, thank you, I'd completely forgotten it.' The landlady hands the haggis over and Her Ladyship thrusts it down behind her seat in such a way that The Asthmatic Barking Dog can't retrieve it. I don't know why he would want to eat it after what it has been through.

'How far are tha goin' today then?'

'The original plan was that I would have reached Bromsgrove last night. But, well, things have happened over the last few days that have rather slowed me down. So as long as there are no further problems, Cheltenham is my target for tonight. I keep off the motorways so I'll have to go straight through Birmingham. I'm not looking forward to that, even though it's this old thing's birthplace.' She looks skywards. 'So please, no incidents today, God, okay? I just want a nice quiet trip.' She turns back to the landlady.

'Thank you again. I had a lovely comfortable stay and an excellent dinner and breakfast, all courtesy of the Golf Club.' The landlady gives Her Ladyship a quizzical look as she starts me up and we roll forwards. 'Bye.'

'Here we go, Old Girl, Chesterfield, Ripley, Derby, Sutton Coldfield and then we attempt to get through Birmingham. Once we're clear of that, well, it's going to be a simple drive to Cheltenham. Let's go then.' She slams her foot on my accelerator and quite soon Rotherham will just be a memory.

We easily pass through Chesterfield and Her Ladyship, managing to avoid all signs to the M1 and M6, points me towards Derby.

'That was pretty straightforward, Old Girl. Here we are, the A61, a straight road all the way. As soon as we're clear of the suburbs I think we'll stop somewhere for a coffee, don't you?'

We drive on a few miles and Her Ladyship spots a petrol station.

'You need some more fuel, Old Girl, and if I'm not very much mistaken there's a little café there as well. Let's pop in and we can both have a drink. Do you agree, Dog?' A snort emanates from my rear seat and Her Ladyship swings me into the forecourt. She fills me up first and then starts to move me over to the parking area for the café. A man comes running out of the door of the petrol station office.

'Oi, you haven't paid.' Her Ladyship bristles.

'Oh I'm so sorry. I thought that since you only had two pumps it would be polite of me to get out of the way of one of them and park here so others can use the pump. I have every intention of paying you. Then I will go into this café for a cup of coffee – if that's alright with you?' The man, now rather deflated since he hasn't just caught an arch criminal, harrumphs.

'My petrol station is nothing to do with that café. So if you'd kindly come with me and pay me now, I'd be most obliged.' There is a rather nasty, sarcastic tone to his voice. Her Ladyship notices it too.

'Of course, Young Man, I'd be delighted,' she replies in a tone suggesting she might have been the lady of the manor speaking to the under-gardener. She takes her time getting herself organised, follows him to his office and returns within a minute.

'No wonder he was so precious about being paid, Old Girl. His prices are at least five pence more than we paid yesterday. I imagine the locals know that too and avoid this place like the plague. Now, will you two be alright? I'm just popping into the café for a quick cuppa. You stay here, Dog.' The Asthmatic Barking Dog, having expected a walk, flops down again with a sort of disgruntled groan, curls up and by the time Her Ladyship reaches the café he is snoring again.

I watch her through the big front window as she pauses to look around and then strolls over to the counter. There must be four or five empty tables and only one is occupied by a gentleman on his own. Remarkably, she goes and sits at that one. Now I wonder why she would choose to do that? The gentleman strikes up a conversation. She seems to be very receptive to what he has to say. She points over towards me and his gaze follows her finger. Then they are in conversation again.

I wish I could hear what they are talking about.

A few minutes have passed and now, accompanied by the gentleman, Her Ladyship comes out of the café. He's quite tall and well dressed. He bends to release a rather lanky dog whose lead has been tied up by the door. All three of them trot happily towards us. Her Ladyship seems quite animated. That is so unlike her, she's normally very suspicious of strangers.

'Here she is. Alexei, this is Miss Daisy. Miss Daisy, this is Alexei.' What am I supposed to say? It doesn't matter, he can't hear me anyway. Mind you, he is rather good looking. What's Her Ladyship up to? I really hope she isn't trying to flirt. Not like her, not like her at all.

'And Dog? This is Boris the Borzoi. Boris the Borzoi? This is Oscar The Asthmatic Barking Dog, better known as Dog.' Boris the Borzoi is so tall he's able to look at Oscar without jumping up on me. This impresses The Asthmatic Barking Dog and he leans his nose against my window to indulge in a mutual nose sniffing exercise. It's all rather pointless really, because there is a side-screen between them. Nevertheless, tails wag vigorously.

'I arm very plizzed to you meet Miss Daisy,' the man called Alexei says as he looks me over. He turns to Her Ladyship. 'I have not sin a motor carr like thees in Roussia.' So, he's a Russian. Her Ladyship used to have a propensity towards Russians. She told me once she loves their accent. He's tall, good looking and on top of that he's accompanied by a tall, good looking Russian dog. No wonder she sat at his table.

'We're going to give Alexei a lift to Birmingham, Old Girl. Oh yes, and Boris. You'll have to make room for him, Dog. Tell you what, it's a lovely day, let's take the hood down.' The Asthmatic Barking Dog takes no notice of Her Ladyship's fiddling with my hood. He's thinking that if Boris's rear end smells as good as his muzzle then he must be an interesting dog to know. Boris seems very interested in getting to know The Asthmatic Barking Dog too. Thinking about what happened yesterday with the corgis, I wonder if this newcomer thinks he's a girl.

'Right Alexei, in you both get. Come on Dog, move over.' She opens my passenger door and Boris the Borzoi eagerly jumps in but discovers that there really isn't very much room. The Asthmatic Barking Dog lets out a yelp of protest as Boris lands on his rear end.

After much protest from The Asthmatic Barking Dog and a lot of shuffling Boris manages to position himself on the seat, but he's facing the wrong way. He turns his head back on itself to look helplessly at his owner. The Asthmatic Barking Dog manages to extricate his rear end and, no longer Boris's cushion, stretches himself up and gives Boris a look that suggests Boris might prefer to jump out and follow us from a distance.

Her Ladyship pushes my front passenger seat back into position so that Alexei can get in. Boris's nose starts to twitch and with tiny movements he manages to turn around. His lanky body stretches across and downwards, his nose following the smell that caught his attention. I should have guessed, he's after that blooming haggis. Fortunately, he can't reach it, but knowing that molesting her haggis would be classed as a criminal offence by Her Ladyship, The Asthmatic Barking Dog attempts to distract his new Russian companion. Her Ladyship spots what Boris is up to.

'Boris, you leave my haggis alone. I plan on eating that when I get home.' Alexei looks quizzically at Her Ladyship.

'Haggis? Vot is haggis?'

'Oh don't you know? Haggis is an ancient Scottish dish. It's sheep's offal mixed with oatmeal I think, and stitched up in its stomach and then boiled. The Scottish rather revere it and always eat it having drunk copious supplies of whiskey on Burns Night. That's towards the end of January. I had some while I was in Scotland and it's rather nice. This one here…' she retrieves the thing, 'this is a haggis. Mind you, the Scottish always address it with a special poem by Burns before eating it.' Alexei's eyes widen.

'Ve haff something like that in Roussia. Ve call it Nyanya. Een Eengish, that mins nurse maid. Eet is the same.' Her Ladyship doesn't like being upstaged when it comes to her spouting some fount of wisdom.

'Yes,' she says dismissively. 'Now hop in, I'm sure the dogs will sort themselves out once we get going.' Alexei has trouble getting in too. He is about six feet six inches tall. In my young day, back in 1934, people weren't as tall as they are now. He eventually settles into my passenger seat but being so tall, his knees are pressing quite hard onto my dashboard. Her Ladyship looks concerned.

'Are you sure you'll be okay? It's a good two hours to Birmingham.' Her Ladyship says this in a way that gives her new Russian friend the option to get to his destination another way, but I have a feeling that she wants him to stay with us. I hope she doesn't flirt, I really hope she doesn't. It would make me feel ill.

'Nyet, I vill be fine. I vill this, get used to.' He shuffles his bottom. 'Vill this seat back, go?'

'Yes, I expect it will a little bit. Reach down the door side of your seat. You'll find a little lever. Pull it back and then push the seat backwards with your legs. Okay? It's a bit stiff mind you, but it will go.'

'No, make it verk, I cannot.'

'Here, let me have a go.' Her Ladyship leans across Alexei's lap and gropes for the lever, trying desperately not to bury her face in his lap. 'Now push yourself back. You may find that if you jerk it back with your feet, it will be easier.' Alexei stabs his feet at my footwell, bouncing rhythmically on the seat.

'Keep going, is anything happening yet?' Her Ladyship's voice is muffled, her face now definitely buried in his lap.

'Aaah, yes I think it moving is, but only a leetle.' If you ask me, he's making a lot of effort to achieve very little. Alexei grabs at Her Ladyship's shoulders and presses down on them as if that will help him push better. The Asthmatic Barking Dog starts to growl as if to say, "Leave my bitch alone." Boris the Borzoi, who just about managed to shuffle himself into a forward-facing position, joins in, but isn't quite sure why.

179

At this point a waitress comes out of the café carrying a newspaper.

'Excuse me sir, but you forgot this… Oh!'

What must she be thinking? That polite foreign gentleman she has just served, bouncing up and down in my passenger seat with Her Ladyship sprawled across his lap.

'Aah, aah, Oh, that, better eez. My legs are no longer jammed.' Her Ladyship, rather flushed, pushes herself up, grabbing at Alexei's thigh as she does so.

'Are you more comfortable now?' A little, high-pitched cough attracts their attention and they turn to see the waitress staring wide mouthed at the apparition before her. She tosses the newspaper towards Alexei and runs back to the café. There is a short pause before shrieks of laughter emanate from the building and all three café staff peer at us from the window, pointing and laughing. This is so embarrassing.

'What's the matter with her? Extraordinary behaviour, don't you think?' Her Ladyship tidies her hair. They exchange glances. Alexei innocently shrugs his shoulders. But there's a look on his face that is anything but innocent.

'I theenk she, as you say in Eengland, bonkers.'

The Asthmatic Barking Dog, deciding all is now well, ceases growling and turns his attention back to Boris who is still struggling to make himself comfortable.

'Birmingham, here we come.' Her Ladyship starts me up and we pull out of the car park and back onto the road south.

'Do you know, Alexei, this road, the A38 is called the longest lane in Britain.' Her Ladyship has to raise her voice so that she can be heard above my engine noise. 'It runs from Mansfield, just back there all the way to Bodmin in Cornwall. Back in the days before motorways, everyone going on holiday to the West Country used to use this road and on Saturdays it could be gridlock all the way. Do you have roads like this in Russia?'

'Oh Nyet. Our roads too long and straight for the jam of traffics. Far too long.'

'Do you know, Alexei, I've always found the Russian accent rather attractive.'

'Have you indeed? Ze Eenglish accent I too like, especially from a posh Eenglish lady.' He gives Her Ladyship a big warm smile and touches her thigh. He's definitely trying to seduce her. 'Can I you call Chunky Lumps? I call all my favourite ladies Chunky Lumps.'

'Oh well, I suppose so,' Her Ladyship says in a shrill and panic-ridden voice. She tries to change the subject. 'It's, it's ninety years since this model of car was first introduced. Just five years after your revolution. There's a bunch of us driving these cars from the very top of Scotland to the very bottom of England to mark the anniversary. But I already told you that in the café, didn't I?' Alexei starts to chuckle. Her Ladyship glances at him, slightly confused, yet amused.

'Why are you laughing? What's so funny?'

'You Engleesh. I try seduce you and you, the subject change.' Her Ladyship attempts to shuffle her bottom to create a little more space between her and him. But I fear that Alexei will persist.

'You no like me?'

'Well, I've only known you for five minutes. You seem very nice, but I mean, it's not appropriate.'

'Vot's not appropriate? Alexei pats her thigh. The Asthmatic Barking Dog, now lying half underneath Boris the Borzoi who has stretched himself right across the seat, emits a long low growl. Boris, more feeling the growl than hearing it, decides to join in. But I don't think Boris knows exactly why he's growling.

'It's just not…' she quickly turns her head back. 'And shut up, Dog. And you Boris.' She turns to Alexei. 'Look, it's just not the way things are done here. We can be friendly, without… without.'

'Oh, you no like intimacy? In Roussia we like intimacy. Those long cold vinters you know.' Her Ladyship decides a change in conversation is necessary, if not essential.

'What about you? What brings you to England and on the road to Birmingham?'

'Me? I verking in London am, and now I on holiday. I veesit friends today, een Beermingham. Then I London, go back.' Her Ladyship gives him a very cheeky look.

'You're not a Russian spy are you?'

'Nyet. I am not zee Roussian Spy. Do I look like zee Roussian spy? Vood you like me to be a Roussian spy?'

'Well,' she ponders this question. 'Well yes, it would be rather fun wouldn't it? Miss Daisy, Dog and I helping an Enemy of the State carry out some espionage with MI5 hot on our tail.' Alexei turns and glances at the vehicles behind us, I think to reassure himself that we aren't being followed. He turns back and gives Her Ladyship a long meaningful look. I can't help wondering, if he was a spy, what would he want to spy on in Chesterfield?

'I am sorry you to disappoint, I just a software engineer, am.'

'Then I'll pretend you're a Russian spy. It'll make you nice and mysterious when I write my diary tonight.'

'Vot, you keep diary?'

'Yes every night, why?'

'You no need write about me.'

'Why not? I write about everything that happens to me in the day. I mean that little incident in the car park back there, for example.'

'I rather you no write about me. Keep me as memory, like Grisabella in ze musical, Cats.' Her Ladyship glances suspiciously at him.

'I can't see what Grisabella has to do with it.'

'I no like having pictures taken and I no like mention in writing. I like memory, being.'

Oh dear, something's wrong with me. Cough, cough, splutter, splutter, cough. I let my engine die and I roll to a standstill at the side of the road.

'Oh no! What now? I tell you what Alexei, this Old Girl always picks the worst times to break down.'

'Vood you like me to have a look?'

'No, it's alright. I think I know what it is.' She climbs out of the driving seat. 'Driving all day every day seems to shake things loose and occasionally they get completely undone.' I can think of someone else at the moment who has shaken a few screws loose and if she's not careful will be completely undone. She opens my bonnet. 'Yes, here we are. The main ignition lead has come off. It won't take long.' Her Ladyship replaces the detached lead, closes my bonnet and gets back in.

'Right let's have a go.' She reaches for my ignition and I happily start again.

'Phew, Thank goodness it was that simple.' Alexei looks at her. He's impressed. I wonder if he's thinking that Her Ladyship is every bit as good as the babushkas that used to service the cars at the KGB school in Moscow. But of course, he's not a spy is he? So he can't be thinking that! Or can he? Her Ladyship pulls me back onto the road. Alexei gives Her Ladyship another long hard look. Her deft action in getting me going again shows her in a new light. Whether or not he's a Russian spy, he definitely wants to make whoopee. But there is no sign of a mutual response. He settles back to enjoy the journey. A slight frown suggests that he is still worried that Her Ladyship will include him in her diary.

They seemed to enjoy the rest of our run down the A38 to Birmingham. Alexei had mentioned that he used to listen to the BBC back in the 1960s and 70s. He and his brother listened in secret, as it was forbidden. Her Ladyship loves the songs of the sixties but I so, so wish that she hadn't decided to start singing some of them. Honky Tonk Woman emanating from Her Ladyship sounded more like a couple of cats fighting. Mind you, Alexei's rendering of a couple of the slower Beatles numbers was quite delightful, that is until Her Ladyship joined in. So The Beatles carried us through Sutton Coldfied, The Beach Boys shot us through Erdington and now Abba helps us towards the beating heart of Birmingham.

'Where would you like to be dropped off, Alexei?'

'My friend, he lives by zee Tyburn Road. Not far from zee Gravel Hill.'

'We're on the Tyburn Road now. I can drop you off anywhere here. Do you know the number?'

'Nyet, my friend, he say to phone him ven I get to Tyburn Road.'

'We're not very far from Spaghetti Junction and I won't be able to stop once we get there, so I'll drop you off here, if that's alright.' She pulls me over to the side of the road, gets out and walks round to the passenger door and opens it so Alexei can extricate himself.

He climbs out with a little difficulty and, snatching the moment, he puts his hands on Her Ladyship's shoulders and pulls her towards him.

'Oh goodness,' is all she can say. She leans backwards to maintain a discreet distance but looks straight into his eyes.

'Listen, Chunky Lumps. I like you, I like you very much. I vish ve meet again, could.' Her Ladyship's defences drop just enough for Alexei to pull her into a full smacking kiss. Ugh, I'm feeling quite sick. This is gross. Where's the fast forward button? Her Ladyship tells me she always uses the fast forward button when there is anything to do with sex on the television. The Asthmatic Barking Dog once more takes exception to this behaviour and a long, low rumble turns into a growl. Boris the Borzoi, finally having succeeded in making himself comfortable without lying on his temporary companion, decides to join in and starts to bark.

Her Ladyship pulls herself free and the two dogs are immediately silent.

'I like you, too, Alexei, but I'm not ready for a relationship or anything like that. Not at my age.' She makes her point even harder. 'Anyway, we won't see each other after today, so.' She shrugs her shoulders. Alexei looks at her quizzically. She realises he doesn't understand and steps away from him. Boris the Borzoi turns to The Asthmatic Barking Dog with a look that says, "if my master can get away with it, then so can I!" The Asthmatic Barking Dog, sensing what Boris is thinking, growls at him to warn him off. Boris gets the message, regretting that his pulling powers are inferior to those of his master.

Alexei slips Boris the Borzoi's lead on and, having attempted one last bid to reach the haggis, he effortlessly leaps out over my side rather than make his exit through the door. Her Ladyship grabs a piece of paper from my glove box and scribbles something on it.

'Look, call me. Call me next week. I'll be home by then.' Alexei looks from the piece of paper to her and smiles. He turns and walks away, Boris obediently walking at his side. Her Ladyship watches them and lets out a little sigh. Then, as if he had forgotten something, Alexei turns back to her.

'Oh, Chunky Lumps?'

'Yes, Alexei?'

'I really am a Roussian spy. Das vedanya.' I knew it!

Her Ladyship climbs back onto my driver's seat and I believe there is a new lightness to her. She starts me up.

'He was nice, wasn't he, Old Girl? I rather liked him.' Yes you did, didn't you, Your Ladyship? Your behaviour has been a total embarrassment from the moment you saw him. All the way from Chesterfield you pretended to be prim and proper and… well, now look at you. For heaven's sake, pull yourself together woman. Her Ladyship gives a long sigh and turns to The Asthmatic Barking Dog.

'You alright, Dog? Did you like Boris the Borzoi?' Judging by the way he spread himself out on the seat as soon as Boris jumped out, I would say not.

'Do you think he really was a spy, Old Girl? Yes I do, but I don't think you do. Her Ladyship restarts my engine and turns me back into the traffic.

'Come along, Old Girl, let's get on through Birmingham.'

Well, that was awful. We've just driven beneath Birmingham.

'It's the quickest way to get through the city, Old Girl, honestly,' Her Ladyship shouted as traffic raced past us, then suddenly we were in a tunnel, and before I could switch on my headlights, we were out the other side and now the city centre is behind me.

'There you are, Old Girl, that was easy wasn't it? Birmingham wasn't like that when you were born was it?' It certainly was not.

'Right, Old Girl, I think I'll take you past your place of birth. You'd like that wouldn't you?' If you say so, Your Ladyship.

'I'm getting peckish too. We really ought to find somewhere to stop for lunch and then get on to Cheltenham this afternoon. We're on the Bristol Road now, which means we'll even be going past where I used to work. It should be just up there to the left, just down Pebble Mill Road. I worked there, at the BBC, for ten years. I have many happy memories. Oh my God, they've knocked it down!' I really don't know what she's talking about. Her behaviour is quite odd since she met this Alexei fellow. We drive on.

'Here's Selly Oak, now I remember a few short cuts through here. So let's try one.' She swings me off to the left and we embark on a journey through some suburbs. It reminds me of when we got lost somewhere around here in 2005. We'd come up to celebrate the Austin centenary. Her Ladyship pulls me up at the side of the road.

'They've changed the roads, Old Girl. I don't remember this one.' Could it be, Your Ladyship, that you are lost? No, of course not, it's Birmingham City Council's fault it. They have only knocked down all the houses and changed all the roads.

'We'll have to back-track Old Girl. This isn't the way.' She turns me around and we start weaving through a series of side-roads.

'Here it is. This is the one we want.' There is some sort of sign lying face down on the road's surface which Her Ladyship has to swerve to avoid.

'Who put that there? It's dangerous. This is definitely the way, Old Girl, I told you I knew where we were.' Her Ladyship is triumphant and starts to accelerate. Up ahead a man steps out into the middle of the road and holds his hand up. Her Ladyship snorts.

'What now? What the hell now?' She slows me down but

continues to roll deliberately towards the man, who isn't sure whether he should step aside or not. He holds his ground and lowers his hand. Her Ladyship rolls me right up to his toes. He's a young man, holding a clipboard and wearing a deaf aid with something I recognise from all of my television appearances as a microphone worn along the side of his face. This is connected to a device on his belt.

'Oh for heaven's sake,' says Her Ladyship, spotting the clipboard. 'You are one of those damned market researchers aren't you? You must be a pretty desperate one to stop me in the middle of the road. What do you want, Young Man?'

'I'm sorry, but, didn't you see the sign?'

'Sign? What sign?'

'This road is closed today. We're filming just up there.' He points vaguely behind him.

'Who are "we"?' Just a hint of growing irritation is emerging. No, maybe more than just a hint.

'The BBC. We're filming a sequence just up there and the road's been closed. You'll have to find another way round.' He is trying desperately not to be unpleasant but I suppose he has to be firm. This isn't going to be a friendly conversation from now on I fear.

'What? WHAT? I'm asked to pay an extortionate license fee just so the BBC can close a road that I wish to legally progress along? When I worked at Pebble Mill we never put members of the public to inconvenience.' Oh dear, I do hope he'll be polite. This conversation could go horribly wrong.

'We've had permission from the city council…' Oh no, that's really not what she wants to hear. She snorts again, this time more obviously.

'The council. THE COUNCIL? Councillors are a bunch of layabouts without the talent to get into real politics. They're there to take our Council Tax, spend it on ridiculous schemes, and then make life difficult for everyone.' She pauses briefly, 'Just like the BBC, it seems. You both take my money and then make my life very difficult. What do you say to that, Young Man?' He reaches for the transmit button on the device on his belt, but then changes his mind. I expect that if he wants to advance himself and become a famous film director, pressing that button could reverse his career plan.

'I'm really sorry you feel this way. But it isn't that far to go left up there. There's a road parallel to this one, it's called Tiverton Road. You can go down there and then you'll be able to get back onto this one further on and continue on your way.' Her Ladyship's nostrils are expanding and contracting rather like a thoroughbred after winning a race. However, Her Ladyship hasn't won this race yet.

'Well, Young Man. I am not going to go down that other road. So what are you going to do about it?' The young man puts his hand to the earpiece he is wearing. Something else has caught his attention. He presses the transmit button.

'Yes Fiona, I've got it here. Hang on.' He steps away towards the pavement where he has a chair and a large bag of bits and pieces. Her Ladyship, grabbing her chance, slams me into first gear, clutch out, and we are away.

'Hey, you can't go down there! They are...' The sound of my engine and the growing distance between us prevents me from hearing any more. I fear that this young man will find himself in the Job Centre tomorrow, his dream of being a world famous film director in tatters. Of course, Her Ladyship will have no sympathy or concern whatsoever.

'Cheeky Little Hitler. Who did he think he was? Oh what now?' We are hurtling, if you can call it a hurtle at twenty miles an hour, towards a group of people in the middle of the road pointing cameras and microphones at another group of people, apparently in conversation around a car, which it seems has driven into another car, and there's a police car and an ambulance parked nearby. There is a bloodied body in the road. A policeman sits on the bonnet of his car picking his nose and the ambulance crew are playing cards. They show no interest whatsoever in the injured man lying in the road.

'Get out of my way! I have to get through!' The group with the camera turn to hear where the shout came from and I think this is the first time I've ever seen a group look of terror. Well, of course they cannot get out of the way, so they stand frozen to the spot. Her ladyship applies my brakes and, I'm proud to say, we glide to a standstill. She attempts to stand up behind my steering wheel, but ends up clinging to the top of my windscreen for dear life.

'CUT.' The voice that shouted that is nowhere to be seen, but everyone reacts to the command. The ambulance men look over towards the action while the policeman examines his finger.

'I say, can you move off the road please. I wish to get through. No-one moves. They all simply stand and stare at us. Finally, a woman wearing a similar set up to the young man we passed earlier presses her transmit button.'

'Piers, we asked you to stop all vehicles coming down this road. Now there's an old jalopy with a woman who looks she is in some sort of pain peering over the windscreen.' She presses her finger to her earpiece and then presses the transmit button again.

'What? Say that again?' She puts her finger to her ear and turns to a rather agitated man who seems to be in the centre of them all.

'Apparently this woman objected to being stopped. What's that Piers? She refused to turn back and…' She presses the transmit button again.

'Piers? Did I hear you right? Mmm, mmm. Yup. Okay. I'll talk to you later.' She turns back to the agitated man who is now quite flustered.

'Xavier, Piers says that whatever we do we mustn't mention the BBC or Birmingham City Council. It seems that this lady gets rather irritable at the mention of either.' The man called Xavier turns to the woman.

'What? Fiona, we go to a lot of trouble to get the cou…' He stops himself, remembering Fiona's advice. 'We go to a lot of trouble getting permission to close a road for the best part of a day. We pay god knows how many householders in this street a hundred quid a head to not take their cars out until after five o'clock and in the middle of a most crucial scene, a mad woman tries to run us down with, with, with a, I don't know what it is.'

The Asthmatic Barking Dog, who has been sleeping through all of this, emits a yelp. He's having a dream, chasing rabbits probably. Realising that we've stopped, he wakes up, stretches himself to his full height and eyes up the group of film people in front of us. Xavier gives him a look of horror.

'Oh my heavens, Fiona, she's got a mad dog with her as well. Get it away, get it away!' The Asthmatic Barking Dog looks on, somewhat confused.

'I can't take this, Fiona, I just can't take this. I need to go and lie down in a darkened room.' He starts to walk around in little circles as if looking for somewhere to go.

'Leave it to me, Xavier. You go and sit down with Patricia. I'll deal with this. Take five everyone. We'll run this scene again in five minutes.' The lady who I presume is Patricia takes Xavier by the arm and leads him away to a chair. She sits him down and pats his hand. Fiona then comes over to us. Her Ladyship has returned her bottom to my driving seat and is watching her with growing indignation. Fiona decides it might be better to address all three of us from the front of my bonnet.

'I'm very sorry, but Xavier is highly strung and he can't deal with the unusual.' She changes tack. 'You really shouldn't have come down this road. It's been closed by the… closed for the day. There was a sign at the entrance diverting traffic another way.'

The Asthmatic Barking Dog, hoping that Her Ladyship won't notice, slowly eases himself over my side and waters my rear wheel.

'There was no sign on display, but there was something that might have been a sign, flat on its face in the middle of the road. I had to swerve around it. Do you mean that?' There is a tone of sarcasm in Her Ladyship's voice.

'I imagine that must have been it. I am sorry.' We are interrupted by a scream.

'Get it away, get it away!' It's Xavier crouched on his chair, which is unfortunate as it's a swivel chair. The Asthmatic Barking Dog is looking up at a slowly revolving Xavier and thinks he wants to play. The rest of the group are trying to entice him away with a chorus of "Here Doggy, Here Doggy" and offering their sandwiches. But for The Asthmatic Barking Dog, Xavier is the most interesting person he's met all day. The swivel chair is giving him a "now you see me, now you don't" effect. There's no way he'll be tempted away by offers of half eaten cheese and ham sandwiches.

'Dog! Get back here, right now!' The Asthmatic Barking Dog turns to see where that familiar voice came from. 'Get back here – now – I say.' He looks from a slowly spinning Xavier towards the "Here Doggy" people holding out their sandwiches, and then towards Her Ladyship. Realising that perhaps he shouldn't have jumped out in the first place but wanting to salvage something from this situation, he trots over to take a closer look at the offered food. He grabs at a sandwich, spits it onto the road and flips the bread off with his nose. He inhales the ham and swallows it whole. He glances back towards us and since Her Ladyship hasn't repeated her order, decides that another piece of ham or even a piece of cheese would be most welcome. Eventually, his taste buds satisfied he trots back towards us in no hurry whatsoever. Xavier is helped down to ground level and is escorted away to the ambulance. The blood spattered corpse has got up and is sipping a cup of coffee.

Her Ladyship clambers out and gestures to The Asthmatic Barking Dog that his place is on my rear seat and not terrorising neurotic directors. Fiona watches this unhurried performance and shrugs her shoulders.

'Look,' she says. 'Why don't you drive off down this road now and we can get on with our filming? I'm not sure Xavier can take much more.'

'He is rather highly strung isn't he? Is he any good at directing?'

'Actually, he's brilliant. But if anything goes wrong he just loses control.' Fiona looks back at the crash set up. 'Do you think you can squeeze through there?'

'Oh, I expect so. We'll manage, won't we Dog?' The Asthmatic Barking Dog couldn't care less. He's still licking his chops and enjoying the lingering taste of ham and cheese. Her Ladyship clambers in, starts me up and slowly rolls me forwards.

'Oh, by the way,' Fiona waves us down again. 'We do a lot of period filming. Have you registered this old car with an agent? I'm sure there will be productions that would like to use it.' Use me? Yes, that is a good idea. I'd like to be driven by Sir Laurence Olivier. But he's dead isn't he?

'Certainly not. I have enough trouble coaxing this Old Girl to head in a direction that I want her to go. No, she's far too moody to be driven by anyone else. Anyway, taking part in a film would make her unbearable.' Speak for yourself, Your Ladyship. I seem to remember you with those news people in Llandeilo.

'Come on, Old Girl, let's go and find your birthplace.' She pulls me past all the film paraphernalia and we continue our journey.

She couldn't find it. My birthplace, that is, she couldn't find it. She couldn't find it because it's all gone and they are building houses on the site. Her Ladyship wasn't pleased so she decided to take me to see Lickey Grange, the home of the man who designed us, Sir Herbert Austin. I met him you know, just after I was born and had been taken for a test drive. He was a rather imposing man, but I do remember his kind smile.

So here we are now, heading into Evesham, Her Ladyship having partaken of a late lunch as we left Lickey.

'Only fifteen miles now to our overnight stop. What on earth is going on here then? Asparagus Festival? Whatever will they think of next? An asparagus festival indeed.' Her Ladyship slows us down. The town is crawling with people, some in fancy dress, others with their faces painted green. They all seem to be having a good time. A man waves us down and Her Ladyship pulls up. She is so intrigued by what is going on around us that she hasn't had enough time to become irritable again.

'Are you here for the classic car run?' He checks his clipboard. Why do officials always have clipboards? I wonder if they think it makes them important. And why do they always appear to check them, having asked a question? He looks up again.

'Because if you are, you're three days too early. It's on Sunday.' Her Ladyship decides to play with the poor man.

'What on earth makes you think we're taking part in a classic car run?' The man laughs nervously and checks his clipboard again.

'Oh hang on. No, of course. You're one of the Morris Dancers aren't you?' He seems quite satisfied that he's got it right this time.

'Do I look like a Morris? Indeed does it look like as if I can dance at my age? Anyway this car is an Austin not a Morris.' She's decided to be obtuse now and the man is completely confused. He's flipping through the pages of his clipboard as if to buy time, searching for inspiration.

'What are you here for then?' The clipboard drops down by his side.

'Absolutely nothing. I'm on my way to Cheltenham to stay the night. But yes, in answer to one of your questions, I am on a classic car run, a one thousand mile run for Austin Sevens. I'm on my way to Land's End with Dog and my car, which incidentally is called Miss Daisy.'

'Oh, good gracious. All that way. Why?' Her Ladyship gives this question some serious thought.

'Because it's there?' That isn't a good answer. 'And I have to get to Cheltenham before it gets dark. Headlights, you know.' He nods sagely but like most people Her Ladyship engages in conversation, he hasn't a clue what she's talking about.

'Are you sure you can't find the time to stay a while?' He then adds hopefully, 'There's an event at The Bretferton Arms. You'd be very welcome.' Her Ladyship ponders whether or not to stay. She's thinking that a large G & T would be just what the doctor ordered. Then she recalls her rather frantic day.

'No, very kind and all that. But I've had quite a day, transporting a Russian spy. Well, he told me he was a Russian spy, from Yorkshire to Birmingham.' A brief smile falls across her face as she remembers Alexei. The Asthmatic Barking Dog winces at the thought of Boris the Borzoi.

'Then my dog here was the cause of giving a film director a near nervous breakdown. No, as much as I would like to stay and share the thrill of your Asparafest,' she forces a tight lipped smile. 'I really must get on. So where do I go from here?'

'Straight through town and follow the road. It's signed all the way.'

'Thank you. Settle down now, Dog. You can have your evening walk when we get to Cheltenham.' Her Ladyship's phone rings. She stabs at the answer button.

'Hello? Oh hello Arthur. Where are you? Land's End? Already? Me? I'm in Evesham and will be stopping in Cheltenham for the night. Launceston tomorrow night, hopefully. What? Why am I only in Evesham? Well how long have you got? Miss Daisy got stolen yesterday. Yes, some kids took her and she was involved in a robbery. The police found her up on the Yorkshire Dales with a petrol pump filler hose stuck in her tank. Apparently she looked as though she had a tail. I'd have loved to have seen that. Yes, that's right, a creature from the dark side. Anyway today we got held up by a film crew in the Birmingham suburbs. They wouldn't let me pass. What? No, I was extremely polite to them. You know me, I always am…' Oh yes, you are always so polite aren't you, Your Ladyship?

'What? No I was momentarily distracted by Miss Daisy. Anyway I will be in Launceston tomorrow night. So I might see you guys on the way home. No? You are staying another couple of nights? Where are you staying, Land's End? No? You're staying in Penzance? Oh then I probably will see you there. I'll try to catch up with you tomorrow night. Bye.' Her Ladyship stabs at her phone once more and tosses it onto my passenger seat.

'Come on, Old Girl, let's get to Cheltenham.'

'Right Old Girl, that's Wells. Let's get to Glastonbury. There's a lot that I can tell you about Glastonbury Old Girl.' I rather thought there might be, but I'd prefer it if you didn't.

~~Launceston~~ Cheltenham to ~~Land's End~~ Launceston

'Morning, Old Girl. Isn't it a lovely day? Sleep well?' Well no actually. I haven't slept a wink. It's very noisy here in the centre of Cheltenham. Perhaps it was something to do with the fact that you picked a B&B in the heart of what I believe is called the town's "club land," and I always thought Cheltenham to be refined.

'Good, good. So how's your oil level?' How would I know? She opens my bonnet to check my water and oil.

'Pretty good, Old Girl, well done. Okay Dog, your turn now. Let's top you up too. But first of all, as it's a lovely day I think we'll take the hood down.' I know they say that dogs understand a few words, but it seems that The Asthmatic Barking Dog knows every single word that relates to food. Her Ladyship fills his bowl and once again he all but inhales the contents. Her Ladyship has started to fold down my hood when the landlady appears at the door. She's holding Her Ladyship's haggis in her hand and for some reason, I think I know why, she's holding it as far from her face as possible.

'Excuse me?' Her Ladyship turns her attention to the newcomer.

'Oh, hello Mrs Peters. Did I forget something?'

'You forgot…' Mrs Peters peers disapprovingly at the battered object in her hand, 'this.'

'Oh goodness, my haggis. Thank you, Mrs Peters.' Her

Ladyship goes over to take it. 'That's the second time I've nearly forgotten it in the last few days and I can tell you, it's been through an adventure or two.' Mrs Peters clears her throat.

'I'm not surprised. It was walking around in my fridge last night.'

'It was what?'

'It's a bit ripe, you know. Would you like me to throw it out?'

'Oh no, don't do that. It's become my mascot, ever since I crossed the border into Scotland last week. I was told by a Scotsman that travelling with a haggis would help to ease my path through his country. So I'm seeing if it will help me all the way to Land's End. It hasn't done so well since we crossed back into England. But it did prove very useful while we were in Scotland. It even helped when someone tried to steal my purse. Perhaps it wants to go home,' she adds thoughtfully.

'Excuse me,' replies Mrs Peters. 'A haggis is just a mixture of a sheep's offal. It doesn't have magical powers.' Her Ladyship chuckles.

'I would advise you not to tell my hitchhiker friend Duncan that. Anyway, I'm stopping for lunch in Glastonbury so if it does have any magical power that's the one place where it will work.' Her Ladyship reaches out to take the offending article and tucks it down behind my driving seat. She returns to finish off fixing my hood down and stowing away my side screens. The landlady is right about that haggis, it is getting a bit ripe.

'Thank you, Mrs Peters, a lovely stay, but I must get on. I want to make it to Launceston by tonight. I'm a day behind as it is.'

She starts my engine and as we roll to the end of the drive, we are stopped by a crocodile of school girls chatting happily away to each other.

'Typical,' Her Ladyship snorts. The girls notice me and start to point and giggle. What cheek. The two-by-two crocodile collapses as some girls take out their mobile phones to take pictures.

'What a funny little car,' says one.

'It's so cute,' says another. They both have rather posh voices. The Asthmatic Barking Dog, having settled down for a snooze, suddenly reacts to the word "cute" and gets up to see what's going on. Anticipating attention, he wags his tail vigorously.

'Aah look, it's a dog. Aah.' More girls cluster around and some are actually spilling into the road to get a view. Others come up to The Asthmatic Barking Dog and start to pet him, something he loves. Her Ladyship is very quiet, realising, I presume, that there is absolutely nothing she can do about this. She forces a smile through gritted teeth.

'Look,' she says finally. 'I'm on my way to Land's End from Scotland. I really need to get on. I'm already a day late. Would you please get out of the way so I can leave?' The girls ignore her. They are not interested in Her Ladyship, nor are they interested in me anymore. Just the blooming dog, who is lapping up all this attention.

'What's its name?' asks one girl?

'Oscar,' Her Ladyship replies reluctantly, realising that she's not going to get them to move. 'His full name is Oscar The Asthmatic Barking Dog. I just call him Dog. He seems to prefer that.' All the girls are now reaching for The Asthmatic Barking Dog and he's loving every minute of it.

'Girls, girls!' A shrill voice rings out from behind this gathering crowd. 'What is going on? Stop girls, wait here. Let me through, let me through.' A rather prim woman wearing a tight fitting suit materialises through the crowd and stands in front of me. She appears most displeased, evidenced more when her hands move to her hips.

'What is going on here?' Her Ladyship shrugs her shoulders.

'Aah Miss, we saw this funny little car,' says the first girl to have noticed me. 'And then this really cute doggy.' She bends to rub her face against Asthmatic Barking Dog's head. He in response belches with delight. Judging by how quickly she pulls her face away that cannot have been a very nice experience. The Asthmatic Barking Dog doesn't mind though, because there are at least another five hands petting him. The prim woman turns her attention to Her Ladyship.

'How dare you invite my girls to come and look at your, your car and your…' she glances at The Asthmatic Barking Dog. 'Mongrel.' The Asthmatic Barking Dog did not like that description. He looks at the woman most disapprovingly.

'I didn't invite anyone to come and look at us as you suggest. I was waiting to pull out when your crocodile blocked our path.' Her Ladyship's starting to get annoyed. 'Why, would you prefer it if I'd mowed them all down?'

'Of course not. But you must have done something to get them to break away from the crocodile. Girls, come along. Get back on the pavement at once.'

'They're driving all the way to Land's End, Miss,' says another girl. They've come from Scotland. How far is that, Miss?'

'It's about a thousand miles,' interjects Her Ladyship in answer to that question. 'But I had to drive another seven hundred and fifty miles to get to the starting line at John O'Groats.' She turns back to the teacher.

'As I have said, I did nothing to distract them. It's obvious to me that you don't have any control of your pupils. In my day…' Oh no, she's off now. 'In my day at school we obeyed our teachers without question. But now in this modern age of total indiscipline, you can only hope that your charges will go along with what you want. In this case they obviously didn't. So please, get a grip, take control, and get them out of my way.' The woman harrumphs at Her Ladyship's criticism. Being made to look in the wrong in front of the girls is not good for her authority, whatever is left of it. The teacher flicks her head upwards, letting out another harrumph as she does.

'Come along girls, get in line and let's go, or we'll be late at the museum.' She turns back to Her Ladyship. 'It occurs to me that the museum is the place for you, that old car of yours and your… mongrel dog. Come along girls.' She spins on her heel and marches off up the pavement happy to have had the last word, the girls obediently follow.

'Cheeky cow! Who does she think she is?' Her Ladyship lets out a sigh. 'Come on, Old Girl, let's get going before anything else happens to mess up our journey.'

Her Ladyship has navigated me through Gloucester and, still avoiding the motorways, we are now in Bristol.

'Look, Old Girl, there's Bristol Zoo. I used to come here with my mother. If I remember correctly, there was a famous gorilla here called Alfred. I wonder if we've got time to stop. Maybe not. There again, I need a pee.' She pulls me into a car park and The Asthmatic Barking Dog arises from his slumbers.

'You won't be allowed in Dog, anyway, I'll be right back.' With that, The Asthmatic Barking Dog settles down and she heads off to the Zoo entrance. She's back almost immediately and apparently not in a good mood.

'Bloody cheek. They wanted fourteen pounds. I told them I just wanted to use the loo but they didn't believe me, I'm not blooming paying that. I can wait a bit. Come on you two, let's go and find that bridge.' We pull out of the car park.

'There it is, Old Girl, come on then. It's just across the Down.' We manage to find a public convenience on the way to the bridge and then arrive at the toll booth. Her Ladyship tosses a fifty pence piece into the bin.

'This was built some one hundred and fifty years ago, Old Girl,' Her Ladyship announces in her tour guide voice. 'Brunel designed it, but died before it could be completed. Just look at that view. Sensational isn't it? It's a favourite spot for suicides.' I am not sure I really want to know that.

'Come on, Dog, let's find somewhere to park on the other side and we'll take a little walk.' We pull over as we leave the bridge and she parks me. The Asthmatic Barking Dog, aware that he's getting Her Ladyship's full attention for a few moments, eagerly jumps out.

'Steady Dog,' Her Ladyship says as she grabs him to slip his lead on. 'You don't want to get yourself killed.' One of my relatives, in fact a strangely familiar one of my relatives, drives towards us from the opposite direction. Seeing us he slows down and pulls over in a little parking area on the other side. Oh dear, I thought it was him. Her Ladyship recognises him too.

'YOU!' The Asthmatic Barking Dog, although alert, jumps out of his skin at this sudden outburst. He looks anxiously at Her Ladyship, thinking that he is being blamed for something, but he knows not what.

'YOU!' comes from over the road. Well I hope the conversation gets a bit more interesting than this monosyllabic start. Her Ladyship takes a couple of paces towards the other driver. A passing car blasts its horn and she steps back quickly. Forgotten the Green Cross Code, I fear. Her Ladyship decides she can handle this situation better if The Asthmatic Barking Dog is not in tow, so she grabs him and plonks him back on my rear seat, much to his annoyance. The other driver decides to cross over to us.

'You sabotaged my car,' Her Ladyship shouts across the passing traffic. 'In fact, you sabotaged it twice. Uh, uh, uh, umm… and you sabotaged it in front of the Queen!' Dodging the cars, the other driver reaches me.

'What do you mean, I sabotaged your car? You sabotaged mine first and that was after having been so rude accusing me of lying about my car, when you were too stupid to recognise your own!' Her Ladyship takes a step towards him.

'That was a simple mistake. But you had to make something rather big out of it, didn't you?'

'Big out of it? It was you that made something big out of it when you rammed something up my exhaust. You could have damaged my engine.'

'Oh, could I? Well I didn't, because I saw it – it was a haggis, by the way – fly out over the North Sea. Serves you right.

'A haggis?'

'Yes, they're supposed to ease your path through Scotland, didn't you know? They've certainly eased mine. Look!'

Her Ladyship reaches behind the seat and extracts the pungent haggis, advancing on him with it raised above her head.

'You wouldn't leave it would you? Oh no, no, no. You had to sabotage my car in the middle of nowhere. Not just once, but twice. I could have been stranded in that car park with just a pair of rotting kippers.'

The other driver, deciding that further conversation with this deranged woman is pointless, retreats back across the road, luckily through a break in the traffic. Her Ladyship is not letting it end there. She too crosses the road, haggis in hand.

'You deserved it!' He shouts as he reaches his own car.

'And your blooming kippers. After two days they were humming and the Queen noticed it.'

'The Queen? What on earth has the Queen got to do with this?'

'She smelt them after the police had ordered me to lie in a muddy puddle and pointed their guns at. Look, I'll show you.' Her

Ladyship lies on the ground behind my relative and shoves the haggis up the exhaust pipe.

A broad grin spreads across the man's face.

'Police? The Queen? Forced to lie on the ground? My my, what a busy time you've had since we last met! He chuckles and Her Ladyship, standing back up and satisfied that the haggis has found a perfect home, starts to grin too.

'It's actually been quite an adventure so far. That old thing was stolen in Yorkshire, we stayed at a very spooky B&B the night before and yesterday we disrupted a television programme being shot in the middle of Birmingham. Hopefully from now on it'll be trouble free. Are you on your way home?'

'Yes, I am. I reached Land's End yesterday afternoon. They had a big welcome for us. You'll have to hurry though, the welcome party packs up at midday tomorrow.'

'I'll be there. I plan to get there tomorrow morning. It should have been today, but all the holdups. You know what I mean.'

'So, how's she gone?' He looks across at me, 'She looks great, can I take a look?'

'Yes, of course.' Her Ladyship turns her back on him to negotiate the traffic. He dives behind my relative and retrieves the haggis from the exhaust pipe. He holds it behind his back as Her Ladyship, still talking, makes her way across the road. He follows.

'She's had a full engine rebuild over the winter and has gone like a little bomb all the way. But Scotland's roads are a bit rough, aren't they? I've had things shaking loose on me.'

'Me too. One of my headlights actually dropped off.' He squats down behind me and shoves the haggis up my exhaust pipe. 'That's a really nice luggage rack isn't it?'

'Yes, a friend made it for me and it's been most useful on this trip.' He stands up again.

'Yup, very nice.' He looks at his watch. 'Well, I'd better get going. I want to be home by tonight. Are we friends now, all forgiven and forgotten?' Her Ladyship smiles. How could she be angry with him now that she's rammed a haggis back up his exhaust? If only she'd seen what I've seen. I have a strange feeling that this entente cordiale isn't going to last very much longer.

'Yes, forgotten and forgiven. Have a safe journey home.' She grins.

He returns to his car and starts it up. Her Ladyship looks baffled, and then shrugs. As he pulls away he shouts across the road, 'You too!' Then he starts laughing.

'Strange man. Sorry Dog, we'll leave your walk for a little while. We'll stop when we get clear of Bristol.' Back on my driving seat Her Ladyship makes herself comfortable. Ignition on and she pulls my starter control.

Wurrr, rurrr, rurr, rurr, rurr.

'That's funny. What's wrong with you, Old Girl?' Wurrr, rurrr, rurr, rurr, rurr. Wurrr, rurrr, rurr, rurr, rurr.

'He didn't do anything to you Old Girl, did he?' She clambers out and checks my rear end and turns towards the departing relative now halfway across the bridge.

'BARSTAAAAARD!' Somehow I don't think he heard us. Oh yes he did, he's waving. Her Ladyship squats down and pulls the haggis from my exhaust pipe.

'The swine. Had to have the last laugh, didn't he?' She carefully stows the haggis away and climbs back in. My engine starts straight away.

'Come on you two. Glastonbury, here we come.'

We've made it to Wells, a trouble free trip and Her Ladyship has parked me in front of the cathedral so she could take The Asthmatic Barking Dog for a good walk in the grounds. I'm glad of the rest. All the way from Bristol we've been travelling along parts of her childhood stamping ground and she's become quite a bore about it all. On our way out of Bristol she got very excited about a flipping public park.

'That used to be Bristol's Airport, Old Girl, it was built back around the time you were born,' she'd remarked so excitedly. 'I remember seeing aeroplanes take off from there when I was tiny.' I mean, do I care? Uh-oh, here she comes, perhaps we can get on now.

'Right, Old Girl. Let's get to Glastonbury, then I can have an early lunch. It's ages since I was there. There's a hell of a lot that I can tell you about Glastonbury too, Old Girl.' I rather thought there might be, but I'd prefer it if you didn't. Her Ladyship settles The Asthmatic Barking Dog, climbs in herself and starts me up.

'Hippieland, here we come. Do you know, Old Girl, there are more old VW campers to the square inch in Glastonbury than anywhere else in Britain?' How utterly fascinating.

'You'll love it. It's a really mystical place. We'll have to see how the haggis reacts, won't we?' If you say so.

It doesn't take us long to reach Glastonbury and we park close to the abbey. I cannot see a single VW camper. Her Ladyship's usual nonsense, then.

'You'll have to stay in the car, Dog. Sorry. They probably won't let you into restaurants here. They don't even let meat into most of them. I'll put the hood up so you don't get too hot.' While she does that, I look around. It's rather a smart car park surrounded by lawns and flower beds. The only things spoiling the view are the plethora of signs asking people to "Keep off the Grass." With the hood and side screens fixed, she strolls off in search of sustenance and The

Asthmatic Barking Dog, having been deprived of a walk, flops down and goes to sleep.

'Hey man, look at that cool motor.' The voice comes from a man walking towards me in very loose fitting cotton trousers and a Kaftan top. He has long hair and sports an equally long beard. There are three other similarly attired people with him, two women and another man.

'Wow man,' said one of the women. 'That is so far out! Would you like one like this, Alisha?' Both of the women come to look inside.

'Hey, Serenity, this is so, so, wow. Kestrel, like, come and have a look.' The first man looks up.

'In a moment, Baby. Like I'm busy?' Kestrel? What sort of name is that? Anyway, he's more interested in rolling himself a cigarette. He must be quite poor, not being able to afford proper ones. The woman called Serenity looks annoyed.

'Keep cool man. Like, there's no need to be irritable. Hey Flight, like isn't it cool? What do you think?' Flight strolls over and peers in.

'Okay, groovy, it's better inside than out, like.' He peers at the door handle and tries it. 'Is it like, locked?' My door opens.

'Like, there are no locks, man. This car is free and open to the world.' Alisha spots The Asthmatic Barking Dog. 'Hey, far out, the car's got a dog!' The Asthmatic Barking Dog, as usual failing to do his duty by protecting me, happily welcomes the new arrivals. Alisha climbs in onto my rear seat next to him. Kestrel has now lit his cigarette and comes over. He takes a long, slow draw, inhaling the smoke deep into his lungs. He holds it before letting it out again.

'Anyone wanna share my stick?' Flight, who has also clambered in onto my rear seat, reaches out to take it.

'Like thanks, man.' He too takes a long slow draw on the cigarette, holds his breath as he passes the so-called stick to Alisha.

The Asthmatic Barking Dog is wedged in between them. In ecstasy, he stretches himself across their laps.

'Wow man,' says Flight. 'That is some giggle weed. Come on Kestrel, like get in.' Kestrel clambers into my passenger seat and slams my door. The Asthmatic Barking Dog starts to sneeze because of the fug building up inside me. Serenity, now in the driver's seat, draws on the cigarette and passes it back to Kestrel who takes another long draw.

'Oooh, man. That is sooo good.' He passes it to Flight. Serenity starts to wiggle my steering wheel and then looks round.

'How old do you think this car is, man?' She glances back at Flight.

'Like, who cares? Man, this stuff is good.' I really don't know what these strange people are talking about. I wonder if they are from somewhere foreign.

'This car is so small, but the whole world is in here,' Serenity announces to the others, staring out of the windscreen.

'Do you think, like, the people who own this car like, are little people?' If only you knew dear lady, if only you knew. Alisha, who seems very happy at the moment, starts to look around in the footwell. Flight's eyes are half shut and he lets out a long, low sigh. The Asthmatic Barking Dog is now flopped, fast asleep across his lap. I have to confess that I am feeling a little light headed.

'Oh man.' It's Kestrel this time and he has a simple, happy smile across his face.

'Like what's this?' Alisha holds Her Ladyship's haggis up for everyone to see. Kestrel looks around.

'Pass it over, babe.' Alisha complies.

My driver's door flies open and Serenity falls out onto the ground. She attempts to stand, but can't.

'What the hell are you doing in my car?' Her Ladyship's returned and she is not best pleased. I am, I am very pleased, but I don't really know what I'm pleased about.

'Moreover, what the hell are you doing with my haggis?'

Kestrel stares at the haggis quizzically.

'Like, what's a haggis?'

'It is sheep's offal stitched up inside its stomach lining, what do you think it is?' A look of sheer horror appears on Kestrel's face.

'Like M-m-m-meat?'

'Of course it's meat, you silly man.' Kestrel throws the haggis at Her Ladyship who deftly catches it in her right hand.

'What on earth are you panicking about? A haggis has magical properties.' She sniffs it and pulls a face. 'Well maybe this one's starting to lose them.'

Kestrel pushes my passenger door open and stumbles out, standing briefly before, like Serenity, falling down. He starts rubbing his hands on his trousers in an attempt to remove any vestige of the haggis. The other two passengers follow suit and they fall over too. Her Ladyship can't see The Asthmatic Barking Dog. He is now half on his seat and half on the floor. He cannot summon up the strength to get back on.

'What have you done with my dog?' Her Ladyship pokes her head inside, takes a sniff and then slowly extricates herself. The Asthmatic Barking Dog slides gracefully to the floor.

'You've been smoking Whacky Baccy, haven't you? In my car! And you've gone and drugged my dog!' The Asthmatic Barking Dog, on hearing reference to himself, thwacks his tail very slowly on the floor. He can't be bothered to do any more.

Flight, Kestrel, Serenity and Alisha again attempt to stand up, but only get as far as their knees. It's Kestrel who speaks first.

'Like, there's no need to get riled man. We were only adm, adam, adm.' He gives up. Apparently his tongue cannot cope with words of more than one syllable at the moment.

'Yeah, Man,' the others chorus. 'Yeah like.' They look at each other, wondering what they are agreeing about. Her Ladyship walks to my passenger side and shuts the door. She returns to the driver's side and examines everything to see what else has been messed with. Apart from a stoned Asthmatic Barking Dog everything seems in order. She extricates herself to addresses the four, still on their knees.

'You can push off. Go on, push off – now – before I call the police. You should all be arrested but I can't be bothered to disturb them.' All four begin to crawl in different directions to look for something to grab hold of to help them stand up. Kestrel looks back over his shoulder.

'Like, you need to be cool, Babe.'

'Don't you dare call me Babe,' Her Ladyship calls after them. 'Anyway, can't you read the signs? They say "Keep off the Grass." You should take notice of them.' She turns her attention to me.

'Honestly, Old Girl, who the hell do these people think they are? I ask you, smoking cannabis in my car without so much as a how do you do.' Like, keep cool Your Ladyship. Keep the faith.

'To make things worse, I haven't had a proper lunch either. I ended up in some ghastly vegan place, so expect me to sound like a bassoon factory in an hour or two. Come on, let's get the hell out of here. I still want to get us to Launceston tonight.'

Having previously determined not to use a motorway on this trip, Her Ladyship changed her mind at the M5 near Taunton and joined it. It's not like her, I think her courage to use this road is inspired by the lingering fug of that "Whacky Baccy" as she called it. She's certainly still distracted by our experiences in Glastonbury and as a result I have endured a diatribe of moans and complaints ever since.

'Anyway, Old Girl, this little diversion should save us some time. The weather's getting warmer isn't it? Next time we stop, I'll take your hood down again. Oh, look over there Old Girl. That's the Wellington Monument. They started to build it in 1817 to commemorate the Duke of Wellington's victory at Waterloo.' Oh do shut up. Talk about being the fount of useless knowledge.

We carry on down the motorway. I am feeling a little odd. No not odd, decidedly strange actually.

'Can you smell hot oil, Old Girl? I can. It's quite strong. Oh blooming hell, there's smoke coming out the sides of your bonnet.' Her Ladyship glances at the dashboard. 'Your oil pressure's falling too. Right. Emergency action. Clutch in, neutral gear, engine off and there, we'll coast onto the hard shoulder.' We roll to a standstill and rather a lot of smoke starts to pour out of each side of my bonnet. She bangs my steering wheel in exasperation.

'This is all we need on a motorway. I knew we should have avoided it.' She clambers out and opens one side of my bonnet.

'Flipping Henry, your petrol pump's nearly come right off. It's those Scottish roads again. You know you have two nuts holding your pump in place? Well now you've only one and that's worked itself so loose your pump is sitting half an inch away from the engine.' She stands up and peers back up the motorway. 'And you've left an oil slick along the road. I hope there's a nut somewhere I can use to replace the missing one. I know,' says Her Ladyship, 'we'll use this one holding your fan assembly in place. We are not needing that anymore.'

She tightens the pump back into place. 'Right, how much oil have you lost?' She removes my oil dip stick and examines it.

'Bone dry, not a drop.' She reaches in to grab the can of oil and pours it into my engine for several minutes before the dipstick tells her that all has returned to normal.

'Crikey, Old Girl. Four pints of oil scattered down the M5. I think we should get out of here, don't you? But not before I take your hood down.' She glances up and down the motorway.

'Just making sure no police are around, Old Girl. They might get a bit iffy if they saw me doing this.'

She's just stowing away the last side screen as a car rolls up behind us. For once it isn't a police car. The driver gets out and comes over.

'Are you all right?

'Yes, we're fine thank you.' Her Ladyship smiles politely at the newcomer. 'We had a little oil leak, but we're okay now.'

'I thought someone was having a problem. There are blobs of oil down the motorway from about a mile back.'

'That's lucky then.' Her Ladyship packs away her toolkit. 'I'm afraid I can't stop for a chat, I need to be in Launceston before dark.'

'Hmm, that's a bit of a way. Where are you from?'

'I am doing the John O'Groats to Land's End run.'

'I did that once, I was on a bike. I'm heading for Exeter. Are you sure there's nothing I can do for you?' Her Ladyship gives this offer a little thought.

'Well yes, actually, I need to get through Exeter and on to the Crediton road. I don't know my way around here. I'm also keen to get off this motorway, it's not an ideal place to break down. I don't suppose you could guide us through?'

'I'd be delighted. I'll pull in front and lead the way.'

'That's very kind, thank you. I just need to check her oil pressure.' She starts me up. 'All's well, Old Girl.' She gives a thumbs-up to the car behind, he pulls past and we follow him down the motorway towards Exeter.

'You'll like Exeter, Old Girl. There's a castle there which was built for William the Conqueror.' Oh do shut up.

I do wish people would realise that at my age I cannot keep up with modern cars. We've nearly lost our escort three times, but Her Ladyship is managing to at least keep him in sight. We roll up to some traffic lights which have just gone red.

'Why is it, Old Girl, that when you're following someone through a town you don't know, the traffic lights let the person you're following, go through and then stop you? If I don't catch up with him soon we'll lose him completely.' She peers through my windscreen. 'He's turned off to the left up there, I'm sure of it. Hopefully he'll wait for us. Ah, here we go.' The lights change back to green and we pull away as quickly as I can manage.

We get to where Her Ladyship thought our escort turned left and there is no sign of him. She swears under her breath.

'We're on our own now Old Girl, slap bang in the centre of the city and we don't know where to go. There's a turning over there, let's take that.' Her Ladyship thrusts her arm out to indicate we are turning right and turns us straight into a pedestrian area. Her Ladyship slams on my brakes as people scatter in all directions.

'Blast and dammit, Old Girl. I'll give it five seconds before some officious little toad materialises. Five, four, three. Ah, here he is.'

'You can't take that thing up here. This is a pedestrian precinct.' A uniformed gentleman, not a policeman thank goodness, walks over to us.

'Well there's a surprise. I'd never have known.' Please don't, Your Ladyship. Don't start.

'Didn't you see the no entry sign?

'No, Constable, I did not. Because if I did, I wouldn't have turned up this road, would I?'

'I'm not a constable, I'm a Civil Enforcement Officer, and...' Her Ladyship butts in.

'A what? What did you call yourself?'

'A Civil Enforcement Officer, and as I was about to say...' Her Ladyship interjects again.

'And what do you Civilly Enforce? Mass deportations?' Oh dear, she's off. The nostrils are beginning to go and I fear he might take offense at that remark. The important question is whether he can keep his cool. Her Ladyship will do her best to destabilise his confidence now. The pedestrians who had been scattered start to gather around us, obviously hoping for some sort of a confrontation.

'There's no need to be offensive, Madam. We enforce the safe flow of traffic through this city, and as I was about to say...'

'Why do you need to enforce it? Surely most motorists are just like me, naturally keen to keep our roads safe and clear of hindrances. Let's face it, Civil Enforcement Officer is just a new, fancy name for a traffic warden.' This banter is rather like a tennis match. I'll be the umpire. Mr Civil Enforcement Officer serves.

'Civil Enforcement Officers have new powers, madam.' Fifteen – Love. A good start, he's keeping his cool. The crowd starts to murmur. The tension is rising here at Centre Court.

'Go on lady, hit him one.' Someone in the crowd shouts out from the back. Quiet please!

'For instance,' says the Civil Enforcement Officer. 'I have the power to immobilise vehicles.' Thirty – Love.

Her Ladyship rallies. 'Look get to the point,' she says. 'We've been sitting here for the last few minutes and we've agreed that I – accidentally – took a wrong turning and have driven into a pedestrian-only street. Realising my error I have stopped.' Thirty – fifteen, I believe.

'I'm anxious to find the road to Crediton. Perhaps you'd be good enough to enforce me in that direction. Because if you can't, I'll leave my car here and go and have a cup of coffee while you decide what you're going to do.' Thirty – All. This brings a ripple of applause from the gathered crowd. The man's shoulders drop, then drawing himself up to his full height, he tries another tack.

'I would be more than happy to help you, Madam. Please, just do what I advise – not enforce.' Good one Mr Civil Enforcement Officer – Forty – Thirty.

'So, what do you advise?' Her Ladyship's eyebrows rise in anticipation.

'I'll guide you back to the turning and then if you go back up the street you came down, you'll find a road sign which will put you onto the Crediton road. Okay?'

Game, set and match to Mr. Civil Enforcement Officer. Her Ladyship, recognising defeat, puts me into reverse and the crowd disperse, obviously unhappy that the situation was defused quite so quickly.

We ease ourselves back to the road junction and Mr. Civil Enforcement Officer gestures us on our way.

'Thank you, Constable,' Her Ladyship shouts as we accelerate away. She has to have the last word, doesn't she?

As we head up the road we see the man who had been escorting us. Her Ladyship applies my brakes and we glide to a standstill about ten feet past him. She clambers out.

'There you are. We'd lost you.' He nods his head in the direction of Mr Civil Enforcement Officer, who is watching us rather suspiciously.

'What was going on down there then?'

'Oh nothing, I took a wrong turn and a rather officious little man who calls himself a Civil Enforcement Officer engaged me in a meaningful conversation. Now I'm heading up here, hopefully to find a sign for Crediton.'

'Yes, that's the turning up there. Would you like me to show you?'

'No, I'll be okay now. Look, thanks for your help, but I'd better go. I don't fancy my chances if I upset him again. Come on, Old Girl. Hopefully we'll now have a safe, unhindered run to Launceston.'

We've made it to Crediton, but here we are, stuck in the centre of town. We are stuck because they are having some sort of Tudor festival. Her Ladyship sits impatiently waiting to pass through and a young man dressed in Shakespearian costume dances across to us.

'My mistress with a monster is in love,' he addresses Her Ladyship, who is taken by complete surprise.

'What? What are you on about, Young Man?'

'Near to her close and consecrated bower, while she was in her dull and sleeping hour, a crew of patches, rude mechanicals, that work for bread upon Athenian stalls, were met together to rehearse a play, intended for great Theseus' nuptial day.' Her Ladyship is obviously irritated by this bizarre confrontation.

'Excuse me, Young Man, but will you get to the point? And then perhaps you'll get out of my way.' He starts to dance around us.

'The shallowest thick skin of that barren sort, who Pyramus presented in their sport, forsook his scene and entered in a brake. When I did him at this advantage take, an ass's nole I fixèd on his head.' Her Ladyship watches in total astonishment.

'Should you be allowed out on your own, Young Man?' Her Ladyship asks with genuine concern. 'Or am I a victim of one of those Candid Camera programmes?' She looks around nervously.

'Nay, Fair Lady.' Now I know he's off his trolley, or perhaps he's blind? Fair Lady indeed! 'Nay. We are but humble actors and performing arts students presenting A Midsummer Night's Dream for your delight and delectation at this Springtide festival.'

'Well that's very nice isn't it?' Replies Her Ladyship, trying to be polite. 'But I really have to get on my way. Will you kindly let me through now?' He continues his dance around us.

'Anon his Thisby must be answered.' He's off again. 'And forth my mimic comes. When they him spy.' Her Ladyship, seeing that he has disappeared around the back of me, manoeuvres me forwards.

'Forsooth, Young Man, 'tis time to say good bye. Parting is such sweet sorrow – not.' She presses my accelerator pedal and we leave Crediton at more than my normal speed.

'For heaven's sake, Old Girl, what a palaver. Shakespearian performances indeed, holding up the flow of traffic. I ask you. Not too far to Launceston now. Uh oh, that's a sign for a steep hill.' We swing round a bend and there ahead is indeed a rather steep hill. Her Ladyship drops me into third gear. But it's still a struggle.

'Come on, Old Girl, you can do better than this.' That's fine coming from her. If she had gone on a diet before we left Pembrokeshire this particular hill, not to mention most of Scotland, would have been much easier.

We are just over half way up when a large group of cyclists in stretched Lycra shorts and tops, wearing those ridiculous helmets, start to overtake us. It wouldn't be so bad if they weren't passing on both sides. Her Ladyship is horrified.

'Get out of my way!' She cries. 'Get out of my way!'

'You get out of our way,' cries one of the cyclists dressed in bright yellow and black, slowing down to ride alongside us. 'You're blocking the road and anyway, power gives way to sail.'

'You're not sail, you're pedal power.' Her Ladyship shouts back.

'So we may be, but we're faster than you, so just slow down and let us through.'

Angrily, Her Ladyship slams on my brakes. We stop, but unfortunately a cyclist who is directly behind us isn't paying attention and his front wheel hits my rear end and now he's head first in my rear seat being lovingly licked by The Asthmatic Barking Dog.

'Oh for heaven's sake, says Her Ladyship as some of the other cyclists come over to see if they can help.

'Sorry Missus, I didn't see you stop.' He unravels himself from the tangle he's in and hops out over my side, much to The Asthmatic Barking Dog's consternation. He was enjoying the company.

'Are you alright?' Unusually Her Ladyship seems quite worried.

'I'm fine, a bit bruised, that's all.' He sniffs the air. 'What's that smell?' Her Ladyship takes a sniff too.

'What smell?'

'That smell, of something going off.'

'Oh, that's my haggis. It has magical powers you know, and it has eased my path through Scotland.' The cyclist decides that perhaps it's best not to take this matter any further. He examines his bicycle which was lying where it fell.

'The front wheel's a bit out of alignment but I can fix that. Sorry Missus, I should have been looking where I was going.' He starts to adjust his bicycle and the leader of the group, the one in yellow and black, comes over.

'Look, Lady, why don't you just drive on while we fix Charlie's bike? It's a long downhill run after the top up there. You'll be well on your way before we start again. Her Ladyship satisfies herself that I am well too and we are on our way yet again.

We've got to Launceston and guess what? Her ladyship is lost, yet again. I'm beginning to wish she hadn't disposed of her Satellite Thingy. This is not a big town, so why doesn't she just ask the way? We drive up and down just about every road that Launceston has to offer and some of them are rather steep.

'It's got to be somewhere near here, Old Girl. When I phoned he said it was a sharp turn and then up a little hill. Hang on, what's this? That's a sharp turn, let's try it.' It is sharp and Madam has to do several manoeuvres to get me up there. Fortunately, there are no cyclists.

'This is it, Old Girl. Look, there's the B&B up there. My, this is a steep incline isn't it? At least we're here.' We pull up near the kerb and the owner of the B&B comes out to greet us.

'Hello, hello. Welcome, welcome. A good journey? Her Ladyship remains seated and peers irritably up at him.

'Well no actually, it's been a bit fraught. First of all a load of schoolgirls held us up. That was in Cheltenham. Then someone tried to sabotage my car on the Clifton Suspension Bridge. He was a complete pain.' The B&B man is beginning to wish he hadn't asked about the journey and turns to go inside to be stopped in his tracks by Her Ladyship.

'I haven't finished yet.' He turns back with a resigned look on his face. 'When we got to Glastonbury, a bunch of hippies hi-jacked my car and started to smoke dope in her, knocking out my dog and for all I know the car as well. Then we had a problem on the motorway with her oil.'

'What, did she have the Munchies?' He gives a little chuckle

'What? Munchies? What are you on about?' He shrugs his shoulders.

'Never mind. You're here now aren't you and I expect in some need of refreshment. Are you able to park just there? I'm afraid it's a bit steep.' Her Ladyship looks at the parking space the B&B man suggested.

'It is very steep here, Old Girl. I think I'd better turn you around.' Her Ladyship does a neat 3-point-turn and firmly puts my brake on.

'I don't think that'll be enough,' says the B&B man. I'd put something under your front wheel as well if I were you. Just to be sure.'

'I have just the thing,' announces Her Ladyship and she reaches behind my driver's seat and produces the haggis. 'This'll do the job. It'll mould itself to fit.' She rams it under my front nearside wheel. The B&B owner looks unconvinced.

'Are you sure that will hold?'

'Oh yes. The handbrake is on, and my organic wheel chock is in place. What could go wrong?' He shakes his head and goes back into the B&B.

Her Ladyship expertly puts my hood back up and lets The Asthmatic Barking Dog out. She waves at me.

'Good night, Old Girl, sleep well. See you tomorrow.'

For some reason, I have the most enormous headache.

Chapter Ten

Her Ladyship looks up. I follow her gaze and about twenty feet above us is a helicopter hovering. Then to our amazement, Asthmatic Barking Dog makes a mighty leap and lands precariously on my roof.

Land's End – At Blooming Last!

There's a blasted cat examining the haggis that is presently my wheel chock. Every now and again it whacks at it with its paw. I am surprised it can't smell it. I can and it stinks. I wonder if it has no sense of smell. Uh oh, it's gone and ripped it open with its claws and is having a good sniff. Now that is a pong! It has lost interest and has wandered off to examine my other wheels, perhaps looking to see if I have any more haggis-styled wheel chocks which project less pong than the one at the front. On discovering that it is the only one, the cat has come back, settles down and is eating it. All I can say is that it must be really hungry. At the rate this cat is eating it I reckon I have about half a minute before…

'Good morning, Old Girl.' Just in time, Your Ladyship. Please attend to that cat. There, the one eating your haggis. Because if you don't, disaster is looming.

'Sleep well, Old Girl? I did. Apart from Dog snoring all night and dreaming about being sat upon by that blasted Borzoi.'

Excuse me for interrupting, Your Ladyship. Will you just for once, just once, LISTEN TO ME! There is a cat slowly eating my wheel chock and, oh. Did we move then? I'm sure I rolled forwards a little. That blasted cat has gone and thrown up. Serves you right cat. Now it's eating more of the haggis! FOR GOODNESS SAKE WOMAN LISTEN TO ME AND SORT THAT CAT OUT! Or

I cannot be held responsible for the consequences. Her Ladyship finally spots the activity by my wheel.

'What are you doing, cat?' Get away from that. That's my wheel chock. I was going to eat that when I got home. Leave it.' She looks around. 'Dog! Dog, where are you, when I need you? I've got a job for you.' The Asthmatic Barking Dog trots over, very pleased with himself. He probably thinks he's being offered breakfast. Somehow I think not.

'Dog? Look, it's a CAT! See it off. Pssssst. Go on.' The Asthmatic Barking Dog looks up at Her Ladyship as if to say "Wot? Wot d'ya want now?" Her Ladyship points at the offending feline and the shrinking haggis. He spies the cat eating it and trots over to join in. I imagine he's thinking that Her Ladyship wants him to have some haggis too. Oooh I don't think I like this. I inch forward downhill again. Her Ladyship prods the cat with her foot and it runs off.

'Grrrr, arf, arf, arf!' The Asthmatic Barking Dog is off too, straight after the cat. The haggis, which is now half its original size, creaks and oozes an obnoxious mixture of goodness knows what as my wheels slowly but surely start turning again and I move forwards once more, continuously this time.

'Oh shoot. Bloody hell, Old Girl, where do you think you're going?'

Talk about stating the blooming obvious, I am going down this hill, woman! She grabs my driver's door handle and leans backwards in the vain hope that she can stop my progress. The door swings open but Her Ladyship hangs on for dear life. Your Ladyship, you do realise that there are only four wood screws between you, my door and me? Oh yes, and I also weigh rather a lot more than you.

There is the sound of four corks being slowly pulled from four bottles and Her Ladyship is left holding my door while I happily roll slowly down the hill towards…? Yes, that's right, towards the rear end of a parked car, and a rather expensive one at that.

'Come back this instant Old Girl,' shouts Her Ladyship. Do you know, there is nothing I'd rather do more at this very moment. But when gravity demands, well there isn't much I can do. Let's face it, you really haven't been much help have you? Her Ladyship drops my door on the ground and totters after me. She reaches me just as my front wheels make contact with the other car. It jumps, much as anyone does when being suddenly awoken from a peaceful sleep.

'Oh my God! What have you done now?' Me? I like that. I am an inert object that can only do things when a human physically makes me do so.

'OI! What's going on? What have you done to my car?' A rather irate man is coming out from the house next door to the bed and breakfast. Other doors up and down the street start to open as people come out to see what's going on. The man who shouted at us looks rather angry. He marches over. Her Ladyship, trying to ignore him, examines the place where my wheels met this vehicle.

'What the hell have you done to my car? You'll pay for the damage.' He tries to nudge Her Ladyship out of the way to take a look himself. She stands firm to get a first look at what sort of damage there is, then she steps backwards with a smile.

'Absolutely nothing, look! Not a mark. The old girl merely rolled gently into the rear valance of your car.'

'Get out of my way, let me see. Come on, give me a hand pushing this old heap back from my car.' Old heap indeed. Do you know, I've had to put up with rather a lot of derogatory references on this trip and I'm getting rather fed up. Her Ladyship and a couple of neighbours push me back from my resting place. She looks around for something more effective than a rotting haggis as a wheel chock. Finding a brick, she wedges it under my front wheel.

'There you are. A slight tyre mark that's all.' She goes to retrieve a duster from the glove pocket in my driver's door but there's nothing there. She's left the door several yards back up the road.

'Hang on,' she cries and strolls up to retrieve my door, pulling a duster out as she returns. She plonks the door on my roof and polishes away the mark on the other car.

'There. No tyre mark. Satisfied?' I don't think he is, he climbs underneath the rear of his car to check if there is any internal damage.

'Hmmph, it seems alright,' he says as he extricates himself from underneath his vehicle.

'Told you so. Now if you don't mind, I need to fix this door and get to Land's End before lunch.'

'You'm be'er be careful my Bird.' Another voice chirps in. 'Weather forecast says there's a sea mist comin' in. They'm unusual this time o' yur. T'will be a devil o'er Bodmin Moor an' tiz always turrible at Lan's End.' I don't think Her Ladyship wanted to hear this. She looks round to see where this new voice has come from. He's an elderly man with a wrinkled face and bright pink cheeks. He wears a rather tattered jumper. With a knowledge of the weather, I expect this is a man who's spent his life at sea.

'Oh really? I expect we'll be fine,' she says, brushing off that bit of news. She starts to examine my door and how she might put it back in place.

'On yur own 'ead be it than. But don' say I didn' warn ee.' The gentleman turns and goes back into his house.

'What does he know, Old Girl?' Probably a lot more than you, Your Ladyship. She continues to examine my door. 'Tell you what, Old Girl, I'll strap it onto the hood for now. I can manage without it.' She fits the erstwhile door into its temporary home and secures it with bungee cords.

'Right, we're ready for the off. Where are you, Dog?' The Asthmatic Barking dog had soon lost interest in chasing cats and returned to the remains of the haggis. But he's been sick too and is looking very sorry for himself.

'Your own fault, Dog. You shouldn't have eaten it if it was bad for you. Come on.' The Asthmatic Barking Dog clambers to his feet and walks slowly towards Her Ladyship.

'Here, have some water. That'll make you feel better. I don't want you being sick in the car, okay?' They both hop in and Her Ladyship starts me up, engages gear, clutch out and… Nothing.

'What's the matter now, Old Girl? It's downhill and you can't pull forwards?' If you had bothered to remember, Your Ladyship, there is a brick against my nearside front wheel.

'I know, I'll give you a bit more wellie.' Her Ladyship revs my engine and lets my clutch out too quickly. I leap into the air and neatly hop over the brick. Her Ladyship slams my brakes on again. My number plate, having finally lost a securing nut, drops one end down on the road and to top it all, my nearside headlamp assembly drops off my wing, pulling its connecting cables out with it.

'What have you done now, Old Girl? Do you want to get to Land's End this side of Christmas or don't you?' Her Ladyship clambers out and comes round to my front.

'Blast and dammit. I haven't got time to fix your headlight, but I do have a bit of wire I can fix your number plate with.' She grabs a length of wire from under a seat and secures my number plate back into position.

'We'll sort out the lamp at Land's End. Come on, let's go before anything else happens.' She tosses the headlight onto my passenger seat, puts me back into gear and we're off, but not before my rear nearside wheel jumps noisily over the very same brick that she'd failed to take out of the way.

What a sight we must be on this final part of our journey. Me with a door strapped to my hood, a missing headlight and Her Ladyship sitting primly on my driver's seat, exposing a profile of her rear end for all to see.

'Tell you what, Old Girl,' Her Ladyship announces after a long thoughtful silence. 'That haggis has proved quite useful on this trip, but the one thing it isn't, it's not a wheel chock. I feel another letter to the Scottish government coming on. First it's their rough roads and now it's their national dish. Or is that deep fried Mars bars? Mind you, I don't suppose a steak and kidney pudding would have held you back either. Nor, come to think of it, would a bowl of cawl. The moral of all this is, Old Girl, never trust your national dish to act as a wheel chock.' What on earth is she on about now? There have been times on this trip, no, not just on this trip, there have been times when I have really worried about this woman's sanity.

We start to cross Bodmin Moor and a light mist rolls across the countryside leaving tiny globules of water on my bodywork.

'Is this what they call sea mist, Old Girl? Because if this is all it is, we aren't going to have any problem, are we? This isn't going to hold us up. Come on then, only about 65 miles to go. The moor seems very barren, a sort of flat version of Snowdonia. There is the odd farmstead dotted around and about, but they are very few and far between. There is a real sense of desolation. I wouldn't like to break down here, I can tell you.

'On the whole, Old Girl, I think we've done really well. We've only been delayed about twenty four hours and look, look there. There's one of our lot coming back from Land's End now.' A relative approaches and Her Ladyship waves vigorously.

'Hello!' she shouts at them. 'How is it in Land's End?'

'Hellooo,' comes a voice from the other side of the road. 'You'd better hurry. It's getting miss...' A lorry roars up behind us and slams on his air brakes, so we are unable to hear the rest of what he was shouting. Her Ladyship waves and we move on.

'Getting Miss? What do you think he meant, Old Girl? Getting Miss what? I wonder if they'll be doing lunches at Land's End. Oh come on, let's speed up and get there sooner rather than later.' She presses her foot down on my accelerator and I speed up.

'I'll be happy when we get off this moor though, Old Girl. It's giving me the creeps.' Cough, cough, splutter, splutter and my engine dies.

'Oh for heaven's sake, what's wrong with you now?' Fortunately there's a parking area just ahead and we roll into it with ease. Her Ladyship smacks her hands against my steering wheel.

'Oh damn and blast it! Come on, Old Girl, you're not going to die on me so close to our finishing line are you?' She fiddles with my ignition switch and tries my starter again. Nothing. I know what's wrong, but I wonder how long it will be before Your Ladyship realises we've run out of petrol? Forgetting that my driver's door is fixed to my roof, Her Ladyship falls out onto the ground. She clambers to her feet and opens one side of my bonnet.

'Right,' she says rubbing her arm. 'Let's test your ignition. Leads tight,' she removes one of the spark plug leads, props it close to my cylinder head and cranks my handle. 'And you've got a spark, good. So it must be your fuel supply.' She walks to my other side and opens my bonnet. She tries my petrol pump.

'That seems to be working, so what about your carburettor?' She removes my float chamber. 'Hmm, bone dry. Let's check that pump again. It may sound as though it works, but we may have to change it over to the spare.' Her ladyship reaches down to the pump and operates the manual control.

'Well Old Girl, that seems to be working, but there's no petrol coming through. Umm, no petrol? I know.' She hops back onto my driver's seat, switches on my ignition and taps at my petrol gauge. The needle stays firmly at zero.

'How could I be so daft?' Quite easily, I would suggest, Your Ladyship. 'We're out of petrol, Old Girl. How silly of me, I should have filled you up in Launceston and do you know? I packed every possible spare part, I packed oil and I packed antifreeze, but I didn't bloody pack a spare can of petrol.'

A white van pulls into the layby just in front of us. The driver gets out and stretches himself. He is a middle aged man, dressed in a T-shirt and jeans. I think he is probably a plumber. He has that sort of look on his face that says, "Whatever you want, I can't help."

'I say,' Her Ladyship walks over to him. 'I don't suppose you know where the nearest petrol station is?'

'Yup.'

'Well?'

'Well wha'?' I definitely think he's a plumber, but he could be a jobbing builder.

'Well, where is it?'

'Well, where is wha'?' He's definitely a plumber. His van is too clean.

'Well where is the nearest petrol station?'

'Oh that. You'll find 'n back there about a mile. Tiz good petrol thur. Allus stop thur missel' when I need to fill 'un up.' He gestures to the van.

'Thank you, that's all I want to know.' She starts back to me and then stops, pauses and looks back at the man.

'I don't suppose you could give me a lift back up that way could you?'

'Nope. Can't stop. You'll get me the sack. Gotta get on.' Her Ladyship is not pleased at this brush-off and comes back to me.

'Definitely not a knight of the road, Old Girl. Selfish swine. It wouldn't take him two minutes. I suppose I'll have to walk now. It shouldn't take too long. You'd better come along too, Dog. You'll enjoy the walk.' She slips the lead over The Asthmatic Barking

Dog's head, grabs her bag and they plod off in the direction pointed out by White Van Man. As Her Ladyship disappears off into the mist, the man settles down to light himself a cigarette. His mobile phone rings. He whips it out to answer.

'ello Bolventor Plumbing?' I knew it.

'Oh 'ello Mrs Cooper. Wha'? You wan' wha'?

'Oh no Missus can' do tha'. Oi'm terrible busy at the mo. Wha'?'

'Water all over where?'

'Yus, Oi knows oi wus thur lass' week and you fought oi'd sorted it. Oi told un oi ha' to cum back. Oi can be thur nex' Toosday. Alroight?'

'Now Missus Cooper thur's no ned to cum over all 'igh an' mighty. Oi canna' get thur today. Orl roight? Oi'll see you on Toosday.' He switches his phone off, pulls out a paper, folds it in two and produces a pen.

'Roight, seven down. "Fault, water main breaks". Eight ledders. Oi knows. Tiz Plumbers. Easy.' He scribbles on the paper.

It's over half an hour since Her Ladyship wandered off with The Asthmatic Barking Dog and our white van plumber finally drove off about five minutes ago. I am sure this sea mist is getting thicker. Oh do hurry up, Your Ladyship. It's lonely here. A car transporter pulls up in front of me. The driver and his mate hop out and walk back to look at me.

'What do ee think o' this 'un then Jem? Nice liddle car.'

'Yur tiz noice innit Kitto? Whassit doin' yur.'

'Oi dunno.' The man called Kitto touches my radiator. 'Tiz

Cold. Bin yur a while I reckons.'

'Twasn't yur yesterday Kitto.'

'Wan'it? Do ee reckon sumun dumped 'n, Jem?'

'Could've, s'pose. T'would be worth a bob or two, wouldn' un Kitto?'

'T'would. Tiz a good bit 'o steel. Tha's worth a bit, even if th' car ain't. C'mon, less haul 'un onto th' low loader.' Excuse me for interrupting gentlemen, but I'm not a candidate for the scrap yard. Leave me alone, do you hear? Oh where's Her Ladyship when she's needed? The two men fit some ramps to their low loader and the man called Jem hauls back a cable which he attaches to my front axle. Kitto winds a handle and I slowly approach the ramp.

'Jem, th 'and brake. Is'n on?'

'ang on Kitto, oi'll check.' Jem peers through into my driving compartment. 'Yeah 'ur tiz. Ang on, oi'll let 'n off.' He releases my brake and I roll forward with greater ease.

'I say, what the hell are you doing?' Oh thank heaven, it's Her Ladyship and The Asthmatic Barking Dog. They're back, with petrol. 'Will you kindly unhand my motor car, immediately?'

'Tiz yur's is'n Missus?' Kitto is decidedly sheepish. 'We thought 'un was dumped, honest.'

'Well, "un" wasn't dumped. If you care to examine the contents of this motor car you will see my luggage. And other things. Do you really think anyone would dump a car like this? We'd simply run out of petrol and I had to go back to get some more.' The Asthmatic Barking Dog, sensing the atmosphere, decides he wants to join in. It starts as usual with his low rumble and crescendos into a prolonged growl followed by:

Grrrr, 'Arf Arf, Arf!' then the long, asthmatic intake of air followed by more arf, arfs. He leaps forwards, jerking at his lead and almost pulls Her Ladyship off her feet. Kitto and Jem might have thought they could handle Her Ladyship, but with his hackles up,

234

The Asthmatic Barking Dog is something different to contend with. Kitto lets go of the winch handle and Jem, trying to avoid The Asthmatic Barking Dog, circles round to undo the cable from my axle. Kitto throws the ramps onto the low loader, both men jump in and they are off down the road with the winch cable still in tow.

'Well done Dog. We saw them off didn't we? Right, let's get going to Land's End. I only hope that the reception committee will still be there.' Her Ladyship pours the contents of the petrol can into my tank. She looks to see where she can pack the used can away, but finding nowhere she tosses it into a rubbish bin.

'We won't need that again, Old Girl. We'll fill you up when we get to Bodmin. I'll stop for a quick sandwich and a coffee there as well and we should make it to Land's End in less than two hours.' Her Ladyship opens my bonnet to tickle my petrol pump.

'We'd better pull the fuel through before trying to start your engine, Old Girl. There, that'll do.' She closes my bonnet and hops into the driving seat, rolling her backside around to get comfortable.

'Come on then, let's go. This mist seems to be getting worse and we don't want to get lost.' She starts me up and we are off, heading on the last leg of our journey.

We found a petrol station just outside Bodmin and Her Ladyship ate a quick lunch of goodies she'd bought in the shop. She didn't hang around because that mist wasn't going away.

'This could be the proverbial pain, Old Girl,' she'd said. 'Once we pass Penzance the roads get quite small and we could easily get ourselves lost in this, especially if it gets much worse.'

But we've made it to Penzance and the place is crawling with my relatives, unsurprisingly parked outside pubs with their occupants enjoying a celebratory pint of beer.

'Oh look, Old Girl, there's Arthur and the others. Let's go and say hello.' It is indeed The Nice Mister Arthur.

'Hello you lot. Have you been waiting for me so we could get to Land's End together?'

'No we got there yesterday afternoon. We thought we'd spend a couple of nights here in Cornwall before going home. What happened to you then?' He asks, wandering over to us and observing my door-less and one headlamp-less state. 'You've been through the wars, haven't you?'

'It's a long story,' says Her Ladyship. 'And if I could be bothered, I'd write a book about it. Tell me, are they still at Land's End, you know, the reception committee?' The Nice Mister Arthur looks doubtful.

'I think you'll find they've packed up and gone home. Anyway, it's not a good idea to head to Land's End now. We left there this morning and the mist was rolling in then. It'll be pretty awful by now.'

'I've got to. Seven hundred and fifty miles to John O' Groats and nigh on a thousand miles back down to here. It would be a shame if I didn't finish it properly. Are you staying here in Penzance?'

'Yes, until tomorrow and then we're going home. Would you like us to come with you to Land's End, if only to take a picture of you by the signpost?'

'No, no need. It's less than ten miles now. Look, I'll pop there, someone will take a picture for me and I'll come back here to see you all. We can have a little celebration tonight. See you later.'

'Okay, but be careful with this weather. You don't want to get lost.' The Nice Mister Arthur grins. But is that a grin of reassurance or of pity?

'Me? Lost? It's only a few miles, there's no way I could get lost. I'll be back in a couple of hours, have a large G&T waiting for me.' She puts me into gear and we head off west for the last time. But with this mist, we are not going very fast and Her Ladyship is leaning towards my windscreen. I've always wondered why when driving through mist or fog, Her Ladyship thinks that by leaning forwards a few inches, she will improve her view.

'Have you noticed Old Girl, that when we're driving through a village or town in a mist, one's visibility is much clearer than when in the country? Still, we're on the right road... I think. What am I saying? Of course we're on the right road.' She decides to change the subject. 'Well, Dog, nearly there. Not far now.' There is little certainty in that last statement. Personally, I think she made a wrong turning back there.

We've gone a little way now and I really wish that Her Ladyship hadn't disposed of her Sat-Nav thingy. It would have been much easier to navigate ourselves in this mist. She could have bought another, or accepted being accompanied by The Nice Mr. Arthur. But no, "it's only 10 miles, Old Girl, we can't get lost." Well I'm sure we have. Ah, there's a farmer up ahead, he's escorting a couple of cows into a field. Her Ladyship spots him too.

'Excuse me? Can you help me?' She pulls us to a standstill beside the farmer. He briefly watches his cows run off into the field. He turns to Her Ladyship and then to me. He notices that my door is missing, but doesn't react. It's almost as if he's quite used to seeing cars driving around this part of Cornwall with no doors.

'Oi'll try m'dear. What do ee want?'

'I'm heading to Land's End. How much further is it? The farmer rubs his chin and looks up in the direction we are going and then back to the direction from which we came. He shoves his thumbs into the pockets of his ragged waistcoat.

'Well now.' He looks up and down the road again. 'Goin' the

way you'm goin', tiz about twenty five thousan' mile. But, if ee turns roun' and goes t'other way, tiz aboot two.' He almost spits out that last word.

'Twenty five? Two? Oh, I see what you mean. Oh very funny.'

'I thinks so too. Ee can turn roun' just up road thur an' head back. When ee gets to junction ee needs to take a right an' Lan's En' is a couple o' mile doun thur.' Her Ladyship looks thoughtful.

'Back down the way I came, then right for two miles and I'm in Land's End? Is that it?'

'Yup, s'right. T'ain't far now. Are you'm on tha' ol' car rally?'

'Yes, why?'

'Well, they'm all gone.'

'Gone? Who's all gone?'

'Them 'ol car people, they'm all gone 'ome.'

'Oh, that's a shame. Will anyone be there?'

'Oi dunno. Mebe, mebe not.'

'Thank you. I'd better be off.' Her Ladyship puts me into gear and we drive off into the mist once more.

'Well, we've made it, Old Girl,' says Her Ladyship as she peers into the mist. 'Land's End. Here we are... D'you know, I think this mist is starting to clear a bit.' We inch slowly forwards. Occasionally the shadow of a large building looms up beside us as we look for somewhere to stop. In the distance a fog horn bellows out trying to attract the attention of passing shipping.

'This is rather creepy, isn't it Old Girl? That forlorn foghorn blasting out through the mist like that. It makes this whole thing really eerie, especially as we can barely see where we are. Oh look, here's a turning, let's go up here.' Her Ladyship turns me left across some sort of courtyard. A momentary breeze swirls and confuses the remnants of the mist making our visibility a little clearer.

'Look, Old Girl, I'm going to park you up here and have a wander around on foot. I think it'll be easier.' Her Ladyship gets out and looks about us. 'This mist is definitely clearing and somehow it's only a few feet high off the ground. It's much easier to see when I'm standing. It's almost as if I am looking above a cloud.' She peers down. 'You must be on the right spot. We've parked by a big letter "H". There has to be someone about somewhere.' A gust of wind comes up and the last of the mist swirls around and clears.

'Hey!' A voice cuts through from somewhere. 'You can't park there!' Her Ladyship peers towards the direction from where that voice came.

'What? What did you say?'

'I said you can't park there. You've got to move that thing.' An approaching whirring sound diverts our attention briefly. It seems to be coming towards us. The owner of the voice appears beside us.

'You've got to...' He is drowned out by the noise of the whirring, which is by now directly above us. I can feel a strange wind buffeting down onto me. The Asthmatic Barking Dog wakes up, obviously annoyed at the noise. '...rescue helicopter...That car!'

'What?' Her Ladyship is shouting now. 'I can't hear you!' Suddenly we are lit from above with very bright lights. Are we being abducted by aliens? The Asthmatic Barking Dog obviously thinks so. He leaps out off my rear seat, out through where my door used to be and dives underneath me.

'We have to move that bloody car now, unless you want a helicopter to land on top of it!' Her Ladyship looks up. I follow her gaze and about twenty feet above us is a very large helicopter hovering. The bright lights dazzle us and a man leaning out of its side is shouting at us but we cannot hear him.

'Here!' shouts the owner of the "Hey" voice. 'Help me push it out of the way!' With the man's help she pushes me away from the big "H". The Asthmatic Barking Dog is revealed lying flat on the ground with his paws over his ears. Her Ladyship bellows at him and he rushes with uncharacteristic obedience straight over to her. Then to both our amazement, he makes a mighty leap and lands precariously on my door which is still strapped to my roof. He regains his balance, gives Her Ladyship a look of triumph and happy that he is now safe from the helicopter, settles down to watch it arrive.

'Good grief Dog, what on earth are you doing? You'll damage the door.' The Asthmatic Barking Dog glances at the ground and looks at Her Ladyship is if to say "Did I just do that?" Her Ladyship turns her attention once more to me.

'Guess what, Old Girl, you'd only parked on a helicopter landing pad.' Oh that's a relief then. Mind you, after nine days with her, being abducted by aliens might have been preferable.

'Careful now,' shouts the man. 'There's a sheer drop ahead. We don't want to push it over the edge.' CRUNCH! Somehow I have a feeling that we've just found Land's End. To be more precise, it's not so much a feeling, more a lack of feeling because I cannot feel anything in particular under my front wheels. Her Ladyship spots this, and so does The Asthmatic Barking Dog. I might be about to plunge to my death, but he's having no part of that. So he leaps off the roof and finds himself a suitable position from which to watch developments.

'Don't let go! And whatever you do don't push! Gently, pull her back.' I feel myself edging back a little, but my front wheels are still precariously perched at the edge of the cliff. The helicopter lands on its chosen spot. With so much swirling of the air, the mist has completely dispersed. I can see a few buildings, and the nearest tells me it's the Land's End Hotel. Thank the lord for that, despite Her

Ladyship's attempts to the contrary, we've made it. But what could have been a nice calm trip has, with Her Ladyship's help, turned into a veritable nightmare.

The helicopter pilot comes over to join us.

'That was a close one,' he says. 'I nearly flattened that sardine can of yours. How do you do, I'm Squadron Leader Warner. You were in my parking space.' Oh at last, a military man, someone responsible with an air of authority. I feel a lot better now, but one little point Mister Squadron Leader, I am not a sardine can. Her Ladyship looks sheepishly at him.

'Yes, well, sorry. But when I arrived, I couldn't see where I was, let alone where I was going.' Her Ladyship's phone rings. She fumbles for it in her pocket.

'Hello? Who's that? Alexei?' Madam's face brightens. 'Where are you calling from?' She turns and looks around. 'Land's End? Where in Land's End?'

'Right here, Chunky Lumps,' Alexei emerges from the hotel, Boris the Borzoi trotting happily along beside him. Boris is very pleased to see The Asthmatic Barking Dog and both dogs embark on the "Ello Mate" routine with noses once more examining each other's nether regions in the finest detail.

"You made it, Mate." Sniff, sniff.

"Yes Mate, but I can count on my four paws how many times we nearly didn't." Sniff, sniff, lick.

"What do you mean, Mate?" Sniff, sniff.

"Put it like this, Mate. Mine shouldn't be allowed out on her own, she's a danger to everyone and everything, especially me." Sniff, sniff.

"What do you mean, Mate?"

"She only tried to poison me with that haggis this morning. Do you remember it Mate?" The Asthmatic Barking Dog decides to move to Boris the Borzoi's other side.

"Yes I do, Mate. It stank a bit when I was travelling with you."
Boris the Borzoi manoeuvres his position too.

"Well Mate, by this morning it wasn't even fit for the compost
heap. Mind you, it made a feline sick too, so it wasn't all bad." They
continue to indulge in the smells of each other's anatomies.

'What on earth brings you to Land's End, Alexei?' I don't think
she really cares. She's just pleased he's here.

'You, Chunky Lumps. I vanted to velcome you at the line,
finishing.'

'That's wonderful, how nice. Oh, I'm sorry I'm being rude.
Alexei, this is Squadron Leader Warner. Squadron Leader, this is
Alexei. He's a Russian spy you know. Oh whoops!' They all laugh,
Alexei more nervously than the others.

They're ignoring me and I think they've forgotten me.
CRUNCH, another lump of rock falls away from under my front
wheels and it takes a long time to reach the sea. I feel I've been in
scenes from several films and TV shows over the last nine days and
now it seems I'm in "The Italian Job".

'Oh my God, it's Miss Daisy. Quick everyone give me a hand
to pull her back.' Her Ladyship, followed closely by Mister
Squadron Leader, Alexei, the man who told Her Ladyship off for
parking me where she did and another man from the helicopter rush
over. Between them they successfully haul me back to safety.

'Gosh Old Girl, that was a close one. I don't know what I'd have
done if you'd gone over the edge.' That's one of the nicest things
she's ever said to me.

'I mean, how on earth would I have got home?' Why does she
have to ruin a beautiful moment?

'Come on Chunky Lumps,' says Alexei. Miss Daisy vill be fine
now. I've got a bottle of champagne vaiting for you inside.'

'Mmm lovely, but you go on in Alexei, I'll just sort the Old Girl
and make her safe for the night and I need to call my friends in

Penzance to tell them I'm staying here. I'll join you in a few minutes.' Alexei and the others wander into the hotel, leaving Her Ladyship alone with me. She leans closely towards my radiator.

'Welcome to Land's End, Old Girl. Well done. We did it.' Her phone rings. She looks at the dial to see who it is and taps a button.

'Hello? Oh hello Arthur, I was about to ring you. Yes, we've made it, safe and sound.' She glances at me. 'Well, fairly safe and sound. What? That gin and tonic? Actually I won't be coming back to Penzance now. Alexei's here and is opening a bottle of champagne. What did you say? Who is Alexei? Oh just someone I met on the way down. He's a Russian spy you know. He's here with a couple of RAF people. What do you mean are they spies too? I was only joking about Alexei. He's not really a Russian spy. Look I've got to go. I'll get away early tomorrow and catch up with you before we all go home. Bye.' She puts the phone in her pocket.

'Where was I, Old Girl? I was congratulating you wasn't I. I know I don't always appear to appreciate you, but I am so very proud of you. Once again you did it.' Yes I did, didn't I? But Your Ladyship, why all these niceties? Are you after something?

'The thing is Old Girl, it's been suggested that we take part in the Peking to Paris run next year. I think it would be rather fun, don't you?'

Oh no, not again. Why can't you just settle down Your Ladyship? I am not going. You can. I'm staying at home! But then, I have a funny feeling that I might be persuaded to change my mind by this time next year. I wonder what the petrol is like in China.

Oscar, The Asthmatic Barking Dog 1999 – 2013

(Picture Sue Tanguay)